LYCOPOLIS

LYCOPOLIS

Ali Luke

Aliventures

For Mum & Dad, with love and gratitude.

The Players and their Lycopolis Characters

Seth Harrington – Lord Cyrric and Remegius the Demonologist

Katherine "Kay" Blake – Sir Tristram, leader of the knights

Edwin Mitchell – Benedict, squire to Sir Tristram

Mark Webster – Roderic Revelry, a thief

Hannah Webster – Matilda, warrior-woman, leader of the Haven

Robert Stephens – Heidi of the Plains, an academic

Brandon Starchild – Sir Wilhelm, a knight

Chapter 1

Kay sipped uncertainly at her hot chocolate. Seth was taller than she'd imagined him. His blond hair hung perfectly, parted in the middle to fall to his chin, just like his profile picture on Messenger. She'd brushed her own hair into fierce plaits as usual, but the wind had whipped strands of it loose.

"So." He poured his coffee from a tall chrome cafetière. "How are you finding it?"

"It's all very ..." She trailed off.

"Give it a bit of time. You'll find your feet."

"I just feel so out of place here." By *here*, she meant the university – but she found herself glancing into the huge wall mirror to her left, taking in the crowded Grand Café. There were a few other students, most of them with parents, and a couple of guys in suits. She felt under-dressed in jeans and a polo-neck.

Seth tilted his head slightly, as though inviting her to continue.

"Everyone else is so confident. They seem like they should be here."

"And you feel like you shouldn't?"

"I know it's stupid, but I always thought Oxford was full of geniuses." Her cup clattered as she put it down on the saucer.

"Kay. Come on, look at me."

She lifted her head, and met his eyes. They were a greyish blue, like stonewashed denim, like the pebbles on the beach back home. For a long moment, he just gazed back. Her cheeks were hot. She was sure she was blushing.

"First, everyone feels like that. Second –" He leant forwards across the table, and lowered his voice, as though telling her a secret. "This is Oxford. They don't let people in by mistake."

That actually made her smile. "Did you feel the same way, though? When you were at Cambridge?"

"No. But I had a rather well-developed sense of entitlement."

She wasn't sure whether to laugh or not.

"Anyway." He picked up his shoulder bag. It was light brown leather – definitely in a different league from her battered rucksack. "You've been great. I've appreciated all your help with Lycopolis."

At the start of the summer, while she was waiting for A-level results, he'd declared her his assistant. She had a badge against her name on the forums, and a few administrative powers in the game. She'd been surprised, though no-one else had. He'd noticed her. He trusted her.

"Thanks," she said. "I enjoy it."

He passed her a wrapped box; she hesitated, then untied the ribbon. The shiny silver paper slid off easily. Chocolates. Rich, glossy chocolates, beautifully packaged.

"Oh! You didn't have to ..."

"I wanted to," he said, and smiled, easily.

This was awkward. She wasn't going to be put off, though; she'd decided what she was going to say, and she wouldn't talk herself out of it just because he'd given her a present. "It's really kind of you, but look, what I told you, about this new storyline for the game –"

"Hey. We can talk about that later. I didn't come up to Oxford to argue about Lycopolis." Some of the warmth had left his voice, though. That *was* why he'd come – but she tried to make herself believe his next words. "I came to see you, Kay. To find out how you're doing."

"Thanks. I'm all right, really." Her throat felt tight. She'd thought that Oxford would feel like a new home; had pictured friends, laughter, deep and meaningful conversations. She'd been promised dreaming spires – but she was surrounded by thick stone walls and daunting courtyards.

"You're settling in? Making friends?"

"Yeah." That wasn't really true. She'd tried. But everyone else doing Archaeology and Anthropology was dismayingly clever, and all the girls on her corridor existed in a constant whirl of clothes and parties. She'd spent most of her evenings hiding in her room, losing herself in Lycopolis.

"You don't sound too convinced," he said.

2

"I suppose I thought it would be easier."

To her surprise, he reached out and put his hand over hers. For a brief, silly, instance, she wanted to flinch away.

"Hey, you have me," he said. "And everyone in Lycopolis. We're there for you."

"Thanks." Her voice came out so small that she couldn't even hear herself over a sudden laugh from the table next to them. She said it again. "Thanks."

For a while, they talked about easy, inconsequential things: books, films, the dismal weather. Kay gazed out at the street. The sky was darkening.

"We'd better get moving," Seth said. "Looks like rain."

He was facing the back of the café; her confusion only lasted a moment before she remembered that there was another mirrored wall behind her. She slid the box of chocolates into her bag, and rummaged for her purse.

Seth shook his head, retrieving the bill from a waitress and putting a handful of coins down. "It's on me."

"Are you sure?"

"Absolutely." He was already standing, pulling his coat on.

They walked out onto the High Street. The wind was even stronger now, tugging at Kay's coat and flattening strands of hair across her face.

"Let me walk you back," he said.

"Oh. Thanks."

Cyclists darted along the road, seeming oblivious to the traffic. She would never get up the nerve for that.

"So," Seth said, as they crossed over in a gap between buses and cars and bikes. "You'll join us tomorrow?"

He'd said it as there was no doubt, but – "I'm still not convinced it's the right direction for Lycopolis."

"I think I'll be the judge of that."

It was the same every time she disagreed with him: he'd point out that Lycopolis was, after all, his game. He'd created it. He paid for the servers. He decided who to let in and who to kick out.

"What about the no magic rule?" she asked.

"That's to stop newbies flying around on dragons – I can quite happily ignore it."

3

"But why this? Why do we even need something on Hallowe'en? It's not like we have anything for Christmas or Easter or –"

He stopped abruptly, turned and looked at her. His eyes were colder now, though his tone stayed pleasant. "You're over-thinking things. It's just a game."

Three years ago, she'd promised herself she'd never believe that again. Not with something like this. "It's not in-character for Tristram. Human sacrifice – summoning a demon – no."

He didn't say anything for a moment. "You're shivering."

"I'm okay." Dusk was falling and it was cold, the coldest Oxford had been since the start of term, but that wasn't what had sent a shudder through her.

"Here." Before she'd quite realised what he was doing, he'd unwound his scarf and looped it around her neck. It was slate grey, and soft against her skin.

"Everyone else has agreed to be there, you know. Even Hannah." He stopped, letting a group of teenagers go past. They were on the bridge now, the river Cherwell murky below them. Her halls were just a little further – but he'd reached out and taken hold of her arm. "Seeing as you're my assistant, I'd rather hoped I could count on your support."

"Does supporting you mean I always have to agree?"

He hesitated. "Well, no. Of course not. But I can't very well have an assistant who's refusing to go along with my storyline, can I?"

That felt like a threat. She pulled her arm away. "You mean, you'd sack me."

He frowned, as if to say that she'd misunderstood him.

"Seth, I don't want to spoil the game." She loosened the scarf, which was pressing too hard against her throat. "You know, we've got something good there."

"It won't spoil it, I promise. This is what Lycopolis is *for.*"

The wind was blowing harder now: she hugged her arms around herself. Perhaps he was right. Perhaps she was overreacting, and it was all just harmless fun.

"Come on, Kay, be there tomorrow night. I'm asking it as a favour." He smiled at her. "I really want you to be part of this."

Now he was making her blush. It seemed churlish to refuse. "Well, okay, then."

4

"Thank you." He reached out and touched her shoulder, lightly. "It was good to meet you at last."

Her face was hot, despite the cold sting of the air. "Thanks, you too."

"I should go and catch my train. See you in Nottingham."

"Yep. Looking forward to it."

She fumbled at the scarf, but he put his hand over hers. "Keep it."

"Are you sure?"

He nodded, then turned and strode away, back across the bridge. For a minute, she just watched him; walking fast, his hands thrust in his pockets, the hem of his coat trailing over the top of his boots. She was suddenly angry – at herself, rather than at him. She'd been determined not to have any part in this, and now she'd just gone along meekly. But he was Seth. Lycopolis was his creation: a game of words, of rich, meaningful stories and people to share them with; a world where she belonged, where she had friends. She couldn't throw that away.

The first drops of rain began to fall as she swiped her entry card and walked in through the gates to the Waynflete halls. Tomorrow, she'd be braver, and unswayed by chocolates and warm words and blue eyes. Tomorrow, she'd be Tristram.

* * *

"I have deep misgivings about this." Sir Tristram strode over to where Lord Cyrric stood, in the doorway leading down to the Temple of Shadows.

"I don't care." Cyrric leant towards him, the city's insignia glinting from the medal around his neck. "All I care about, Tristram, is your loyalty."

There were footsteps on the road, slowing, then halting. A lantern pierced the gloom, illuminating a pale face and blonde hair. "Lord Cyrric. Sir Tristram."

Tristram frowned. "Miss Heidi. Are you sure you wish to be here?"

"Of course." She glanced at Lord Cyrric, and Tristram saw her wait for his nod before continuing. "I will not be participating, merely observing."

She should not see such things. No-one should.

5

There were louder footsteps now, accompanied by a jangling of metal, then a whooping battle-cry. Matilda. She came over, dragging a chained slave girl no older than Tristram's squire.

"Stay and join us," Cyrric said, to Matilda.

Tristram hoped she'd refuse. Matilda was a law unto herself – along with the sprawl of streets that she ruled over.

She shrugged. "Why not?"

From behind him, another voice came: "You require my service, Lord Cyrric?"

Roderic. A slippery character, ringleader of a gang of thieves and muggers. Tristram turned, and was surprised – and angry – to see his squire there too. "Benedict, go back to the Keep at once."

"Oh, I think he can come with us too," Cyrric said.

"Ben," Tristram said, but the boy pretended not to hear.

Cyrric said, "Roderic, open the door. Without damaging it. I would prefer the priests not to know we were here."

As Roderic set to work, Tristram stepped over to Benedict. "Go home. That's an order."

"Done it," Roderic said, and the door creaked open.

"Tristram, if you're quite ready?" Cyrric said.

Benedict turned away, back to the road. Tristram took a long breath, and walked with the others down the stone steps into the crypt. They huddled on the two rough pews, and Tristram fought mounting horror as Matilda chained the slave girl to the altar.

"Defenders and citizens of Lycopolis," Lord Cyrric said. "We do this for the greater good. For the glory of our city. For the safety of our citizens. We have gathered here at the Hour of Darkness, on the night when the realm of demons comes close to our world. We have gathered to call for aid, to summon the one spoken of in the ancient legends of our city. The one who can shape reality for us."

Cyrric lifted the knife. The girl didn't even flinch. Her face was turned towards them, and her eyes were blank.

Then he paused, and pointed towards the back of the Temple. "Stand up!"

Sick dread weighed down Tristram's heart. He stood, turned, knowing as he did so what he would see. "Benedict, leave! Get out of here."

6

"It's too late," Cyrric said. "Come forward, boy."

Benedict walked forwards and edged into the pew next to Roderic, well out of Tristram's reach.

"We call the Prince of Nightmares!" Cyrric thrust the knife down.

The girl's blood ran down the altar, spilling into the ancient channels carved into the floor, a red stain winding across the white stone. She shrieked as her body was engulfed in blue flames.

A mass of black smoke, coiling like something living, appeared behind the altar. Cyrric stumbled back, one arm up to ward it off. The flames died, and a pack of wolves snarled around the altar, eyes glinting yellow. They tore the slave girl's body to pieces, more blood running.

The smoke thickened.

The wolves turned.

Tristram vaulted over the pew, sword already in hand. He thrust it through the throat of the nearest wolf, almost severing its head. Behind him, Matilda shouted a warning. A second wolf came at him. He fought it off, yelling "Keep back!" to Benedict and Heidi.

When he turned, he saw Matilda clubbing one wolf while another snapped for her throat. He ran the sword into it. Both Cyrric and Roderic were cowering against the wall. He'd have cursed them if he'd had breath enough to spare.

The remaining wolves let out a howl. The smoke swirled around them for a moment, then they vanished.

Cyrric edged forwards to address the cloud of smoke – which, Tristram realised, *was* the demon prince. "You are bound within these ancient lines until our contract is agreed. We are representatives of Lycopolis. We have summoned you and request your aid against the forces which threaten our city."

There was a long silence. Then the room echoed with a laugh, deep and jarring. *"You will all kneel to me and serve me as your lord and master."*

Tristram grabbed Benedict's arm and pulled him close.

Cyrric was already covered by the thin haze of black smoke at the edge of the cloud: slowly, he knelt. Roderic joined him. Heidi left her notebook. The black smoke drifted around them all. It whispered at the corners of Tristram's mind: *kneel, obey, it's easy...*

He steeled himself against it and held Benedict more tightly. "No."

7

Matilda was still standing, but her gaze was fixed on the demon. "You'll give us strength? Victory in battle?"

"Yes."

Tristram had never seen her submit to any form of authority. But now, he watched her kneel.

The smoke drifted towards him. It smelt like soil and musk and blood. *"You will serve me too, Tristram, you and your squire."*

He stayed silent. A long moment went by.

"You have no choice." A tendril of smoke snaked out and Benedict was pulled out of Tristram's grip by some invisible force. The smoke curled around his throat.

Too late, Tristram reached for him. "Let him go!"

"Knight." The voice was quiet, the words, somehow, intended just for him. *"Serve me."*

Tristram swung his sword up and lunged. It crackled, as though lightning stormed through it. The blade crumbled to dust, and the hilt fell from his numbed hand.

"You will kneel and serve me, as will your squire. The souls of all here belong to me."

The smoke seemed to tighten around Benedict's throat. The boy made a sound, almost a cry.

"Do not harm him!" Tristram shouted.

The Prince of Nightmares released Benedict's neck, the curling smoke looking solid for a moment. Tristram reached for the boy, but a gust of wind, like a blow, forced him back.

A thin trail of smoke reached Benedict's forehead as he knelt. The boy gasped as though in pain. Tristram forced himself to watch as the smoke slithered through the air, touching each of them in turn – marking them.

"Stand," the Prince said, and the smoke curled around Benedict's arm and pulled him to his feet. *"Take your squire, Tristram. And do not doubt that we will meet again, and that you will do my bidding."*

There was a rush of wind that rang in Tristram's ears and shook them all. Benedict stumbled. Tristram reached for him. A crack tore through the crypt floor.

When the noise and the tremors stopped, the demon was gone.

Chapter 2

Seth watched the computer as a progress bar inched forwards.

Nothing. Just like before, nothing. No sign of any interference with his game. He jabbed a few keys and set a final test running, then flicked to Messenger, wanting a distraction.

Kay had vanished straight after the role-playing, but Edwin was still online. A few months ago, Seth hadn't wasted any time on him, leaving him to be Kay's little sidekick. Recently, though, Edwin had become more interesting. He had potential.

"Ed. Try this." It was a track by some obscure Norwegian death metal band: after listening to it once, he'd decided not to subject himself to it ever again.

"Okay, thanks!" As usual, Edwin was typing in an almost unreadable Gothic font. "Hey, thanks for letting Benedict be there. It was so cool tonight, properly creepy."

"Glad you enjoyed it."

"Yeah, I could really *see* it all ... the girl and the blood and the temple. And the wolves, wow."

Normally, Seth lurked invisibly in the game, watching; he'd get involved where necessary as Lord Cyrric, but without any particular attachment. Today, he'd found himself hunched over the keyboard, typing almost without thinking, his mind full of stone and shadow.

"So, what's the Prince of Nightmares gonna do next?" Edwin asked.

An unexpected shiver ran up Seth's arms. He shrugged it away, irritated at himself. "I'm not at liberty to reveal the Prince's plans."

"Heh, okay."

The test was still running. He pulled the conversation back onto safe ground. "Are you coming to the meet-up?"

"Yeah. Well, I'm trying to get Mum to agree. She's being so unreasonable."

Seth pre-empted the usual whinging with, "You'll talk her round, I'm sure."

"Yeah. I'll be there."

"Good good. Here, I've got another song for you." He sent it through Messenger. It looked like a perfectly innocuous file.

"It won't play."

Seth knew it had installed just fine. It would record everything – Google searches, Messenger chats, emails. "Let's try it again. Here."

A couple of minutes went by. "Cool, I really like it."

The interface was a little clunky, but the program worked perfectly, showing an echo of Edwin's words to him. Excellent. It'd be even better if he could get the spyware onto Kay's computer too, but he never sent her anything other than text files, and she wasn't as blindly trusting as Edwin. In fact, she was getting more and more uncooperative. He should've gone ahead without Tristram there.

The test was still running. The progress bar ticked on. Restless, he went over to the window and looked out at the lights across the Thames, a sprinkling of reds and greens reflecting from the grey water. The Eye was stilled for the night. He drew the curtains and shut out the dark. He didn't feel like sleeping yet.

After making a coffee, he returned to the computer. The test routine was still trawling through the files. If there was anyone screwing around with his game, he'd find them.

In Messenger, Edwin was asking him, "Kay's going to be there, right?"

"In Nottingham? Yep. Looking forward to meeting her?" Seth sipped his coffee. It was a strong Javan blend, with a distinct kick to it. He appreciated that. It had been a long weekend.

There was a long pause before Edwin's reply popped up. "Yeah, I guess."

"You role-play with her all the time." He could've added, *And talk about her. Constantly.*

"Yeah. I know. But it'll be a bit weird to meet her in real life."

"You like her, don't you?" A month ago, he wouldn't have asked it so directly. But now, Edwin trusted him, brightened up every time Seth favoured him with a special item in the game.

"Well, I like everyone in Lycopolis."

"You fancy her." Seth checked the progress bar again. Another five minutes to go.

"Maybe a little bit."

"Just a little bit?"

"I don't even know her, really. Seth, you won't say anything, will you? Don't tell her, don't even hint or anything."

He finished his coffee before typing, "Of course I won't."

The computer beeped. The test was finished – and, once again, there was nothing.

No unusual activity in the game. No suspicious logins. No tampering, no hackers, no bots, nothing at all that shouldn't be there. Just him, with power over everything, Kay with a few administrative functions, and thirty-four bog-standard players.

Well, now he knew.

For so long, he'd wanted this. But he'd hadn't let himself dwell on it. He'd thought of the game and the storyline; he'd concentrated on winning everyone over, Kay especially. He'd been prepared for nothing to happen – a let-down for everyone, an anti-climax.

But the Prince of Nightmares had appeared.

He took a couple of deep breaths. Just for a moment, he wished there was someone he could talk to. It was a childish and pointless thing to want: in any case, there was no-one. The other players assumed that he'd been pushing the story along last night, that he'd been writing the Prince of Nightmare's lines. Edwin thought he'd brought the wolves snarling in. They all knew he could shape the game world like that. He often did.

Except this time, he hadn't.

Rain was beginning to fall outside, cold specks landing on his face. He didn't bother going back up to his flat for an umbrella. He strode to the South Bank, drinking in the cool night air, a breeze tugging at his coat.

Most of the buildings along the Thames were still lit up, pouring squares of light towards the river. It was busy for a wet Monday night:

zombies and ghouls and witches walked past, along with Londoners in suits and jeans and little black dresses. Tacky Hallowe'en decorations festooned the restaurants.

He turned left, and paced past The Globe, then the Tate Modern, their fame made ordinary by long acquaintance. He should be excited – jubilant. What he'd seen all those years ago had been *real*. The Prince wasn't a lonely child's imaginary friend. The journal he'd started when he was seven wasn't a creative writing exercise.

And Lycopolis wasn't just a game.

He realised how fast he was walking, and deliberately slowed to a saunter. Under the Southbank Centre, kids were skateboarding and spray-painting. It was a cold, ordinary November evening.

He wasn't a child any more. He was twenty-four. He'd conquered his fears long ago, thrust them away, and learnt to turn the nightmares aside. Yet tonight, every breath seemed to catch in his chest. Things were already slipping out of his hands: the ritual should have worked. Cyrric should have had control. The Prince should never have been able to stroll past those carved channels of blood.

And, of course, Cyrric should not have knelt. That hadn't been in the plan at all. But in the heat of the role-playing, it had seemed exactly right. Had it felt that way to the other players, too? It was hardly in-character. Heidi had been there as an observer. Matilda never recognised any form of authority. And yet they'd knelt.

Only Tristram hadn't – only Kay hadn't.

Leaning on the wall, he looked into the Thames. Water pouring into water, rain streaming into river. His hair was wet now, and he kept having to blink his eyes clear. He turned, and began to walk back.

Half-a-dozen girls swayed towards him, heels clicking on the path, a bottle being passed between them as they pressed together under umbrellas. One of them – flimsy dress, witch's hat, too much lipstick – nudged her friend, and they looked at him, unabashedly eyeing him up.

Any other night, he'd have smiled, started a conversation, amused himself a little. Tonight, he just raised his eyebrows at the one who'd pointed at him and held her gaze, relentlessly, until she blushed, looked away and hurried on with her friends.

Back home, he unlocked the bottom drawer of his desk and took out his journal. The first few pages held the list, beginning with three names in careful cursive:

Michael Harrington (my father)
Victoria Harrington (my mother)
Richard Harrington (my big brother)

It went on: names from the playground, from boarding school, from university. Some of them had been struck through long ago. The first three names remained, along with a handful of others sprinkled throughout the list. Soon, though, he'd be able to cross off every single one.

In the bathroom, he washed the rain from his face and hair. The mirror had clouded up. He swept the towel across it, to see his reflection. His hair was darkened by the water, heavy around his face.

There was a mark on his forehead. It was so faint he could've walked away and convinced himself it had just been imagined, conjured up by tiredness and not-quite-conquered nerves.

He pulled the plug from the sink and watched the water spiral away. There was no backing out now. Not even if he'd wanted to. He'd known for years what he was playing with. When he'd created Lycopolis, writing the code line by line, building the world line by line, he'd known what he was doing. He wanted the Prince, and all its power.

Later, as he lay in bed, he reminded himself that he hadn't expected it to be easy – hadn't dared hope it would be easy.

He closed his eyes, and braced himself for sleep.

Chapter 3

Edwin slammed the front door, kicked his trainers at the wall, and was half-way up the stairs by the time Mum called, "How was school?"

He didn't know why she bothered asking. What did she expect: that he'd stroll home, announce that he loved Year 10, that his teachers were the most intelligent and sympathetic people he knew, and that Darren Miller was his new best friend?

He slammed his bedroom door so hard that a bit of paint flaked off the wall.

"Edwin!"

After bolting the door, he flung himself face-first onto the bed. It had been the worst day yet. Darren Miller had started getting the bus to school, and had chucked spit-balls at him the whole way there. Then, in Chemistry, Darren and a couple of his cronies had decided it'd be really fucking amusing to waft a Bunsen burner near his hair. Of course, it was Edwin who got yelled at for messing around.

At lunch, he'd thought he was safe, hanging out round the back of the art block in the grey November drizzle. But they'd found him.

He pulled off his blazer, then his shirt, examining his upper arm. There wasn't a bruise, yet. He dropped the blazer and shirt on the floor and dug through his wardrobe for a black sweater. It was hard to feel properly Goth in school uniform, even now his hair was nearly down to his shoulders. He wanted to re-dye it – the roots were starting to show – but Mum had gone on and on about the streaks he'd left on the bathroom sink last time.

When he stared into the mirror on the back of his wardrobe door, he saw a reddish bruise on his forehead, right in the middle. He didn't even remember getting that one.

He lay down on the bed, and pressed his face into his pillow. Another three days till the weekend: that meant fifteen lessons, six bus journeys and three lunchtimes to somehow survive through. And it would be the same week after week, for almost seven whole weeks till the Christmas holidays.

If he told Mum he was too ill to go to school, she wouldn't believe him. Even if he could convince her – by faking a temperature or pretending he'd been sick – she'd want to stay home with him. And then he'd have to lie in bed, rather than playing computer games.

His medallion was poking into his chest. He sat up again and pulled it out from under his shirt. After he'd started at the new school in September, he'd come up with a sort of routine. He'd put on the medallion every morning and clasp his hand all the way around it, and concentrate really hard on not getting punched or kicked or beaten up. Until now, he'd almost managed to convince himself that it was working.

On his bookshelf by the bed were the twelve wolf figurines. Apart from the medallion, they were the only things he had that'd once belonged to Dad. The only faint thread that linked them.

At the far end of the shelf, the empty space still waited for birthday cards, Christmas cards, postcards, any cards signed "Dad".

None ever came.

He switched the computer on and it chuntered into life. He opened Media Player, even though he didn't have any playlist heavy enough for a day like today. Messenger logged him in automatically, and he looked for Kay. She wasn't online. He found himself gazing at her profile picture, wondering what it'd be like to actually see her for real.

A message popped up from Seth. "Hey Ed. Meant to say, great role-playing yesterday."

Edwin sat down and spun his chair all the way round – which was totally un-Goth, but there was no-one to see him. Seth saying "great role-playing" made the day a little less crap. Seth owned Lycopolis, Seth had written it all, from the crooked streets in the Thieves' Quarter to the mansions and gardens where the Nobility lived. And the demon-summoning had been so creepy and intense that, for a couple of hours, Edwin had forgotten about half-term being over.

"Thanks," he typed, but didn't add a smiley face. They weren't Goth, plus, Seth never used them.

"Didn't give you nightmares, did it?"

"No." His flicker of a good mood vanished. He wasn't a kid. He could cope with the violent, nasty stuff, it didn't bother him. He liked the darkness of Lycopolis. It made it real. Better than life, where people pretended everything was okay, even when they were cracking apart.

He pulled up Media Player, shoved the volume up and set the "Crap Day" playlist on shuffle. Avenged Sevenfold's *Nightmare* began.

"Good good. Check your game inbox, Benedict has a message."

Curious, Edwin loaded Lycopolis, typed "Benedict" and his password, "creepingdeath." Once he was into the game, he typed, "Hey all," to the Chatroom.

"Hey Edwin."

"Welcome back!"

It was so different from school. People liked him here, even though he was younger than them all. They cared about him.

He opened the message.

Benedict,

You impressed me last night. You showed courage and spirit. It is clear to me that you are an intelligent young man – one who I would be glad to have in my employ.

I require your assistance on a matter of great importance to the city.

As I am sure you noticed last night, Sir Tristram and I do not always agree about the correct course of action. With our city under threat, I need to know that all of my subordinates are acting in accordance with my mandates.

This is what I task you with. Watch Sir Tristram closely. Note the places he goes to, the people he talks with, and the orders he gives. If you suspect he is planning any form of rebellion, any dissent, you will inform me immediately.

Lord Cyrric
Governor of His Majesty's City of Lycopolis
High Judge of the Lycopolis Court

Edwin read it through several times, wondering how Benedict was going to react. Lord Cyrric had never taken any interest in him before. And Ben was usually deeply loyal to Tristram. But this wasn't the sort of order you could disobey.

In Messenger, he asked Seth, "Cyrric wants Ben to betray Tristram? What if he won't?"

"I'll leave that to your imagination. And Ben's."

Edwin grinned.

"Anyway. I've just sent an email about the meet-up."

"Oh cool!" The weekend in Nottingham – so long as he could talk Mum into letting him go – was the one thing in his life that he could look forward to.

Hello all,

Saturday 12th approaches rapidly. So, some plans:

We'll meet at The Pit and the Pendulum (pub, centre of Nottingham, google it) at noon on Saturday. I owe you all a drink as a thanks for helping make Lycopolis what it is.

Seth.

"The Pit and the Pendulum?" he asked Seth. The name sounded familiar.

"You'll like it. It's named after one of Poe's short stories."

Edwin hadn't actually read any of Edgar Allan Poe's stuff yet, though he kept meaning to: if there was a reading list for Goths, Poe would be right at the top.

Messenger showed that Kay was online now.

"Did you get Seth's email?" he asked her. "You're coming, right?"

"Yep!" She added a smiley face. "I definitely need to escape from Oxford for a weekend. How're things for you?"

"School's really shit at the moment."

"Oh ... I guess everyone feels like that a bit, at times."

"No they don't." He found himself suddenly annoyed, typing fast, the letters jumbling in his desperation to make someone understand. "*Everyone* doesn't get spat at or kicked in the corridors or have their homework ripped up. *Everyone* doesn't get smacked in the eye by some stupid Neanderthal bastard thug. It's just *me*. They all hate me."

18

He sent it, then sat looking at the words, wondering if they sounded pathetically emo.

A single word appeared in response: "*hugs*"

His throat tightened up, as though there was a hard lump of misery lodged in there. As he typed "*hugs*" back, he wondered if she'd actually hug him for real, or if she just meant it virtually. It didn't matter: hugging wasn't very Goth.

"I'm sorry, Ed. That does sound shit."

"Yeah," he typed, "It is. And it just gets worse all the time."

"Have you told your mum?"

"Not really." He didn't want to worry Mum, not now that she seemed to be better.

"How about your form tutor?" Kay asked. "Head of year? They'll know how to handle it."

"Yeah. Maybe." There was no way he could say anything to a teacher. He'd just get beaten up for being a snitch. Plus he knew exactly what Mr Thompson would say. *"Perhaps if you got a hair-cut and didn't wear jewellery ..."*

He was *not* going to compromise his Goth identity. But for about the millionth time since breakfast, he wished his dad was around. He'd be able to tell his dad anything. He could talk about the bullying, he could say he wanted to move schools. His dad could tell him about girls and stuff. His dad could teach him how to fight. If he could beat up Darren Miller, the rest of them would leave him alone.

"You around for a while?" Kay asked. "Sir T's having a Knights' meeting soon, and he wants Ben there."

"Yeah, sure."

But Mum was banging on his bedroom door. "Edwin. Can you hear me? Switch that music off, please."

He turned the speakers down a bit. If she'd get him some decent headphones, like he kept asking, his music wouldn't bother her.

"What?" he yelled.

"Dinner's ready."

"But Mum! I'm playing Lycopolis."

"Well, just pause the game for a bit, and –"

"I can't – I keep telling you, it's an online game! There are *other people* playing it with me."

"I'm sure they'll wait while you have your dinner. Sausage and mash – I'm dishing up in a minute."

Scowling, he switched off the speakers, and typed a hasty message to Kay. "Mum's making me go and eat dinner."

"No worries, we've not got everyone online yet anyway."

He unbolted his bedroom door. He'd fixed the bolt on during the summer; all Mum had said was, "Well, you are a teenager, I understand you need some privacy."

His new poster, on the back of the door, had come unstuck at the corner. He pressed it down. It was a Led Zeppelin album cover which he really liked – he wasn't so keen on their actual music. He'd found it on eBay, and Kay'd bought it for him, because she had an eBay account and good feedback. When he'd posted her the money, he'd written her address on his arm with a biro: *Katherine Blake, Magdalen College, Oxford*. It still hadn't completely washed off.

He trudged downstairs. There was no carpet on the stairs, and the wooden steps were cold through his socks. He wandered through to the kitchen and sat down.

Mum put a plate in front of him. "How did your maths test go?"

"All right."

"Well, how did you do?"

"Hundred percent." He dug into the mash.

"You don't sound very happy about it." She filled a plate for herself, and sat down opposite him.

He gave his trademark gothic grunt. It was like the "unh" he'd been doing since he was twelve, but with a hint of a world-weary sigh, and a touch of death-metal growl.

Mum leant across the table to touch his forehead with the back of her hand. "You sound like you're coming down with something."

"I'm fine." He picked up *Cult Times* and flicked to an article about a new vampire series.

"I'm sorry I had to work during half-term."

It'd been great, he'd had the house all to himself. And without Mum nagging him to go outside and get some fresh air, he'd been able to spend the whole time on the computer.

"We could watch a film later," she said.

He ignored her, turning the pages of the magazine with his free hand.

"You can pick, if you like," she said, "As long as it's not too gory."

Anything *she'd* want to watch would be rubbish. She wouldn't even rent 18s from the library for him to watch on his own. It didn't matter, though; Seth'd explained how to download films from The Pirate Bay.

"I've got maths homework," he said.

"Well, perhaps I could give you a hand with it?"

"I don't need any help, I'm not a retard." He trudged back upstairs before she could tell him to help with the washing up. Once he'd logged back into Lycopolis, he headed straight to the knights' meeting room.

* * *

The clock out in the courtyard struck seven, and the three knight leaders entered, one by one. They were all big, stern men, with bright tunics in their Orders' colours.

Their greetings were brief. "Sir Tristram. Squire."

Standing, Sir Tristram said, "The danger we face is grave. I am sure you have heard the rumours – these are the facts. An evil, demonic creature, known as the Prince of Nightmares, seeks to control our city. I believe that Cyrric is acting under this creature's influence."

Sir Tristram paused. Benedict felt a slow shiver run up his spine. He'd tried not to think about the demon, or Lord Cyrric, or that girl's blood running across the temple floor.

"Cyrric has barricaded the Lionheart Gate and set guards on almost all the others. The only ways out of the city are the Old Gate towards the mountains, and the southern path through the forest. I believe Cyrric's actions mean that the demon wishes us isolated. We *cannot* allow our city to be cut off from the outside world and its aid – we must reopen a route to the capital."

Before continuing, Sir Tristram glanced around the room. "Matilda has promised the aid of the Haven. I would rather not have to rely upon it, but we will need numbers on our side. I welcome your suggestions."

21

Sir Elliot said, "We should dismantle the blockade. Set fire to it, or dynamite it, if we have to."

"That was my thinking also," Sir Tristram said. "But Cyrric will not turn a blind eye whilst we do it."

They kept talking, discussing tactics. Benedict tried to concentrate, because he didn't want his thoughts to drift back to the Temple of Shadows, and the blood running on the floor, and that black smoke.

"Do we have enough men to take on Cyrric's?" Sir Farrion asked. "Even with Matilda's rabble, we're going to be hard-pressed."

Sir Julian said, "We should pull down the blockade, yes, but there is no bravery or wisdom in risking lives. We should take the gate under cover of night."

There were nods of assent.

"Are you all agreed to this?" Sir Tristram asked. "Let me have your voices on it."

"Aye," they said, together.

"Tomorrow, at midnight, then. We meet just outside the Keep. On foot – we need to move quietly. I will send word to Matilda. Only give your men the details necessary. We need but one loose tongue for this to reach Cyrric's ears."

After a round of hand-shakes, they filed out. Benedict stood up to follow, but Sir Tristram caught his arm. "Benedict. You look tired. What's wrong?"

"Nothing," he said, hastily. "Nothing. Just – it's late."

"Yes. Off you go, then, get a good night's sleep."

Benedict walked slowly out of the meeting room, across the courtyard, through the dim gloom that was barely broken by the lanterns shining through the windows of the Knights' Rest. He went to his room, and huddled under a blanket. He wasn't going to tell Cyrric anything. He wasn't going to betray Sir Tristram.

* * *

"So what's up with Ben?" Kay asked him, in Messenger.

Edwin almost told her, then hesitated and went back to Seth's window. "I can tell Kay about Cyrric and Ben, right?"

22

"No."

Normally, Edwin would've left it at that: you didn't go questioning Seth. But maybe out of curiosity, or because he'd had such a shit day at school, or because Seth had been much chattier recently, he asked, "And what if I do?"

"Well, I'm not always as merciful as Lord Cyrric."

Edwin grinned. A dangerous tingle ran along his arms. No-one crossed Seth, not if they wanted to stick around in Lycopolis. Newbies were always getting banned for pissing him off. But there was a sort of fun in being threatened. Jokingly threatened.

"Heh," he typed, for an amused-but-still-Goth laugh. "Okay."

"Good good."

He told Kay, "I can't really say what's going on with Ben."

"Oh. Right. Well, I'm sure Sir T will figure it out." Then, a moment later, "Ed, last night, did you think Seth seemed too eager about it all?"

"Don't know," he typed, then, reckoning he should agree a bit with Kay, "Maybe."

"Perhaps it's just me. Anyway, I have to finish reading this astonishingly dull article, so I'm going to call it a night."

Bored, he wandered downstairs to the kitchen. There was nothing interesting to eat: the biscuit box was empty and there was only wholemeal bread. He settled for a bowl of frosted flakes. However often he told Mum that proper Frosties really did taste better, she never listened.

He peered out the kitchen window. Back at their old house, he'd spent hours curled up in the shed, reading comics and playing on his Nintendo DS. Now, they barely had a garden at all, just a bit of scruffy grass and a knobbly tree. Mum had told him she was sorry they'd had to move to Milton Keynes, but that was where her new job was.

There wasn't anything he could say to that: he was glad, really glad that she was well enough to work, even though it was only part-time so there still wasn't much money. Even though it meant living in an ugly, concrete city full of chavs and shopping centres. He cupped his hands against his face and pressed closer to the window to watch the wind whip the tree's feeble branches. It had already lost all its leaves.

A murmur came from the living room. Mum had closed the door: he crept up close to it. She was on the phone, probably to Aunty Sue.

"Oh, the course is fine – though I'm going to have to go in on a few Saturdays."

Silence for a moment.

"Well, it's Edwin I'm worried about. He just doesn't seem to have settled very well."

They were talking about him again. He stood in the hall, listening.

"Yes, of course I have. But he's fourteen, he doesn't talk. He just grunts."

That was totally untrue. He'd had an entire conversation with her over dinner, when he'd been trying to read.

"No, he never wants to go anywhere, just spends hours on the computer." Her voice went a bit shaky on the next words. "I wonder if, you know, he needs a father figure."

Edwin didn't stay to hear any more, just stormed off up the stairs and slammed his bedroom door.

He didn't want some stupid *father figure*. He wanted his *dad*.

Chapter 4

Mark slammed off the alarm. Hannah was already up: no surprise there. He could hear Megan chattering in the kitchen below, Denny's feet on the stairs. The clock read seven-twenty, but he felt knackered, like he'd barely slept. Somehow, he pulled himself out of bed and stumbled into the bathroom. He took a shower, letting the water drown out everything else. For a few snatched minutes, it was just him. No wife, no kids, no boss, no envelopes marked *final demand*.

"Shit!" The bills – the postman. He dressed hastily and hurried downstairs. There were no letters on the mat. Did that mean that nothing had arrived yet, or that Hannah had got there first?

He poked his head into the living room. "Has the post come?"

"No." Hannah said, from behind the ironing board. "Could you look for Megan's new jumper?"

"In a minute. I haven't even had breakfast."

He'd just put the bread into the toaster when the letterbox rattled. He shot down the hall, grabbing the envelopes before Denny, hurtling downstairs, could reach them.

"I could've got the post, Dad!"

"There's nothing for you. All boring stuff for me and Mum."

He hurried through the kitchen to the den. It'd once been intended as a study – he'd built shelves and a desk – but for years it'd been overtaken by kids' toys, a couple of broken computers, and bits of furniture that wouldn't fit anywhere else.

He flicked through the envelopes, looking at them properly this time. *Final demand. Urgent. Open immediately.* One looked promising: he ripped it open. *Regret to inform … High volume of applications … We will keep your CV on file.* He crumpled it in his hand, and shoved the lot into the

25

back of the junk drawer, underneath broken remotes and old instruction manuals.

Abandoning his toast, he headed for the door and called a hasty, "Bye!"

Mark was contemplating getting a second cup of awful coffee, just for something to do, when a Messenger window appeared from Seth. "Busy?"

"No, I'm at work, and bored out of my mind."

"Up for some role-playing?"

"Sure." With only a couple of weeks to go, it wasn't like it was going to matter if he got caught playing games on company time. He logged into Lycopolis, typing "Roderic" then his password, "fullmoon".

In the game, a message waited in his inbox, from Lord Cyrric. *"Roderic Revelry. Kindly meet me at the Court."*

Mark wandered over there, found Cyrric, and had a guarded conversation in between checking emails on his phone. He'd hoped for a reply from some of the places he'd applied to, but he had nothing. It didn't matter; there was plenty of time yet.

In the game, Cyrric was offering Roderic a deal, couched in wary terms: go and fetch me Benedict, here's your pay, half now, half later. Mark didn't need to give it any thought. Roderic was friendly with Ben, sure, but he wasn't about to pass up on that sort of money.

"How's the job hunt going?" Seth asked, in Messenger.

"Pretty well. I've got one in the bag, I think, just waiting for an email."

"Good good."

His phone beeped – and there it was, a reply from the job he'd just about met the requirements for. A glance told him all he needed to know. *Unusually high number of applications ... Thank you for your interest.*

He slumped in his chair. There was still one more to get back to him, but he doubted they'd even bother replying. Seth was the one person he could confide in. "Actually, I'm getting a bit worried. I thought I'd have something definite lined up by now. Maybe I should've stuck it out here a bit longer."

"No, you did the right thing. You deserve better."

"It's just," he typed, "I've not said anything to Hannah yet."

"About quitting?"

"Yeah. I thought I'd get something else sorted out and then tell her. I didn't want to worry her, not with the kids and everything." He loved Denny and Megan, of course he did, but whenever he thought of them, it was with surprise: how had his life ended up like this?

"You're still coming to Nottingham?"

It seemed an odd thing to ask – but he knew how keen Seth was for them to all be there. Anyway, Mark was looking forward to the meet-up: a chance to get away from the usual Saturday routine of trailing round parks with the children. "Yeah. We've already arranged to leave the kids with Hannah's parents. But after that, I really need to get some work."

"Anything I can do?" Seth asked.

Mark was surprised – and oddly touched. "Not unless you happen to know anyone in Swindon who's busy recruiting IT workers."

"I might."

Mark had meant it jokingly, but those two words brought an unexpected rush of hope. After all, Seth was the sort of guy who knew people. "Well, if you do have any leads, I'd really appreciate it."

He wouldn't have been able to say that face to face, not to Seth, the best part of a decade younger than him, and already so far ahead in life.

"Perhaps we can have a chat in Nottingham."

"Sounds good. Thanks."

Last month, he'd been so certain he'd have something by now. Seth had seemed pretty sure, too, encouraging him to make the jump, seize the day.

Another message appeared. "Can I ask you something a little personal, Mark? Have you had any nightmares recently?"

What a weird question. He typed, "Why do you ask?"

"Reasons."

"Well, I suppose I've had some weird dreams." When he'd woken up earlier, his brain foggy, he'd not remembered them – but they were coming back to him now.

"Nightmares?"

"I suppose so. If you want to call them that."

"What about?"

He felt stupid, typing it. "A tree – I was trying to pull myself up a muddy bank, holding a sapling, and it broke away."

"Were you in a forest?"

An image drifted into his mind: a thicket of trees, each stretching up for the sky. "Maybe, I'm not sure. Why do you ask?"

Seth didn't reply.

Chapter 5

Kay typed a message to the knights, telling them simply, "Meet in the Keep. T."

It was the first time she'd arranged a large-scale scene without consulting Seth. In fact, she'd gone further than that. She'd asked them all to keep it quiet. They'd talked on Messenger, instead of discussing it in the Chatroom or on the forums. In the game, the Prince of Nightmares had spoken to Tristram several times – and whenever she asked Seth about it, he wouldn't offer any explanation. She was beginning to feel increasingly on-edge.

At least the game was a distraction from college life – she'd had yet another tutorial where she'd felt stupid and tongue-tied, and her current essay consisted of two paragraphs that she'd deleted and rewritten a dozen times. After four weeks, she was still missing Mum and Dad and Tom all the time; she'd rationed herself, strictly, to only phoning home every other night.

There was a knock at her door. She ignored it, but then it was repeated six times in quick succession.

"Come in, it's unlocked," she called.

Somehow, she wasn't surprised to see Brandon, the one person on her corridor who fitted in even worse than she did – though he never seemed to care or even notice. Today, he was wearing a tie-dyed T-shirt, along with grey jeans patched at the knees, and sandals.

"Hey," she said. "Um, I'm sort of busy."

Brandon leant against the doorframe. "I don't mind. I can stay anyway."

"Well ... if you want." Sometimes, he'd show up with a textbook and sit silently in her room while she was working on an essay. He usually wandered off wordlessly after half an hour or so. She didn't mind: she was starting to enjoy the company.

Sitting on the end of her bed, he took a Hobnob from the packet on her bedside table. Crumbs fell onto her carpet as he broke it in half, then into quarters. He pointed at her screen. "What are you doing?"

Elliot, Julian and Farrion, plus a host of imagined foot-soldiers, were at the Keep now, along with Benedict. "It's a sort of game," she said. "All in text, no graphics."

He didn't ask anything else, just looked intently at the screen and said, "They're waiting for you."

Kay was impressed that he'd managed to pick up that much. When she'd tried to explain the game to her parents, they'd been bemused by the lines of text appearing in different places – the gossip and in-jokes in the Chatroom window, the main action in the big Game window, private messages in the Inbox.

"You don't mind if I carry on?" she asked Brandon.

He was gazing at the screen, as though perfectly happy to sit there all evening and watch. Kay set her hands to the keyboard, and turned her attention to the game, to the footsteps and murmurs of the wary knights...

* * *

They walked through the streets, lanterns dimmed low. Tristram hated having to sneak around his own city in the dark, but it was the only sane choice they had. He led his men towards the alleyway that jinked down into Matilda's realm, the Haven.

"Knights." Matilda was waiting, with her ruffians: a dozen men and a few women, plus a handful of children. He'd have protested – but he'd brought his own squire.

He paused, and looked back at the men following him. "Where's Benedict?"

"Shirked it," Elliot said. "He was scared half-witted."

Tristram frowned. Although Benedict had seemed on edge, he'd given no indication he wanted to remain behind.

"Well?" Matilda asked, impatiently, "Can we get going? I'm freezing my tits off."

They crept onwards, under the cover of night. The moon was not even a crescent: only stars lit the sky. Tristram listened for any sound, watched for any movement in the shadows, any sign that they had been spotted.

Matilda fell into step beside him. "Tristram. You seen anything of Roderic recently?"

"No." The less he saw of Roderic, the better. "Why?"

"He's working for Cyrric."

"Damn." Cyrric had dozens of informants in the city – but none with quite the same underground network of contacts as Roderic.

As they turned out of the alleyway onto the only road that led towards the Lionheart Gate, Tristram said "We do this as quickly and quietly as we can. No unnecessary bravado."

They strode up the street to the gate, to the blockade of brick and stone, and started to tear it down. Some of the men, with heavy hammers from the Keep's forge, began to break the biggest rocks into smaller chunks.

Tristram shoved stones aside, his hands protected by gauntlets. The sound was becoming deafening. They made slow progress, but eventually he could see a gap emerging at the corner of the gate, a glimpse into the darkness outside the city.

Over the clatter and rush of stones, the sound of hooves went unnoticed until too late.

"Tristram!" Matilda's elbow caught him in the ribs; he turned.

All he could do for a moment was stare. There was Cyrric, his courtiers, and at least a hundred soldiers.

"Get the bastards!" Matilda yelled.

"Hold back!" Tristram shouted. "Stay your weapons! We do not engage!"

But a battle horn sounded, and the soldiers charged forwards; Elliot and Farrion attacked at once, and Tristram drew his own blade.

It was over quickly. Matilda and her group were cornered by the soldiers; his own men retreated at his command. Cyrric had stayed well out of the fray. He sat on horseback, the light from his guards' lanterns glittering from the plates of armour on his steed.

"Sir Tristram," he called. "Might I ask what you think you are doing?"

Next to him, small and drab in the midst of the bright retinue, stood Benedict.

It took Tristram a long moment to take that in, before he found his voice. "We are here to rip apart this blockade. If we cannot do so tonight, we will attempt it again tomorrow, and the next day, and the next, until the trade route is opened again."

"Aye!" yelled Elliot. The other knights – and Matilda's rabble – joined in the cry.

"That might be a little difficult, Sir Tristram, if I have you all thrown into prison."

"Fuck this!" yelled Matilda. The nearest soldiers backed away. "Let's get this bloody thing down now. A few more rocks and it'll tumble."

"Don't you dare!" Cyrric snapped. "Guards!"

There was a hiss of metal as blades were drawn.

"Stand down!" said Tristram. The odds were overwhelmingly against them. And how – why – had Cyrric got Benedict?

"Stop this instant, or I'll have you all put to the sword!" Cyrric shouted – but his next words were lost in a roar. The stones crashed down like an avalanche.

The men nearest the gate, both Tristram's and Cyrric's, were suddenly scrambling backwards.

A wolf leapt through the gap, followed by another, and another, until a dozen of them snarled in front of the barricade. They pounced indiscriminately: Matilda and Tristram and Farrion were all fighting alongside Cyrric's terrified soldiers.

"Drive them back!" Tristram yelled, "Drive them out of the city!"

It was only once the immediate heat of the battle was over, once the wolves, some wounded, some dying, limped away, that he saw the carnage. The grey light of morning made even the blood look colourless. A dozen or more of Cyrric's men were dead. Three of his own. Several of Matilda's, including one boy barely any older than Benedict.

Benedict. Tristram sought him anxiously. He was no longer at Cyrric's side.

That voice from the Temple, and from his dreams, spoke through the dawn. *"Missing someone?"*

At the edge of the road, smoke pooled around Benedict.

"Let go of him! Lord Cyrric, tell your demon to release my squire."

"This isn't in my hands any longer. You went against the Prince's wishes in trying to destroy the blockade."

"Good Sir Tristram." The Prince's words carried above the groans of the injured and the dying. *"What nightmares do you have? Perhaps treachery and betrayal number amongst them?"*

Next to him, Matilda gazed with a disturbing intensity at the black smoke.

He strode forwards: the smoke curled threateningly around Benedict's throat. He stopped. Cyrric, he saw, was urging his men away, gesturing them back towards the road.

"Tell your men to go home," the Prince of Nightmares said.

Tristram turned to Elliot. "Take everyone back." His voice sounded strained to his own ears. "See that the injured are tended to."

"Aye, sir."

They left – all his knights, all his men – and the Prince watched them as they walked away. Matilda said, "Scram," to her people; they went without a word, carrying their wounded.

What unspoken, unholy, agreement did he, Cyrric and Matilda have?

"Your little traitor was magnificent." The Prince spoke quietly now, his voice playing through the dawn like silk. Cyrric still kept his distance. Matilda watched, poised almost as though ready to spring.

"He wormed his way into your confidence. He pleaded to be allowed to come with you tonight. And then..." The voice turned hard. *"He told Lord Cyrric everything."*

Tristram felt a dark wave of anger. He'd loved Benedict like a son. He'd trusted the boy just as he trusted Elliot and Julian and Farrion. And now, a dozen of his men were badly injured, and three were dead.

"I believe that the Knightly Orders are hardly tolerant of traitors."

They couldn't afford to be. The Code, ancient yet living, demanded unswerving loyalty.

"Lord Cyrric." The demon's voice was suddenly directed away from Tristram. *"Would you like me to spare this child?"*

"Do whatever you please. I have no further purpose for him, unless you do."

"You bastard," Tristram said, and Matilda gave a low noise, something like a growl.

It was to her that the demon spoke next. *"You knelt to me, Matilda."*

"Yes." She was still tense, ready to fight – or, Tristram realised, to run.

"I promised you power. The expansion of those dark streets where nightmares can fester, which you call the Haven. You have your share of runaways there. Murderers. Slaves. Traitors. Children."

"No," Tristram said, sharply. "No!"

"Shut up, Tristram," Matilda said, and it wasn't the coldness in her voice that shook him so much as the greed in her eyes. To the Prince, she said, "I take anyone."

Benedict was trembling in the demon's grip, and Tristram wanted to stride forwards and snatch him back, but he did not dare, in case it could snap the boy's neck.

"No," he said again. "I don't care what's he's done. He pledged himself to the Knights, and I am not abandoning him."

But a trail of smoke rose and curled upwards, as if beckoning Matilda. She walked towards it.

"A gift. Use it well, it bears my mark."

Benedict stumbled forwards as the smoke faded; Matilda took hold of him. A thunderclap tore the dawn sky, and clouds opened, rain pelting down.

* * *

It was only when Kay blinked her way back into the real world, dragging herself from a place of knights and blood and broken promises, that she realised that Brandon was gone.

So were her Hobnobs. Oh well.

A Messenger box popped up, from Seth. "Why did you refuse to kneel to the Prince on Monday night?"

"Hello to you too," she typed, and added a smiley face.

"I'm serious, Kay. Why didn't you kneel?"

She was struck that he'd said *you*, not *Tristram*. Seth was normally rigid about the character versus player distinction, insisting that nothing in the game was ever to be taken as a personal attack. She suspected this was an excuse for Lord Cyric to be more of a bastard than Seth could otherwise get away with.

"Tristram sees it as selling his soul. I'm just trying to role-play consistently."

"Where consistently equals defiantly?"

That made her blink. "Who are you accusing of defiance, me or Tristram?"

"You." The word hung there on the screen, like a challenge.

"It's just a game, Seth, you said that yourself." But he was taking it far too seriously; they'd barely spoken since Sunday, and when they had, he'd been unusually curt.

"I don't want you screwing around with my plans."

"Perhaps it'd be easier I knew what your plans actually are. Why did Cyric close the gates? Why does Tristram keep hearing the Prince's voice? Why did you give Benedict to Matilda?"

"The *Prince of Nightmares* gave Benedict to Matilda."

He was behaving as though it had nothing to do with him. Her chest felt tight, her heart thumping fast. "You role-played it, though. Didn't you?"

"This is my game. I do whatever I fucking like."

The aggression didn't distract her: he'd not answered her question. But now he'd gone offline or more likely, blocked her.

Kay's room was cold at night, even with the radiator turned up high. She unfolded her old Guide blanket, badges still sewn along one edge. *Camper, Survival, Outdoor Cook, First Aid, Traditions.*

When she finally managed to sleep, she tumbled straight into dreams. There were black trees all around her, close together, branches grasping at one another. She backed away from them. The ground was slippery underfoot, sodden leaves sliding on mud.

She began to walk, lifting her feet carefully, setting them down slowly, the thud of her heartbeat echoing in her ears. The trunks rose like thin spines to tangled balls of branches and dying leaves. A leaf fluttered down into her hair: she grabbed it, and it crumbled to ash. There was a black stain across her hand.

"Kay."

She didn't know where the voice came from. It seemed to be part of the forest, pressing in like the trees.

"Kay."

There was something both compelling and terrible about it. She couldn't move. When she tried to answer, her mouth made no sound. The mud was oozing up around her ankles, gripping tight.

The trees were getting closer.

She watched them come towards her, moving in the corners of her vision.

"Kay."

She woke in the dark, one arm clutching her pillow. There was an odd scent in the room, like freshly turned soil. When she flicked on the bedside lamp, she was sure she saw a black smear in the air.

Once she'd blinked and rubbed her eyes, it was gone.

Chapter 6

"The Pastor will be disappointed." Robert's father put on his coat.

"I'm sorry. But I do need to study. I've got an essay due next week." As always, Robert kept his tone respectful. He hid anything like defiance or fury deep inside, smouldering in a locked box.

His mother sighed, picked up her purse. "Don't work too hard, Robert."

He knew what she was thinking. They'd told him often enough. *You don't need to do that well to get into Texas Bible College.*

"I'll try to make it next Saturday," he said.

His father nodded, mollified.

"There's pecan pie in the refrigerator," his mother said.

Robert waited. The front door closed behind them; the car sputtered into life and growled out of the drive. He walked through the kitchen and out into the back yard, glancing all around for watching neighbours. No-one was outside, and the trees and woodshed screened him from most windows. He stood beneath the ash tree, on a carpet of autumn leaves. As he reached into his pocket, his fingers were shaking with the promise of forbidden pleasure. He pulled out a single, squashed cigarette and a lighter.

He flicked the lighter and watched the flame flare for a moment, before touching it to the end of the cigarette. His mother would be horrified if she found out. His father would be furious. Greedily, he inhaled; he'd got the knack of it now, no longer ended up doubled over coughing. If they knew, they'd stop his allowance, but that wouldn't matter; he had his job at the bookstore. They'd ground him, for sure, even though he'd turned eighteen last month – but it wasn't like he ever went out anyway.

Smoking was just one silent way to rebel. Last week, he'd listened to an illegally-downloaded Black Sabbath song, *Heaven and Hell* – before deleting all evidence from his computer. He knew exactly what his parents would've called his behaviour: piracy *and* Satanism.

In less than a year, he could leave home. He wasn't going to go to Bible College. He was going to head as far out of state as possible. Maybe even to England, if he could get funding. He would study physics and philosophy. On Sunday mornings, he'd stay in bed. He'd smoke and drink. He'd do anything he wanted. And it was starting to look possible now. Upstairs, in his closet, in an unmarked folder, at the bottom of a box of papers, lay his first ever passport.

He stubbed out the cigarette on the patch of earth beneath the tree, the forbidden wisps of smoke mingling with the clay soil. Scratching the dirt with a stick, he buried the stub and brushed leaves across to cover it.

Back in his room, he switched on his computer and logged into Lycopolis, typing "Heidi" and his password, "agnosticism". Adopting Heidi's persona was a relief, a release: she could voice the thoughts he hardly dared acknowledge. But last Sunday, he'd not been able to get the afternoon's demon-summoning off his mind. He'd lain awake long into the night, thinking about the posters around his room: *I am the Way, the Truth and the Life. No-one comes to the Father except through Me. The Fruits of the Spirit are Love, Joy, Peace...*

It was nine o'clock his time, three in the morning, UK-time; he'd set up two clocks on his computer so that he'd always know at a glance what time it was for Kay and Hannah and Mark and Edwin and Seth, who lived six hours in the future, thousands of miles away.

From another hidden folder, he pulled up an email he'd saved, with an invitation to the Nottingham meet-up attached:

"Heidi,"

Doubt you can make it over here, but you're the only one of my favourites who doesn't live in the UK, and I didn't want to leave you out of the invites.

Feel free to send me your thoughts on the game – what improvements you'd like, what new areas you want to see. I value your input.

Seth.

For a few days, he'd thought about flying over to England – but his parents would never agree. Lycopolis was his secret, the place where he was accepted, no questions asked. And if he went to meet up with them all, he'd have to let them know that he was a guy in real life. He'd never *lied* about it – he'd just let their assumptions stand uncorrected. He knew all of their real names, but none of them knew his.

The Chatroom was silent, and when he typed "who?" into the game, he saw that he was the only person online. He felt a twist of disappointment, somewhere between his chest and his stomach. Even though it was late, he'd hoped some people would still be around. It was a Saturday, after all. He wanted to argue morality with Tristram, or banter with Roderic, or try yet again to be a civilising influence on Matilda.

"Evening, Heidi." The words appeared in his game window, in the cyan out-of-character text, with no indication of who was speaking.

Which meant it could only be one person. "Seth?"

"Indeed. You're not usually about at the weekends."

"My parents are out."

"Ah. Illicit gaming, then?"

Robert hesitated. He'd tried, for several months, to keep quiet about real life. He didn't want to talk about his family, his faith – his *parents'* faith. "They wouldn't like Lycopolis."

"Because of the religious thing?"

Robert must've given away more than he'd realised. "Yeah. How do you know?"

"Educated guess. It pulls some pieces together."

"It's difficult sometimes." He wanted to write more, but he was struggling to control the sudden wave of anger that had seized him. It'd welled up in him more and more recently, threatening to break out of that locked box.

"So what do *you* believe?" Seth asked.

Slowly, he typed, "I don't know any more."

There was something chilling, and something very liberating, about seeing it on the screen, blue text on black, stark and irrevocable.

"Good."

"You think? I feel pretty lost." That didn't begin to describe it.

"Is that because you're finally starting to find your way?"

Perhaps it was. Robert found his gaze drawn back to the posters on his wall, though. *I am the Way...*

He typed, "I shouldn't keep you. It's the middle of the night over there, isn't it?"

"I'm not tired."

Robert hesitated, not wanting to get too personal. Not wanting to get too *involved* with the people who he'd have to abandon if his parents ever found out about Lycopolis.

But all the same, he found himself asking, "Is everything okay with you?"

"Yes. Just not tired. Figured I'd stay up, finish organising next weekend. Sorry you can't be there."

"Me too," Robert typed, and he felt that anger again, almost like a pain, an ache, somewhere above his stomach. He wished he could be one of the group, able to join in their conversations in the Chatroom without second-guessing every word he typed.

"Seth, you don't believe in God, do you?"

"No. But I know there is something in this world that goes beyond the everyday, though. Power which most people shy away from."

A year ago, Robert would've ignored this as heretical and deluded. But now, he was curious. "How do you mean?"

"It's a little late at night to give you an entire thesis."

But Robert found himself eager to know. "Something spiritualist? New-agey?" He wouldn't have thought that Seth would be into any of that.

"No. An ancient power, that runs down the centuries. Real. Strong. None of this love-your-neighbour crap."

Robert could feel the pulse quicken through him as he typed, "Then what is it? Do you pray to it or worship it or something?"

"I don't *worship* power. I intend to *use* it."

"How? To do what, I mean?"

"Does it matter? There are no commandments carved in stone."

Perhaps it was time he turned away, properly away, from the increasing emptiness of his religion. Maybe Seth really did have something that could be used or proved.

But before he could ask anything, Seth had carried on. "Anyhow. Are you around on Thursday? Cyric wants to have a chat with Heidi."

Robert glanced at the calendar, with his bookstore shifts marked on. "Yeah. Before 11pm your time's best."

"Excellent. Well, ta-ta, and sweet dreams."

"Night," Robert typed, feeling awkward about *sweet dreams*, till he remembered that of course, Seth thought he was a girl. He closed the game, took his math textbook out of his bag, and finished off his homework. He left it out on his desk: his father would check up on him.

His parents weren't due back for another fifteen minutes. He looked up flights from Houston to London, to see how much it would cost.

He had enough in the bank.

Chapter 7

On Thursday, Edwin skipped school, just like he'd done the day before. It was easier this time. After waiting in the park till nine o'clock, making up bits of a song in his head, he walked home and let himself back in.

He got a sheet of paper, lay on his stomach on his bed, and scribbled down the first few lines of the song. It took him a while, and he got distracted trying to figure out a guitar riff that'd go with it, but eventually he was happy.

Perhaps it involved the words *nightmare* and *blood* a few too many times, but it was better than anything he'd managed to write before. He sat up. What would a Goth do? A shiver ran across the back of his neck and down his spine. A Goth would, surely, read the song out loud, into the stillness of the house.

In the bathroom, he stood in front of the mirror. As he read the lyrics, he imagined a background of screaming guitars, a thudding drum-beat, chanting fans. Once he'd got Mum to agree to Nottingham, he'd ask again about a guitar.

He found himself glancing over his shoulder – as though something might have appeared that he couldn't see in the mirror. Of course there was nothing. As he met the eyes of his reflection, his gaze was drawn fractionally upwards.

There, on his forehead. That bruise was redder than it was before. And suddenly he thought of the mark that the Prince of Nightmares had left on Benedict.

He hurried out of the bathroom and screwed up the song in his hands, feeling shaky, all hot and cold at the same time. The house was really quiet, weirdly quiet. He put his music on, and sat down at his desk, and told himself not to act like a stupid little kid. It was just a bruise.

Slowly, he unscrunched the paper and flattened out his song. It was the best thing he'd ever written; he couldn't just chuck it away. He put it face-down on the desk, and logged into Lycopolis.

It was the middle of the day, so no-one was around, and Ben had been abandoned in a cold underground room in the Haven. Ben was scared. Really, really scared. And Edwin didn't want to role-play with Matilda or the handful of other characters in the Haven. For once, he wasn't in the mood for something dark.

In the game window, Benedict was alone.

A Small Room with Stone Walls
This room is identical to the others along the row. Cold, with a hard bed and a blanket, it smells of damp and worse. There's little light, and no candles. The thick wooden door has no lock on the inside.

Edwin had been playing Lycopolis long enough to pick up on clues pretty easily. He typed "examine door" and was told:

There are deep gouges in the heavy wooden door, on both sides. There's no lock, but the outside has a thick metal ring that matches another on the wall. A chain or padlock could easily be hooked through these.

So it was basically a cell, just used for sleeping quarters. As far as Edwin knew, Matilda didn't actually keep prisoners down here or anything. Seth would've written this area, though: perhaps it was meant to be a dungeon.

An unexpected line of text appeared in the game window.

"Benedict."

There was no-one there.

A few weeks ago, Edwin wouldn't have considered telling Seth he didn't want to play. But they were friends now, and Seth wouldn't say that he was being a crap Goth just for wanting a break from doom-and-gloom.

"Hey Seth?" he typed, in Messenger. "I'm not really in the mood to role-play."

"Well, tell Kay or Hannah or whoever, then."

He frowned. It seemed like they were talking at cross-purposes somehow, though he wasn't sure why. "I mean you, the voice. The Prince."

A pause before Seth said, "Ah."

Edwin felt he needed to offer some explanation. "I only really logged in to chat."

"Bad day? I gather you're bunking off."

"Yeah. I am."

"Excellent. So, what's wrong?"

It was stupid to want to avoid letting Benedict talk to the Prince of Nightmares. It was stupid to want to log out of the game and pretend he wasn't around. But with the bruise and everything, he almost wished he'd never started playing Lycopolis at all.

He couldn't get any of this into words. He just typed, "I don't know."

"Ed, if this is all a bit much, tell me, won't you? Kay keeps reminding me that you're only fourteen."

Why did Kay always have to remember that he was the youngest Lycopolis player? He wondered what she and Seth had been saying about him.

"It's not too much." He pushed the memory of a bad dream to the back of his mind, and when he typed the next words, he tried to make himself believe them. "I'm not frightened or anything."

"Good good. So, on with the game?"

* * *

There was a clatter, a light clink of metal on stone. Benedict raised his head enough to see a chain with a medallion strung on it.

"Take it. Wear it."

The voice didn't allow the possibility of disobedience or refusal. The medallion was a wolf's head, viewed in profile, with a tiny, perfect, blood gem for its eye.

He fastened it around his neck, as though his hands were moving of their own accord.

"Stop it!" Edwin typed.

"Hmm?"

"I don't want him to wear it. Why did you make him put it on?" His heart was thudding hard, and he felt sick. His hand went to his own neck, to the thin chain there. It took him several attempts to unfasten it.

"Why are you so upset, Ed?"

He dropped his medallion onto the desk, not wanting to touch it for a moment longer than necessary. The chain spooled onto the metal wolf's head.

"How did you know about my medallion?" It wasn't in any photo of him – he always wore it underneath his shirt.

"Ed, what the fuck are you talking about?"

"In real life. The one I wear."

There was a long pause, before Seth's next message came. "You've got a real medallion, like the one the Prince just gave to Edwin?"

"Yes!"

But if Seth didn't already know that, how could he possibly have created that identical game item? Edwin typed "examine medallion".

The medallion is silver in hue, strung on a thin chain. The emblem is shaped like a wolf's head, viewed in profile. A tiny ruby is set in the metal for the eye. Two letter 'R's are faintly etched on the back of the medallion.

Letters? Edwin touched his real-life medallion, gingerly. It still carried the warmth of his skin. He turned it over, and traced the scratches on the back with his thumb-nail. They formed faint letters: he'd never realised that before.

R.R. What was that supposed to mean? Initials? Some sort of maker's mark?

"How did you know about it?" he asked Seth, again.

"I didn't."

46

Somehow, that was the most chilling answer Seth could've given – and now he'd suddenly gone offline.

In the game, Edwin typed "remove medallion" but the game told him that the medallion couldn't be unfastened. He'd never seen an item that did that before, never.

His hands shook on the keyboard as he logged out of Lycopolis. The wolf medallion had always been special, his secret. He'd had it ever since he was a tiny kid. Mum had never said much about it, but he knew Dad had given it to her once. He felt protected by it, but more than that, he felt like he still belonged – however faintly and obscurely – to his dad.

It was one of the reasons he'd chosen to play Lycopolis, months ago: the *lyco* part of the name meant wolf. The game had promised a whole world to escape to, somewhere dark and fun.

There was a choking lump in his throat. He couldn't stay indoors. He had to get outside, into the air.

The clouds were heavy with unspilt rain. He headed to the park. As he paced past the deserted tarmac play area, drops of rain began to fall. He kept going anyway. Past the football court, past an ancient shed covered in generations of graffiti, right up to the bushes along the edge of the park.

"Edwin."

The voice was like a fist to the face. He stopped dead, whipped round, but there was no-one nearby. No-one at all, except him.

His heart was thudding hard. He told himself that he'd imagined it. It was just in his head, like hearing snippets of tracks – guitar riffs, lyrics, that sort of thing. But this had been a menacing whisper, so close and real.

Could it have been a trick of the wind, howling across his ears? Or of the rain, coming down like white noise? Yeah. He was just being childish. But the medallion in the game, and the mark on his forehead, and now that voice ...

Edwin made himself stand still in the centre of the park and listen, really *listen,* in case it came again. It didn't. The rain was pouring down, and the wind was plastering his damp hair to his face.

He went home; there wasn't anywhere else he could go. He locked the front door behind him, and remembered to take off his muddy shoes and his wet coat, and crept up the stairs. The house was silent. In the bathroom, he towelled most of the rain from his hair.

He didn't look at the mirror.

Back in his room, he sat on his bed, and tried to slow his breathing. He was just imagining things. Getting over-wrought, Mum would say. He wasn't cracking up. And he definitely wasn't going to think that maybe he was being hunted by something terrifying, something which he caught glimpses of in half-remembered nightmares.

Edwin leant forwards, his hands on his knees. He was okay. He was fine. He switched on the computer, and clung to the normality of it, the beep as it came on, the whirr of the fan and the hum of the hard drive.

Seth was still offline.

But Edwin left a message anyway: "Seth? If you're there, can you come visible? I really need to talk to you." The computer screen was blurry. He drew his sleeve across his eyes.

A window popped up, but it wasn't Seth. It was Kay. "Hey, Ed. Bit early in the afternoon for you, isn't it?"

"Yeah," he typed. And then, feeling the tears rising up from somewhere in his stomach, he added, "Some freaky stuff is happening."

"At school?"

"No. In the game." He told her about it all. The game-and-real medallion, which Seth couldn't possibly have known about. The odd bruise on his forehead, how he couldn't remember getting it. And the voice he thought he'd heard in the park, calling his name. Probably, he sounded like some scared kid. That wasn't how he wanted Kay to think of him. "I know it seems stupid. But I'm not imagining it or making it up."

"I know, I believe you. Did anything else happen?"

"No. But I wish we'd never done that role-play. Summoning the demon." He couldn't bring himself to type the name, *Prince of Nightmares*, couldn't face seeing it on the screen.

"I'm going to talk to Seth about it," Kay said. "In Nottingham. It's gone too far."

"But then what?"

"We get rid of the demon. Banish it, destroy it, whatever." She didn't use the name either.

The front door clicked, and his heart leapt hard. A dozen thoughts flew through his mind: something evil and powerful was after him; it was in his house. He scrambled out of his room, grabbing onto the banisters to look down and ...

"Edwin?"

It was his mum. He was so relieved that he ran down the stairs and flung his arms around her before his brain caught up.

Shit.

He was supposed to be in school.

"Edwin, what's going on? I got a call from the school office."

"Oh," was all he could say, lamely.

"We need to have a talk." There was tiredness in her voice, and that tense note which made his heart clench up.

"Okay," he muttered, and followed her into the kitchen. The clock said it was almost two. He'd forgotten about lunch; he wasn't hungry.

Mum made a cup of tea. "Do you want one?"

"No, thanks."

"Well, like I said. The school rang. Mr Thompson was concerned about you."

"Oh."

"They asked me why you were away yesterday and today."

He shrugged his shoulders. There was nothing to say.

"Edwin, please tell me what's wrong. Is the bullying still going on?"

With everything else that'd happened today, he'd almost forgotten about Darren Miller. He shrugged again.

"Do you know what a shock it was to get that call from your school? How worried I was?"

Edwin imagined a wall of stone around his heart, and stared straight ahead.

"Well, I was terrified, Edwin, I had visions of you involved in all sorts of things. Shoplifting, or ... or drugs, or something."

"Mum! I was just at home, that's all."

"You've got bags under your eyes. Oh, God, Edwin, *is* it drugs?"

"No!" He curled his hands in his pockets, digging his fingernails into his palms.

"Alcohol?"

He kept shaking his head.

"Then what? What?"

"Nothing! Mum, stop it. Don't get upset."

"How can I *not* be upset?" The mug of tea was trembling in her hands, and she put it down. "Edwin, whatever it is, you can tell me. I promise I won't be angry with you. Please just tell me."

He wasn't afraid she'd get angry. He was afraid she'd cry.

"I just wanted to stay away from Darren Miller and those bastards."

For once, she didn't object to his language. She sighed, though. She was going to cry, he knew, she was going to cry for the first time in months and months and it was all his fault.

"There are lots of ways to deal with problems at school. And truanting is not one of them. Promise me you won't ever do it again."

He focused on the table. He wouldn't look at her face, because if he did, all his resolve would just go.

"Edwin, promise me."

"No."

"Fine." There was something brittle and fragile in her voice. "Then you're grounded."

He almost laughed. He never went anywhere, anyway; spent every evening and every weekend in his room.

And then he realised. "But what about Nottingham?"

"If I can't trust you at home –"

"I'll promise not to skip school any more, okay?"

"I didn't think it was a very good idea in the first place, Edwin. I don't even know these people."

They'd been over and over all this. He'd even shown her Kay and Seth's Messenger photos, and given her the list of mobile numbers that had been circulated. "Mum, they're my *friends*. They're my *only* fucking friends."

"Look, we'll talk about this later."

"But –"

"I said, *later*." There was a catch in her voice.

He mumbled, "Okay."

She left the kitchen, and he heard her steps fast on the stairs, heard her bedroom door click shut. He knew she was crying. And he hated her for it, and hated himself even more.

Slowly, he walked up the stairs, and into his own room. He didn't slam the door, just closed it. Then he switched on Media Player, jabbed the mouse at a random album – not caring what; it was all metal anyway – and turned the volume on his speakers right up.

And then the fury which he'd been holding back filled every inch of him. He had no words for how he felt, and no song could ever express it: there was something terrifying and uncontrollable inside him.

He bunched his hand, and struck the side of his fist into his bedroom wall. Again, and again, and again, and the other hand, the whole arm, hard jolts of pain driving out the worst of the anger.

Then he felt an empty calm. He turned the music down. He sat on his bed, and for several long moments, he didn't think anything at all, he just stared down at the floor and knew how alone he was.

His hands hurt. He turned them over and looked at the tiny red pin-pricks beneath the skin on his wrists. They'd be gone tomorrow.

Under his shirt sleeve, there was a hot red mark across his forearm. He looked at it, then pulled the sleeve back down. It might turn into a bruise, purple first, then yellowing. But that didn't matter. He'd keep it hidden. No-one would see.

He lay on his bed, buried himself in the duvet and in the music, and sleep reached for him, wrapped its arms around him and drew him down, and down, and into the forest.

Chapter 8

Kay dreamt about the forest again. She walked, then jogged, then ran along a line of trees, trying to find a way in, but at each gap there was something wrong. A deep trench; stagnant, black water; a wolf that snarled and leapt.

She jolted awake, and clutched her duvet tight, glad to be out of the dream. She looked at her phone. It was three forty-five.

Dawn light was beginning to seep through the curtains before she got back to sleep; when she woke again, it was almost ten o'clock. She couldn't shake the dream from her mind. She had no lectures on Fridays, so she put on her dressing gown, went as far as the kitchen to get toast and Marmite and a mug of milky tea, then huddled back under her covers.

Her toast seemed to stick in her throat. She gave up trying to eat and just sat there, hands wrapped around her mug of tea. None of this would seem so awful if it wasn't for poor Edwin getting dragged in. She'd made herself stay calm when he told her about his bruise, the voice, the medallion. But she hadn't been able to get any of it out of her mind.

There was a knock, rapidly repeated, at her door; she jumped, would've spilt her tea if the mug hadn't been half-empty. She climbed out of her cocoon of duvet and blankets, stepped over the pair of jeans lying on the floor, and opened the door a crack.

"Hey Brandon."

If he'd been anyone else, Kay would've been embarrassed about being in pyjamas and a dressing gown … but she couldn't imagine Brandon expecting a dressing gown to be some sort of fashion statement, and she didn't exactly think of him as a *boy*, just as *Brandon*.

His feet were bare, and he was wearing an inside-out T-shirt.

"Your T-shirt's inside-out," she said.

"I know."

"Oh."

"I didn't like the other side," he said.

She peered at his chest. "Why, what's on it?"

"Nothing. Kay, will you teach me to play that game?"

She felt as though she'd left her brain in bed; she wasn't able to keep up with a Brandon conversation yet. "What game – oh, Lycopolis?"

"Yes."

Her first thought was to keep him out of it; no-one else should get involved. But Brandon could help her – she'd need someone on her side, if she had to stand up to Seth. And the summoning was done with. Brandon couldn't get drawn in by the demon.

Officially, Lycopolis was still in the beta stage: invite only. A few months ago, Seth had manually created everyone's accounts. Now, they had a simpler system of invite codes. And as Seth's assistant, she had the power to issue those – technically speaking.

She hesitated. "Sure thing, I'll come and set you up with an account. I'll just grab a shower first."

Once she was dressed, she generated an invite code and wrote it on her hand with a Biro, before heading down the corridor. She knocked. "Brandon?"

Opening the door, he stepped back to let her in. She'd never been in his room before – as far as she knew, no-one on the corridor had. The walls were blank, and there were no flyers or timetables pinned to the noticeboard: just a straight line of drawing pins, exactly half-way down one side.

He sat at his desk: no paper or worksheets in sight, only a laptop. On the bookshelf above sat a row of maths textbooks; nothing else, no novels, no notebooks. Kay perched on the edge of his bed. Every other room she'd been in was filled with *stuff* – books, rugs, kettles, fairy lights, televisions, wind-chimes, weird gap-year souvenirs.

Brandon looked round at her, expectantly.

"Pull up a browser window," she said, "And go to Lycopolis dot co dot uk."

He looked at the front page of the site. Kay normally skipped straight past it to the forums, but found herself reading it too, trying to

54

remember the excitement she'd felt back in July, the first time she stumbled across this little corner of the internet. She was drawn in by the promise of adventure, of fun, and of something more than that – the sense that Lycopolis was somewhere she might *belong*. She'd emailed Seth, fumbling for words to outline the character she wanted to play: a knight, someone good and righteous.

But had something dark been at work even then, drawing her in – drawing them all in?

The city of Lycopolis, once renowned throughout the Kingdom, has been beset by the forces of darkness for centuries. Adventurers, warriors and ordinary folk rub shoulders in the sprawling streets. Bravery is prized, though lawlessness rages in the southern part of the city. Whoever you are, whatever road you have travelled, you will find a home here.

Once Brandon had logged into the game, she said, "Type in this code," and read out the numbers from her hand.

He put it in, then began filling in his account details. Email address. Password. Date of birth. He stopped at the "Create Your Character" screen.

"Who should I be?" he asked.

"Who do you *want* to be?" That was what role-playing was all about. When she'd created Tristram, she'd tapped into the books she'd loved as a child, the stories and games that she and Tom had invented.

Brandon set the gender of his character to "male", chose the generic "adventurer" class, then paused. "I'll be a knight."

"Okay." She was pleased, even a bit flattered: he'd watched Tristram and the knights in action, and he wanted to join them. He'd be one of hers, someone she could keep an eye on and protect.

Not that she'd done a very good job with Edwin – and he played Tristram's squire. She should've persuaded him to tell her what was happening between Benedict and Lord Cyrric.

Brandon typed in the name "Sir Wilhelm", and a description: "A tall figure in a hooded cloak. Keeps to himself. Armed."

He logged in and looked at the screen, then back at her. "These windows have different purposes?"

"Yep." That was something else she remembered from when she started playing: feeling bewildered by the array of small and large boxes on the screen, text scrolling in each.

She pointed to the biggest window, which ran from the bottom to top of the screen, covering two-thirds of the width. "This one's the game window. It's where you are – the room you're in, you call it a 'room' even if it's a bit of street. It's where the action takes place."

He nodded, then pointed at the small windows down the side. "What are these two?"

"Chatroom," she said, pointing at the top one. Several chats had appeared in response to his arrival: "Hey newbie," from another knight player, and "Welcome to the game, Brandon!" from Hannah.

"Everyone can see the Chatroom. It's for talking out-of-character ... see, your name's set to *Brandon* for it. You can change that if you want. The little window in the middle here, that's your inbox. If someone sends you a message, it appears there."

He nodded, and began trying out commands: "look" "go north" "inventory".

She spent the next twenty minutes watching him, occasionally answering questions. He picked it up impressively fast. He moved around the gardens of newbie central, methodically trying every direction.

"If you go north-westish from here," she said, "You'll get to the beginner quests."

"I'm exploring." He didn't look round, intent on the screen.

"Okay ... did you have any more questions?"

"No. I'm working it out."

He was intent on what he was doing: not offended, or annoyed with her – just focused.

She stood. "I'll leave you to it."

After half an hour, she gave up trying to read: she couldn't concentrate. Her thoughts kept spiralling back to Lycopolis – to Seth, and the Prince of Nightmares. She'd tried to believe that it was just a story, all innocent fun. But after what Edwin had told her about the medallion, and after the weird, vivid, dreams, she found herself convinced that this was anything but a game.

Maybe Seth didn't know what he was doing – maybe he'd stumbled onto something by accident, and had been intrigued enough that he didn't want to let it go. If so, she could explain to him that he *had* to stop. But would he listen?

She needed to check on everyone – make sure that Seth wasn't forcing the storyline further along without her. She logged in. Tristram had a message from Matilda: *I need to speak with you. Come to the Haven alone. Unarmed. Unarmoured.*

In Messenger, Hannah asked her, "Have you chatted to Ed much recently?"

"Yeah. Yesterday. He's pretty upset. I need to talk to you about it – but not right now, tomorrow, at the meet-up." She had no chance of convincing the others over Messenger: she needed to be face-to-face with them. That way, she could show them the mark on Edwin's forehead. She could see how they reacted if she asked about nightmares.

Pushing some of her anger away onto Tristram, she took him into the Haven's dark streets. He wasn't going to back away; he'd go in and get Benedict, take him safely home.

* * *

Tristram strode through the streets, and perhaps something about his expression stopped Matilda's men from stepping forwards to challenge him. As he drew nearer to the centre of the Haven, he saw two thugs bullying a thin little boy who could hardly have been older than ten.

"Stop that," he said, striding over.

The thugs weren't long out of childhood themselves, both gangly. There was a brief flash of fear across their faces before they scowled at him.

"Piss off."

Tristram's hands bunched into fists. But it would be foolish beyond measure to get into a fight here: he was not hubristic enough to suppose that he had any chance of taking on all Matilda's men, and Matilda herself.

57

He was here for Benedict. Nothing more – and nothing less. No doubt horrors went on in here every day, horrors which he knew nothing of and was powerless to prevent. Attempting to intervene on this one particular day would accomplish nothing.

So he walked on, wishing he could not hear the two thugs jeering after him, and the boy screaming "Let go of me!"

Feeling naked without armour or weapons, he made his way on through the narrow streets. The night was bitterly cold, as though winter had set in early; it was almost with relief that he greeted Matilda.

"Tristram. You're unarmed?"

"Yes." He was in no mood for pleasantries, and she was not someone who cared about them. "Let's get this done with. What do you want in exchange for Benedict?"

"He's not for sale. Come in."

There was no choice but to follow her. Instead of leading him to their normal meeting place – her podium above a huge fighting pit – she turned abruptly, stalked down a corridor, and shoved open a badly scarred wooden door. The room had half-a-dozen chairs, one lying broken against the wall.

Matilda slammed the door shut. "Sit down, Tristram."

He sat. There was no point antagonising her unnecessarily. "At least state some terms. What do you want? We can offer money –"

"I told you." She sat opposite, and almost spat the words at him, "He's not for sale."

"Listen to me, Matilda –"

"No, you listen to *me*."

How he longed to settle this with a sword. She wouldn't refuse a match to the death – but, no, that was her way, not his.

"Tristram, get it through your thick skull that Benedict belongs to *me*. It pleased my Prince to give him to me."

That drove frustration from his mind, replaced it with a creeping cold fear. "*My* Prince?"

"I said *the*."

"You said *my*."

They matched glares.

"I know what I fucking said. The Prince gave me Benedict. And he's going to give me far, far more."

The cold feeling spread. "Matilda," he said, slowly, "What are you expecting from this demon?"

Her eyes narrowed, suspiciously. "I'm not about to share my plans with you. Now listen. You're going to ally with me."

"To what end?" he asked, keeping his voice calm, despite the fury that raged in him. He could see where this was going. She would make demand after demand, with Benedict as collateral. And, inevitably, it would escalate, forcing him to a point where it would be madness to carry on. Where he would have to say, *enough*, and abandon Benedict to his fate.

"I want this city. You can help me overthrow Cyrric and take it."

He hadn't been prepared for quite this level of megalomania – or insanity. "And then?" he asked.

"And then you and your precious knights can fuck right off and leave me to it. Unless any of them want to join me."

"And if I refuse?"

She looked at him, holding his gaze for a long moment. He wondered if she would leave all the threats unspoken, but then she said, "I've got the power of life and death over everyone in my Haven. If I executed Benedict, no-one would so much as blink."

That wasn't a direct threat. And Matilda had never, in his experience, been anything other than straightforward. The clenched feeling in his chest relaxed, just slightly.

He said, quietly, "I don't believe you would kill him."

"Why the fuck wouldn't I?"

"Because that's not what the demon wants." It was more than a guess: somewhere, in a place of chill certainty, he knew that the Prince had some greater and darker plan.

She glanced away, at the sawdust on the rough wooden floor. "You should have knelt to the Prince too, Tristram."

"But I did not. And you did."

Perhaps he imagined it, but he thought he saw her shudder.

"Has it talked to you?" she asked, her tone so belligerent that he wondered what she was hiding.

"The demon?"

She nodded.

"Yes."

Her arms were folded. She looked at him for a long moment, then yelled through the door, "Bring the kid!"

They stood there, watching one another in silence, until the door creaked open and Benedict was shoved inwards. Matilda grabbed him, pulled him away from Tristram.

His face was pale – which highlighted the bruise on his jaw and cheekbone all the more – and he looked like he'd not slept. All instincts of self-preservation and prudence overridden, Tristram took a stride towards him.

Matilda glowered at him. "Not so fucking fast."

His fists clenched of their own accord. He had never struck her, had never struck any woman, but suddenly he wanted to lash out, to hurl her into the nearest wall, to *hurt* her. Yet that was, surely, what the Prince had intended – to divide them, irrevocably. Last night, Tristram's dreams had been filled with blood.

"Let me see that he's all right," he said.

"Fine." She pushed Benedict forwards. He stumbled and almost fell. Tristram made himself stand still, though every impulse was telling him to reach for the boy.

"Ben," he said. "Have they hurt you?"

Benedict hesitated, glanced sideways at Matilda, clearly scared to speak.

"He's alive and standing," she said.

"And visibly bruised," Tristram said. "Ben?"

"I'm all right," he said.

He neither sounded nor looked it.

"Sit," Matilda said, to Tristram, and gave Benedict a shove towards another chair. The boy half-fell into it.

Tristram sat, and longed for a blade in his hand. He wished she was a man, wished he faced her on the battlefield. And then a glint of light caught his eye; Benedict was wearing a medallion, a metal emblem on the end of a thin chain.

"What's that?" Tristram asked him, gesturing.

Benedict's shoulders slumped downwards, and he mumbled something inaudible at his knees. Tristram leant towards him, and was horrified, almost sickened, to see dried blood on the boy's neck. As he stared up at Matilda, she said, "That's what we need to talk about."

60

"Then talk," he said.

"He claims the amulet was given to him. By the Prince."

"Then why the hell is he wearing it?"

Matilda said, sharply, to Benedict, "Speak up, tell him."

"He – the demon – put it around my neck. It w-won't come off."

"Try it if you want," Matilda said, leaning back in her chair, tipping it onto two legs. "Seems like the only way to remove it would be to slice his head from his body."

"Have you seen this demon again?" Tristram's concern for Benedict warred with his fears for the city – for what Matilda might do, intoxicated by the lure of power.

"I've not *seen* him," she said. "I've heard his voice."

"And?"

"He makes promises."

"And you trust them?"

She rocked the chair forwards suddenly, the two front legs smacking against the floor with a crash. Benedict flinched.

"I'm not stupid," she said.

"I know."

There was silence for a few long moments.

Cautiously, he said, "We're stronger when we're together, not in opposition. Ask yourself why this demon is trying to make war between us."

She looked about to snap something in response, but then the words seemed to die on her lips. "Did you hear that?"

He shook his head. He'd heard nothing, except the ongoing rain and the wind.

"The voice." She stood, drawing her knives.

Tristram stood too. If this was some new madness of hers, he was quite prepared to seize Benedict and run.

But Benedict was suddenly on his feet as well, backing away into a corner, his arms held crossed in front of him as though warding something away.

"Ben?" Tristram strode over to him, followed the boy's gaze, and met only thin air. What were they hearing and seeing that he could not? Was it the same voice that had woven his dreams, that had drawn blood-soaked pictures in his mind?

He put his arm around Benedict. The boy was shivering.

Matilda had dropped to a half-crouch, eyes darting about the room. "Leave," she said to Tristram.

"No. Matilda, what's it saying to you?"

Her eyes were glazed, as though she was drunk or drugged. Turning to Benedict he saw, with horror, the same look. He reached for the thin metal chain, tried to lift it from the boy's skin – but Benedict gave an "Ow!" and a pinprick of blood welled up.

He let the chain drop.

"Leave," Matilda said again.

"Whatever it's telling you, Matilda, it's a lie. Don't trust it. It's playing you for a fool."

That seemed to get through to her, to his relief. Her eyes refocused on him. She said, with almost a plea in her voice, "Tristram, can't you hear it?"

"No." Damn it; he had no weapon, no armour, and his enemy was invisible and, it seemed, only audible to Matilda and Benedict. "Ben, what's it saying?"

"I don't know, sir, I can't hear it. I just know it's *there*."

So Tristram said, loudly, "If you've got something to say to Matilda, why not say it to us all? What are you afraid of?"

The floor shook beneath them; he was pushed back into the wall, losing his grip on Benedict. Matilda was thrown off balance, smacking into a chair. She crashed to the floor with it.

A column of black smoke appeared in the room.

Tristram stepped forwards. "Benedict, stay behind me."

But the demon's attention seemed to be fixed upon Matilda, who was lying on the ground. Tristram could hear its words now, and not just the words themselves; he could hear the force of them, the way they gripped and pulled. And it wasn't even him they were aimed at.

"I could give you everything, Matilda, this whole city – if only you'd trust me."

She was trying to stand, Tristram could see, but she was struggling – as though the tendrils of black smoke that coiled towards her were holding her down.

"And what've you promised Cyrric and that fucker Roderic?" she asked.

"That's no concern of yours."

"Have you promised all three of them the city?" Tristram asked. "You're lying to someone."

The demon's voice was menacing. *"I told you. Send him away from here."*

"No," Matilda said.

"We had an agreement."

"It's over," she said. And, despite all his earlier fury at her, despite his anger at the way she'd treated Benedict, Tristram still felt a certain admiration for her courage.

"That's not for you to decide."

"Yes it is." She was still trying to stand – he could see the muscles in her arms straining against the floor.

The roar of the wind was suddenly louder. Matilda gave a cry, as if hurt. And, damn it, he had the Code and months of a grudging friendship with her. Unarmed, he stepped forwards, and said, "Let her alone. Whatever agreement you had is over."

The black mist began to seep towards him. Now he could feel its power, the heavy weight it gave the air. *"And wouldn't you rather I kill her? Haven't you seen the terror in that boy's face? Haven't you seen the bruises on him?"*

Unbidden, those dreams of blood rose up in his mind again. He heard himself say, as though from a distance, "You gifted him to her."

The black mist drifted towards Benedict. *"And now he's mine to reclaim. Whenever I see fit."*

"No!"

"If you truly wish to keep him from me, slit his throat yourself. It would be a merciful death."

"Never," Tristram said, and would have said more, but there was a laugh, like the branch of a tree creaking and cracking and about to fall. And the black mist was gone.

Matilda was sprawled on the floor.

Benedict was shaking. Tristram said, "I'm going to take you home."

"I betrayed you."

"It doesn't matter." Though it did, because of the guilt he saw in the boy's downcast eyes. "We'll put things right."

If only he could feel the conviction with which he managed to say that.

Benedict whispered, "Thank you."

Tristram patted his shoulder, before walking over to Matilda. He crouched beside her. She was conscious.

"Matilda?"

Her knives were on the floor, within reach. He could grab one, bring down swift judgement, ensure that she could never harm Benedict, or any of his people, again.

But what would that make him?

Taking her arm, he helped her to sit – and she did not shake him off, which was disturbing.

"Are you hurt?" he asked.

"I'll live," she said, hoarsely.

"Good."

Outside, the rain was hammering down harder.

"Stay till it stops," she said. Her voice was strained with, he suspected, the effort of hiding pain. "You'll drown out there."

Tristram nodded.

Pulling herself to her feet, she said, "Fucking *hell*."

"Want me to get someone?" he asked.

"I said, I'll live." She sounded more tired than angry. "Could do with a damn good drink, though. Where the fuck are my knives?"

He picked them up for her. She took them, sheathed them. "I'll see if we've still got any of that northern stuff."

As soon as she'd gone, he turned to Benedict. "Ben, I am truly sorry I left you here."

The boy sat down, shaking his head. "You had to. It's all right. I'm all right."

"Really?"

Silence.

He picked up one of the fallen chairs, righted it, pulled it round to sit next to Benedict. "They beat you?"

"No..." Benedict touched his hand to his chin. "Couple of punches."

He said it as though it didn't bother him, but Tristram caught the shiver in his voice. The boy wasn't used to rough treatment, and Tristram wished he could've kept it that way.

64

For the first time, he realised how cold Benedict must be, wearing just an undershirt. No tunic of maroon and gold, of course; no doubt Matilda had stripped him of that as soon as she'd brought him here.

"Here." He took off his own tunic and handed it to Benedict.

Benedict looked at him, startled for a moment, then smiled. "Thanks." A pause. "Sir?"

"Yes?"

"Is it ... is it really going to be possible to make things right again?"

How he wished he could just tell some comforting lie. But the boy who looked at him, pale, exhausted, but steadfast despite it, deserved to be treated as more than a child. "I don't know, Ben. But I pray that we can."

Chapter 9

Seth had spent the last fifteen minutes on the phone to Edwin's mother. He was starting to get a headache. "Do you want to read the numbers back to me?"

She did: his mobile, Kay's, and the hotel's front desk. "Thank you – I know I worry too much. But it's not often he goes anywhere on his own."

In the background, Seth could hear Edwin saying "Mu-um!"

"He can give me a ring if he runs into any trouble," Seth said.

"Yes. Yes, and I'll see him safely onto the train at this end."

Edwin was audible again. "No, I'm going to get the bus to the station. Mum, give me the phone. You're really embarrassing."

Pressing the phone closer to his ear, Seth listened to the whispered conversation.

"Please don't talk to me like that, Edwin. I'm sure Seth wouldn't talk to his mother in that sort of tone."

Seth hadn't spoken to his mother for years.

"Let *me* talk to him, Mum!"

"Just a minute, Edwin." Her voice came down the line clearly again. "And you will ring me, won't you, if there are any problems?"

"Of course," Seth said.

"Thank you. Edwin would like a word."

Seth could hear footsteps: Edwin was stomping off somewhere with the phone.

"Sorry about that. She kept going on and on that she wanted to talk to whoever was organising it."

"It's fine," Seth said, rubbing his forehead with the fingertips of his free hand.

"I could find my way there perfectly well on my own."

"I know. Ed, bring your medallion, would you?"

There was a pause. "Why?"

"I want to take a look at it."

"I think it'd be best if I just leave it here. Or throw it away or—"

"No! You need to keep it, Ed, so we can figure out what's going on."

Edwin mumbled something.

"What?"

"It freaks me out a bit."

"I know. But bring it along, yeah?"

There was another long silence before Edwin said, "Okay."

"Good good." The headache wasn't going away. He needed more sleep. "So, looking forward to tomorrow?"

"Yeah."

"Just *yeah*?"

"I ... I don't want to be in the way."

"Ed, you won't be."

"But I'll be the youngest..."

"We *want* you along, okay? It'll be fun. You'll have a great time."

"Yeah. Yeah, I know." A bit of enthusiasm returned. "It'll be really cool to see everyone."

"Exactly. And I'll meet you at Nottingham station, at noon."

Later that evening, Seth pulled up the Lycopolis database, loaded the SQL query which joined *PlayerCharacter* with *Inventory* with *Items*, and searched for "medallion".

It was definitely only Benedict who had one. Seth copied the row of details – not just the description, but the Yes/No flags for various properties – and printed them out. He'd see exactly how close a fit this was for Edwin's real medallion.

Next, he logged into Lycopolis, invisibly. In Lord Cyrric's palace – which no-one else could access – he typed in the command to create a copy of the medallion. The game returned the message he'd expected: *Only one Wolf Medallion may exist at any given time. This item is already owned by a citizen of Lycopolis.*

He'd modify the database live, never mind if it threw an error and booted everyone from the game. He scrolled through to find the row for the medallion – the newest item, ID 2520 – and put the cursor in the column for "Is Unique?"

He deleted the 1, typed a 0, hit enter.

It lasted for a fraction of a second, then changed straight back to a 1.

Seth stared at the screen. Methodically, he altered various settings on other items – Lotus Poison, a Notched Sword, a Torn Leather Bag. The changes stayed: he pulled the items into existence in the game, just to make sure. But whenever he tried to edit the medallion – the name, the description, its properties, anything – it just reverted to the previous settings.

All evening, he stayed invisible in Lycopolis. There was no new activity from the Prince, nothing unusual at all. He watched Tristram meet with Heidi, the two of them forming a wary alliance with Matilda. He watched the other knights patrol the city, and threw an orc raiding party at them. It was swiftly and efficiently dispatched. After that, though, he moved Cyrric – still invisible – back into the palace, away from the streams of scrolling text.

To distract himself from the game, he dealt with emails from his non-Lycopolis websites. There were a few refunds to approve for disgruntled customers: he sent the money back. No point quibbling. For all he knew, it *had* been an inferior batch. He never sampled the merchandise himself.

His thoughts kept tugging towards Nottingham. The Prince. The forest. It'd crept back into his dreams. He'd resisted it, of course, had retained enough lucidity to pull away from it, to turn the dreams back. But every night, the trees were a little closer.

There was a loud beep. He went to the Lycopolis window to see what the alert was: he had several for different strings of text. Nothing in the Chatroom needed his attention – no mention of "Seth" or "Cyrric".

Cyrric should have been alone in his palace. But there were the three words that had trigged off his alert. The same ones that had drawn him straight to Matilda and Tristram and Benedict's scene the previous day.

Prince of Nightmares.

It was the first time it had appeared when Cyrric was alone. The first chance he had to actually talk with it. He switched to out-of-character mode, so his words would appear not from "Cyrric" but from "Seth".

And then he paused, fingers curled at the edge of the keyboard. He had no idea what he should say.

On the screen, two words appeared. *"Hello, Seth."*

He found himself catching his breath.

"I've missed you, Seth."

He forced his hands to move. "I made your world."

"I need more."

"I know," he typed. "Tomorrow, Nottingham, I'm getting them together in real life."

"I need more."

He couldn't force away the fear that gripped at his stomach, but he could ignore it. "What? What more?"

"Come to me."

He smelt wet soil and trees heavy with rain, felt a cold wind on his face. And then it was gone.

Without conscious thought, he'd drawn back from the keyboard, his hands clenched protectively. "No," he said, out loud. "That's not going to happen." Grabbing the mouse, he closed Lycopolis. He hurried out of the room and stood in the kitchen, hands planted firmly on the breakfast bar, taking deep breaths.

He wasn't a frightened little kid now. He could handle this – of course he could. This was what he'd wanted, the Prince's power reaching beyond the game. There was proof now: Edwin's medallion. Mark's nightmares.

The red mark on his own forehead.

He'd written it all into the journal: dates, times, facts, details.

Turning the thick pages, he looked over it again. Perhaps it wasn't, yet, too late to back out. He wouldn't, though. Granted, some events had been unexpected – but he was still perfectly in control.

Leaving the journal, he went and got a coffee. Tomorrow, they'd be together in Nottingham. Mark. Hannah. Edwin. And Kay, who was bringing Brandon – he'd decided it wasn't worth arguing with her about that.

On his desk, a sketch in his journal stared up at him. The forest.

70

He'd closed the book. Hadn't he?

He slammed it shut now, and set his half-empty mug on top of it.

The printer whirred, making him jump. It was just going into standby. He was tired. He hadn't been sleeping well. The headache lingered, like tight fingers around his skull. All of that was making him edgy.

He thought about going out, heading to a club, trying to relive the student days when he'd blotted out the nightmares with vodka and thudding music and girls.

That wasn't going to work, though. Not any more.

Leaving the mug on top of the journal, he went to brush his teeth. He examined his reflection. His hair was tangled: he must have been running a hand through it earlier. When he combed it straight, he could see the mark on his forehead.

Tomorrow morning, he needed to be at St Pancras by ten. Time for bed, even though he was still wired from the coffee.

There was a crash in the lounge. He found the mug broken on the floor, coffee staining the carpet.

The journal stood open again, at the same sketch of the forest: trees he'd drawn years ago towering to the top of the page, tips brushing against the edges of the paper.

He slammed it shut and shoved it in the bottom desk drawer. Locked the drawer. Picked up the broken pieces of the mug and threw them into the bin. Left the room without a backwards glance.

So the Prince was stepping things up a notch. Seth could handle that. He *wanted* that. Because all he needed to do was to keep going, and the whispered promises would all become true. He'd seen only a fraction of its power. Once it was brought fully into the world – under his careful control – then the possibilities were almost limitless.

In bed, he fixed his eyes on the ceiling, staring up through the dark. Sleep tugged at him, eddies dragging his thoughts around and around, fracturing them into a sinking swirl. Lines of computer code. Long sleepless nights. A list of names, waiting for payback. And before all that, a child, lost in a forest ...

Chapter 10

Edwin spent most of the train journey reading the school library's battered copy of *The Selected Works of Edgar Allan Poe.* Since he was going to a pub called the *Pit and Pendulum,* he reckoned he should read the story it was named after.

It held him gripped, right to the last line. It had the sort of imagery, the sort of thoughts behind it that he loved in the metal Seth sent him, in the Goth art sites he browsed online. The rats, the slow swing of the pendulum, fumbling in the dark, getting lost and mixed up, the red-hot walls closing in ... the whole thing was at just the right level of clever and spooky and scary.

He finished the story a little way before Nottingham, then sat staring out of the window, waiting impatiently for the train to finally, finally, reach the station. He slung his rucksack on, followed the crowd off the train, down the platform and up a staircase and out into a wide entrance place with a few shops at each side and a coffee booth in the centre, in front of big glass windows.

He looked for Seth. Lots of people were walking around: men in business suits, old ladies, a woman with a couple of little kids. There were a group of skaters near the benches, their boards upended. Edwin kept a wary eye on them.

He checked the time on his phone: it was five to twelve. The huge station clock agreed. Seth probably wouldn't be here for a few minutes. He took his rucksack off, slipped his hand into the side pocket to check that the wolf medallion was still there. Nothing weird had happened for several days. The medallion was just a little lump of metal. Except when he'd picked it up from the shelf that morning, he'd felt a tingle up his arms. He'd almost decided to just leave it there ... but Seth had asked him to bring it.

He put the rucksack down and as he straightened up, a voice said, "Edwin, I presume?"

Seth was pretty much how Edwin had imagined from his profile picture. He was tall, and his hair was cut longish and floppy without looking gay. He wore dark cords and a grey denim jacket over a shirt which, unlike Edwin's sweater, didn't seem to have spent all week in a heap on the floor.

"Hey," Edwin said, and found himself suddenly nervous. Did he look sort of stupid, with collar-length hair and studded bracelets and head-to-toe black?

"Love the hair," Seth said.

The shy feeling faded, and Edwin had to stop himself from grinning, because there was no computer screen between him and Seth now, nothing to shield him.

"Right. Taxi," Seth said, and gestured towards the doors out into the car park. Edwin followed along. He was a bit relieved that Seth was there to deal with things like talking to the driver. He buckled himself in.

"Pit and Pendulum," Seth said, then, when the driver didn't seem to have much clue where it was, "Never mind, just drop us in the centre, at Market Square."

He sat in the back with Edwin and didn't bother with a seat belt. Edwin wished he'd not put his on either. He wanted to take it off and explain it was just force of habit, drilled into him by Mum's nagging. But if Seth hadn't noticed, that'd just draw attention to it.

"So, having a better week, away from school?" Seth asked.

"Mmm, I'm not bunking off any more."

"Oh?"

"Yeah. The school rang Mum ... she made a load of fuss about it. I had to promise her I'd stop, if she let me come this weekend."

Seth stretched out his legs. "And you wouldn't want to break a promise to your mum."

"Well, not one she'd find out about. Some stuff, I couldn't care less – like, I promised I wouldn't drink any alcohol, but if I did, she'd never know."

Seth smiled. "True. I seem to recall saying I'd take good care of you, though. Anyway, what're you doing about those cretins at school?"

74

"Um. Not much. I dunno what I can do." He liked the word *cretins*. It summed them up, and dismissed them, all in one breath. Cretins. He wouldn't use it to their faces, though.

"Well, we'll get it sorted out."

"Yeah," he said, and found himself grinning, which really wasn't very Goth. Seth had said *we. We'll get it sorted out.* Seth actually cared, unlike the teachers. And understood, unlike his mum. Plus, Seth was the sort of person who always knew what to do.

They drove past shops and houses and the same kind of stuff that was in cities everywhere, then into a more built-up area with bigger shops and taller buildings, and teenagers and students huddled about on the streets. The taxi stopped; Edwin got out, Seth paid the driver.

"This way, Ed." Seth took hold of his shoulders and turned him around. Edwin didn't mind. It was the kind of thing a big brother might do.

They walked past a few shops and restaurants and down a street at the corner of the square. Edwin looked at the metal strip along the middle of the road, and the wire overhead.

"Tram lines," Seth said.

"Oh, right." And then he saw the sign across the street: "Pit & Pendulum" in a big gothic font. On either side of the sign there was a flaming torch in a metal thing. It really did look like something out of Edgar Allan Poe. He'd only actually read three of the stories in the book so far, but that was plenty to get an idea of the atmosphere.

All he could say was, "Wow!"

"I rather thought you'd like it."

They walked across the street. The windows of the pub were full of old-fashioned jars and bottles, like some sort of ancient chemist's shop. The blackboard outside offered "Seven Deadly Sins" and listed each by name, along with things like "grenadine, orange, lime."

Seth saw him looking at the sign and said, "They're cocktails. Want one?"

He'd never had any cocktails – at least, he was pretty sure vodka and Coke didn't really count. "Yeah, maybe."

Pushing the door open, Seth gestured him through. The pub was wonderfully gloomy and decorated with skulls and things that looked like rusted old weapons.

"Downstairs," Seth said, "We'll get a nice quiet booth there."

Mirrors lined the stairs, and half-way down, on the wide bit where the stairs turned, there was a huge chair with carved arms and red velvet cushions. Edwin gazed into the mirrors, watching his and Seth's reflections. His head only came up to Seth's shoulder. And Seth looked ... well, he looked *good*, relaxed. Edwin wasn't too sure about his own style. Was he properly Goth? Did the new bracelets give the impression that he was trying too hard?

"There, that one will do nicely," Seth said, and led him to a table in the corner. It was in a booth, with wooden side walls right up to the ceiling. Behind the table, against the actual wall, was a long bench with a dark red leather seat, and arched seat-backs ending in gothic points. The wall above it was stone, with a couple of metal rings dangling from it; Edwin peered up at them.

"Handcuffs," Seth said.

"Cool!" He slung his rucksack on the bench and sat down. Seth's bag was a lot less battered-looking than his. Which figured. No-one would chuck *Seth's* stuff around.

"What do you want to drink? One of the Sins?" Seth asked. "I'm buying."

"Um." He didn't really drink alcohol much. Back in the summer, he'd had a couple of orange Bacardi Breezers at Aunty Sue's barbecue. And occasionally, when Mum was out or having a nap on a weekend afternoon, he'd put a splash of rum or vodka into his Coke. But that was pretty much it.

"Maybe just a Coke?" he said.

Seth's eyebrows went up, slightly.

Edwin didn't want to look like a complete wuss. "Um, I mean, a Coke and vodka."

"As opposed to a vodka and Coke?"

Maybe Seth was teasing him; he wasn't sure. "Yeah, um, whichever."

"Excellent. We'll start on the Sins once everyone's here."

Seth went off to the bar. In the centre of the table, there was a clear panel – plastic, Edwin thought, not glass – and beneath it there were various Goth-looking things: a pentagram on a chain, an envelope with a wax-stamped seal, and a skull with a rose in its teeth.

"Here you go," Seth handed him his drink and sat next to him, with a glass of red wine. He gestured towards the staircase. "Aha."

"The others?" Edwin turned round, eagerly. There were a couple of people at the bottom of the stairs. Nearest was a guy who wore a long-sleeved T-shirt that looked like two shirts cut in half and stitched together down the middle. It was cool; Edwin would have to try it some time, though Mum would probably moan at him.

He was pretty sure that the girl was Kay. He found himself both wanting and not wanting to look at her. She had her coat on, so he couldn't really see what she was wearing, except for dark blue jeans. Her hair was chestnut brown, plaited down her back.

He gulped down some more of his vodka and Coke.

"Kay and, I assume, Brandon," Seth said, raising a hand slightly. "They've spotted us."

They came over. Kay said, "Hey Seth! And Ed, right?"

He couldn't stare at his drink for much longer. "Um, hi," he said, and stood up.

Unexpectedly, she hugged him. Girls never hugged him, only Mum and Grandma – and he didn't usually let them, any more. But it felt good, really good, to have someone's arms around him. She was hardly any taller than him. He was so close he could smell her hair: it was like coconut. He'd never smelt a girl's hair before.

And then she let go of him, and he had to make himself let go too, because it would be really embarrassing if he ended up sort of clinging to her.

"Good to see you again," Seth said.

"Thanks. Oh, hang on, before I forget, I've got your scarf."

"Ta."

Edwin gazed at the table. So she and Seth hadn't only *met* before, Seth had actually given her his scarf to wear. Did that mean that Seth liked her? Or that she liked Seth?

"Oh," Kay said, "And this is Brandon."

Edwin looked up at Brandon, who didn't seem especially interested in them – he was looking at a chair, tracing a finger around the spiral pattern on it.

After watching him for a moment, Kay smiled at them. She took off her coat, hanging it over the back of one of the chairs. Her jumper was dark purple, and it clung to her chest. "I'm going to grab a drink," she said. "Brandon, shall I get you a Coke?"

Brandon said, "Yes," but didn't turn round.

Edwin watched as she walked away to the bar. Her plait swung slightly, and it seemed more than natural – inevitable – that his eyes drifted down to her bottom.

"Enjoying the view?" Seth asked, quietly.

He jolted back from the lure of a daydream. His face was hot. He reached for his drink, swallowed too fast, and found himself coughing.

Seth slapped him on the back, not quite hard enough to hurt. "You're supposed to drink it, Ed, not inhale it."

"I'm okay."

"Good good. So. You've met her now. And you do like her, don't you?"

It wasn't just that he'd feel bad lying to Seth, it was also that he knew that Seth would see right through it. So all he did was shrug, before looking back at the table again, at the deep scratches in the wood and the ringed stains where glasses had sat over the years.

"Brandon," Seth said, more loudly. "Are you going to join us? I doubt that chair will be especially communicative."

Brandon turned, not seeming at all put out, and sat down.

Edwin was relieved that Seth hadn't gone on and on about Kay. The guys at school would've. But they were really immature. Seth wasn't like that. And Edwin hadn't really been *looking* at her, he'd just happened to have his eyes pointing in her general direction.

He thought he should probably make some effort to talk to Brandon. "This is cool, isn't it? This pub. It's ... cool."

Brandon stared at him. And kept staring at him, without saying anything.

Edwin glanced sideways at Seth for help, but Seth was busy doing something with his phone. There was something really unsettling about Brandon; something that suggested Edwin was about as significant to him as the chair, or the shelves of skulls.

At last, Brandon said, "Why do you wear all black?"

"I'm a Goth," Edwin said, feeling a bit indignant. Wasn't it obvious? Maybe he should've worn black lipstick or something, but he was still a bit weirded out by the idea of putting on make-up, even though a lot of Goths did. He held up his arms, displaying the studded bracelets.

"Why?" Brandon asked.

"Well, I ... it's just ... it's who I am."

Kay came back, setting a Coke in front of Brandon before sitting down next to Edwin with her Smirnoff Ice. "Do you like the pub?"

"Um. Yeah."

Thankfully, he didn't have to come up with anything else, because Seth rescued him by saying, "Ah, this looks like Mark and Hannah coming to join us."

Kay hugged them both. Hannah said, "Great to meet you, Edwin," and sounded like she really meant it.

"I can't believe you're Sir Tristram in-game," Mark said to Kay. He had a flat northern accent, like Mum did when she got stressy and lost the posh voice that she tried to keep up. "Seriously, you scare the hell out of Roddy."

"I don't go around terrorising not-so-innocent thieves in real life," she said, and Edwin could hear the smile in her voice. It was so weird to think that this was the same Kay he talked to online: she had breasts, and hair that smelt of coconut.

Trying to get up the courage to at least look at her properly, he finished the rest of his vodka and Coke, and nodded gratefully when Seth offered to get him another.

Chapter 11

Once the food arrived, Hannah moved round to share a bowl of chips with Kay. "Is Brandon all right? He looks a bit left out."

Kay looked up from her sandwich. "He's fine. Actually, this is about the most sociable I've ever seen him. It's nice to get out of Oxford for a bit."

Hannah tried to remember when she'd last been anywhere, apart from her parents'. This was the first time she'd set foot in a pub for months. And she'd not visited Nottingham since her own student days.

She'd once hoped motherhood would be a golden time of happiness; she still wished she could have some epiphany at the kitchen sink and realise that there was nothing better she could do in this world than bring up two gorgeous children. But more and more, all she could think was how much she was missing.

"Here, have some more chips, don't let me scoff them all," Kay said. She was bright, cheerful, easy to chat to – but Hannah noticed her glance at Seth a few times, almost nervously.

"You look like you've got something on your mind," she whispered.

"Mm. I'm worried about what's been happening in the game. The Prince and everything."

"Because of Edwin, you mean?"

"No." Kay glanced round – as though to check that Seth, Mark and Edwin were still wrapped up in their own conversation. "Well, partly. Did you know Ed has a medallion just like that one in the game, the one the Prince gave him?"

Hannah shook her head.

"And there's no way Seth could've known about it," Kay said. "That's not the only thing – have you been having nightmares?"

"Sorry?" But she'd heard. An image of trees came to her; a dream she'd had a couple of nights before.

"Ed's been dreaming about a forest. So have I."

They were huddled close together now, turned away from the rest of the table. Kay had one hand on her face, almost covering her mouth.

"Perhaps we all need to get out a bit more," Hannah said, smiling.

"I think that – that there could be something going on. Something – dangerous."

Hannah hesitated. Because evil did exist, she supposed; but it wasn't something that she tended to dwell on, and she certainly wasn't convinced that she believed in demons. "I know the role-play has been a bit intense..."

"It's more than that. I mean, how do you explain Edwin's medallion? How could Seth – how could anyone – know enough to make a copy of it?"

"Seth could have a similar one," Hannah said.

"I suppose so. Yeah. I didn't think of that." Kay looked round at Seth, and he shot a smile back.

"Another drink, everyone?" he asked. "I'm buying."

"Go on, then," Mark said, "Cheers."

Hannah caught his eye across the table, frowning. He stared back at her, mouthing *what?*

"That's very generous of you," she said to Seth, "But –"

"It's fine," he said. "My pleasure. So, what do you all want?"

Pointing at the cocktail menu, Edwin said, "If we get all seven Sins, they'll give us a free pitcher. Or a T-shirt."

"Good thinking," Seth said. "Mark, you going to help carry?"

"Sure."

They slid off the bench and headed up towards the bar. Perhaps she should pull Mark aside, have a quiet word – not that she'd get through to him. He'd just say that it was Seth's money and that he clearly had plenty of it: his fancy watch was evidence enough. But that wasn't the point.

"It's great to finally meet you," Kay said, to Edwin.

Edwin mumbled, "Yeah," at his hands. Hannah tried to make out his expression beneath the curtain of black hair. So far, he'd barely glanced at Kay; it was obvious that he had a crush on her. Kay didn't seem to have noticed, though, and Hannah felt it was kinder to both of them not to say anything.

She rooted her camera out of her handbag, and said, "Mind if I get some photos? I thought it'd be nice to have some for the forums."

"Sure," Kay said.

Edwin peered out from under his hair, a bit suspiciously. "Okay."

She took a couple of snaps of the two of them; Kay grinning, Ed looking deathly serious.

"You can smile, you know," she said to him.

"I won't look Goth if I do." He said it so earnestly that Hannah struggled not to laugh.

The next photo she took was Brandon reading his maths textbook, framed against the side of the booth. He didn't so much as glance up.

"Hey, get another of me," Edwin said. When Hannah turned back, he was standing up on the bench, trying to get his wrists through two metal rings on the wall. "In the handcuffs. It'll look really cool."

Hannah was pretty certain that the pub's decor wasn't intended to be taken all that seriously; there was a heavy dose of Rocky Horror camp to it. But if it made Edwin happy ...

"Hang on, I was laughing, do it again." His expression now was presumably supposed to be Seriously Goth. Hannah managed not to crack a smile.

There was a clink of glasses as Mark and Seth returned.

"Into the bondage games already?" Seth asked, deadpan.

Edwin went red.

"Getting photos." Hannah swivelled round to aim the camera at Seth.

He put up a hand in objection. "Not of me."

"It won't eat your soul, you know," she said.

Even through the viewfinder, it was clear he wasn't amused. He turned to Edwin. "Get down, before someone notices and comes over to chuck you out."

"Huh?"

"You're rather obviously underage. Try not to look so bloody conspicuous."

"Oh. Yeah." Edwin was trying to tug his hands free. "Ow."

"Careful," Kay stood, as though about to climb onto the bench to help him. "Move your arm up a bit first."

Looking up from his book, Brandon said, "You need to rotate your wrist thirty degrees clockwise."

Seth put down his tray of drinks and stood on the bench – blocking anyone in the pub from seeing past him to Edwin. Kay slid back down into her seat.

"They'll see you on the bench too," Edwin said.

"*I'm* not underage. And I doubt they care about the soft furnishings." He took hold of Edwin's arms, pulling them free – rather harder than Hannah thought was necessary.

"Ow!"

"It's only skin," Seth said, as Edwin sat back down rubbing his wrists. "You've got seven layers of it, you know. Now, pick a Sin."

Edwin took one of the creamy ones. "What's this?"

"Envy," Seth said, "Note the green."

Hannah took a couple more photos of the group with the coloured cocktails – carefully avoiding Seth.

"It tastes like mint choc chip ice-cream." Edwin's glass was already half empty.

"Go easy on it," Kay said. "It's a good bit more alcoholic than ice-cream."

"It's hardly strong. Finish it up, Ed, and try one of these." Seth gestured to the half-dozen test tubes.

Seeing Kay's worried glance, Hannah said, "How about a game of Fluxx?"

"In a bit," Mark said, "There's no point getting the cards out till the table's cleared." He turned to Seth. "Who's having the T-shirt?"

"Who wants it?" Seth unfolded it and held it up. It was black, the pub's logo emblazoned across the front.

"Oh cool!" Edwin finished his last mouthful of Envy.

Seth grinned. There was something not quite nice there; smug and self-satisfied. "You want the shirt, Ed?"

"Yeah – can I?"

Seth reached over to the rack of test tubes and tapped a couple. "Drink these."

"I think he's had enough," Kay said.

Futilely, Hannah tried to catch Mark's eye across the table; he was leaning back in his chair, watching Seth and Edwin as though amused.

"Down it." Seth handed a tube to Edwin, took another, and demonstrated.

Edwin copied him, then coughed hard and pulled a face. Seth laughed; so did Mark. Kay had her fingers knotted together.

"One down." Seth reached out again.

Leaning across the table, Hannah put her hand in the way. "Seth, just give him the shirt."

For a moment, she thought he was going to shove her aside – but then he leant back, and smiled, easily. "Here you go, Ed. Put it on."

"Awesome!" He pulled the T-shirt over the top of his black sweater. It was a couple of sizes too big. "Cool, thanks."

"Here's to Lycopolis." Seth raised his glass. "And a better bunch of players than I'd ever expected. Cheers to you all."

There was a chorus of clinking glasses and "Cheers." Edwin was looking rather flushed.

Hannah took the Fluxx cards out of her bag, and she and Mark taught the others how to play. After a couple of games, though, Seth said, "Who's for another drink?"

"Go on, then," Mark said.

"You said you'd drive," Hannah reminded him.

"I know, I'll be fine."

Great. That meant she'd be the one getting them safely back to her parents' house, in Leicester. "Just an orange juice for me, thanks."

Kay shook her head when Seth glanced in her direction.

"Ed. Wakey-wakey." Seth snapped his fingers in front of Edwin's face. "Want another Envy?"

"Yeah! No! I want *two!*"

"Good plan," Seth said, heading off towards the bar before Hannah could stop him.

She leant towards Kay. "We should get Ed to slow down a bit."

"Yeah. Can you talk to him?" Kay said. "He keeps clamming up whenever I try to. I'm going to have a word with Seth."

Chapter 12

"Ed's enjoying himself. You don't need to interfere."

"He's had enough." Kay was squashed in next to Seth at the bar, with two heavily-pierced men behind her. "Too much."

"He's fine."

In the dim light, Seth's pupils were so large that only a faint rim of blue iris was left around them. For the first time, she noticed the grey shadows beneath his eyes. Earlier, she'd almost convinced herself that Hannah was right, the medallion was just a coincidence – but then there were the bruises. And the nightmares.

"He's *not* fine," she said, "And you're not either, are you?"

He blinked, and for just a moment, she saw a flash of surprise, perhaps even fear. "Of course I am." An easy smile curved his lips. His grip tightened on her arm.

"Let go of me," she said.

He did, raising his eyebrows. "Take it easy."

The two guys in front had got their drinks and were walking off. She stepped forwards. "Can I get a couple of tap waters, please?"

The bartender – whose buzz cut and tattoo didn't really match the pub's decor – gave an affirmative grunt. Seth leant an elbow on the bar, next to her. "Kay, come on. Ed's been having a tough time at school. Let him kick back a bit."

The bartender set two glasses down in front of her.

"I'll have a couple of Envies," Seth said. When she frowned, he added, "You're worrying too much."

She hesitated, and picked up her two glasses. One, overfull, dribbled icy water across her wrist. She carried them back across the pub to the table.

"Ed, here, water," she said, putting a glass in front of him, and sliding onto the bench next to him before Seth could get there.

"Oh," he said, clearly disappointed.

As soon as Seth got back, he pushed the two cocktails across the table towards Edwin.

"Awesome! Thanks!"

"Go a bit slower on the alcohol, okay, Edwin?" Hannah said, moving one of the glasses away from him. "You don't want to make yourself ill."

Kay looked at Seth. Earlier, she'd almost managed to convince herself that Hannah must be right about the medallion – but now she was considerably less sure. "You said we could talk about the role-play direction today?"

He leant back in the chair, calm – but she could see the tautness in the line of his jaw, the tension in his arms. "If you want."

"Yes," Hannah said. "It would be good to clarify some things. Like where all this is going."

Seth leant in, his elbows on the table. "The Prince wants to rule the city."

"Is Lord Cyrric going to control the Prince?" Hannah asked.

"Cyrric is a coward and an idiot. So no, in a word. Not on his own." He sounded irritated.

Kay watched him, watched for something that would tell her more than his words did. "Well, how do we destroy it?"

"You don't *destroy* it. You control it."

"Tristram wants to destroy it," she said. Across the table, Brandon tilted his head and put down his textbook.

"Well, Tristram's a fool."

Edwin, who'd been twirling a straw in his glass of Envy, looked up suddenly. "What about all these freaky dreams?"

"Ed," Seth said, with a show of patient amusement, "Those aren't part of the game, are they? That's just *you*."

"It's *not* just Ed. And you know it." The words came out more sharply than Kay had intended.

Mark was looking at them all, mouth slightly open.

"I'm sorry that the role-play's giving you nightmares," Seth said, in that same tone of amusement that he'd used on Edwin, "But we're all big boys and girls, aren't we?"

"So the forest doesn't mean anything to you?" Kay asked, loud enough for them all to hear.

"What forest?" he asked – but she'd seen him flinch. He turned to Mark. "You want another drink?"

"It's my round." Mark was digging in his pocket for his wallet. "I'll get them."

"Let me," Seth said, "It's the least I can do."

Glancing up, Hannah said, "I'm sorry?"

Seth leant over to Mark, whispering something. Kay caught the words "... told her yet?" Mark shook his head slightly.

"Mark?" Hannah said. "What's going on?"

Standing, he held his hands up in a *wait* gesture. "Let's just ..."

Kay watched them disappear off to a corner on the other side of the pub. She looked at Seth. "What's happening?"

"Bit of a domestic. Don't worry about it."

Next to her, Edwin slumped against the wall – head tilted back, eyes closed.

"Ed," she said, "Ed, are you all right?"

"Uh-huh."

"Have some water."

"Nah."

"Leave him," Seth said, "Just give him a minute."

Hannah hurried back to the table, her face rather red. "Look, sorry, we're going to have to go."

"Have a safe drive," Seth said.

Kay hugged her briefly and whispered "Is everything okay?"

"Mostly. I'll catch up with you tomorrow."

Lingering several feet away, Mark raised a hand. "Bye."

Kay had to make sure Edwin would be all right. Never mind about the game now – all that could wait. To Seth, she said, "It's getting busy in here, perhaps we should head to the hotel."

"May as well." Seth glanced at Edwin too, half-smiling. She wanted to tell him it wasn't funny, it was stupid and dangerous. But she didn't say anything, just pulled her coat on.

"Oh, let's stay," Edwin said, "Let's get more drinks."

"Come on, Ed," Seth said. "Put your coat on."

"Nah ..."

"Well, come as you are, then." Seth slung his bag over his shoulder, and picked up Edwin's coat.

"Ed, careful!" Kay said, putting a hand out to steady him as they followed Seth up the staircase. "Here, give me your rucksack."

Brandon took it from her, and carried it in one hand. He was staring at the back of Seth's head, frowning a little.

They walked back to the square, Edwin swaying on his feet. Kay took his arm and led him over to the wide rim of the fountain. "Sit down for a minute."

"I'm all right, I'm all good," he said, or that was what she thought he said – she'd hoped the cold air would sober him up, but his words were slurred. "I'm not drunk, I'm just, the world's gone wobbly, that's all."

She turned to Seth. "Why the hell did you buy him so many drinks?"

"He's all right! Stop fussing around him."

"Yeah. I'm not drunk, see!" Edwin clambered up onto the edge of the fountain.

"Ed, don't do that," she said, reaching for his hand, but he snatched his arm away. "Come on, get down."

"You should be careful," Brandon said. "The grip on your trainers may not be sufficient to maintain a secure footing on a wet surface."

Seth had his arms folded, a half-smirk on his face.

"See," Ed said, "See!"

"Yeah, okay, Ed, just get down now –"

He stumbled, one foot sliding backwards. He teetered for a second, then toppled, arms flying up in surprise as he fell. Ice-cold water splashed across her.

"Shit! Ed!"

Behind her, Seth was laughing.

"He'll freeze!" She leant over the rim, but couldn't reach him; the water was deep – and murky, stale-smelling. "Help me get him out!"

Brandon was next to her, kneeling on the rim of the fountain to grasp Edwin's shoulders. They dragged him out. The water splashed across her jeans, plastering them cold to her skin.

Edwin gulped for breath. Strands of hair were clinging to his face.

90

"Give me his coat," she said to Seth – who was still holding it, watching the three of them as though amused. She wrapped the coat around Edwin's shoulders.

"F-fuck it." He was shivering.

"Ed, are you okay?" she asked. "Did you hurt yourself?"

He looked dazed, but she wasn't sure if that was just from being drunk.

"Right, come on, Ed," Seth called. "It's not far to the hotel. You can get warmed up there."

Kay didn't think Edwin had even heard. Leaning heavily against the rim of the fountain, he closed his eyes. His head was lolling sideways. Gently, she put her hand on his arm. "Ed, talk to me, are you okay?"

He didn't say anything, just folded over and vomited on the ground. She held his hair back for him.

"Is he hurt?" Brandon asked.

"I don't know." Had he hit his head on the fountain? She couldn't see any blood. Probably he was just throwing up from all the alcohol. And at least if he'd swallowed any of the water, he'd have got it out now.

Seth strolled over. "Up you get, Ed. You can walk. Let's get you to the hotel and into something dry."

Edwin mumbled, "Sorry."

"Don't worry about it," Seth said, "First time you did shots, right?"

He wrapped an arm around Edwin, pulling him to his feet then propelling him firmly forwards a couple of steps. "See? You're fine."

Kay stepped into their path. "Seth, I'm taking him home."

"Don't be silly. He needs to get in the warm, not stand around waiting for a train."

It was a good point. Her resolve wavered. "Well, I'm calling his mum once we're at the hotel."

"No!" Edwin grabbed at her sleeve. "No, you can't, don't! Don't call her, please."

He was almost crying. She said, "Ed, it's okay. Let's just get you somewhere warm, all right?"

Chapter 13

There were two beds in the room. That made it feel safe. Even after five weeks of college, Brandon still disliked being alone in the silence – though he could sleep if he whispered strings of primes into the darkness, backwards and forwards, until the room buzzed with numbers.

The beds here stood along opposite walls, the gap between them almost exactly square. Brandon pushed his own bed away from the wall slightly, then adjusted Edwin's, to make the square perfect. Sitting down, he opened his book, *Nonlinear Optimization in Finite Dimensions*.

The concepts in the book were not hard, and he could understand them and listen to Seth and Kay simultaneously. Kay paced around the room. For the fourth time, she said, "We should ring his mum."

Seth hadn't answered her the previous three times. He stood by the bathroom door and said, "Try not to drown yourself."

From inside the bathroom, Edwin yelled, "You can't drown in a bath."

Brandon felt that this misapprehension should be corrected. "You can drown in less than six centimetres of water."

"Thank you, Brandon," Seth said, "Very useful. I don't suppose the hotel will be terribly impressed if we ask them to dispose of a dead body."

Brandon decided that his input was not required. While reading, he reached out to experiment with the round switch near his bed. Between "off" and "on" there was a gentle, binary, click; then the light level increased rapidly.

"Brandon, knock it off," Seth said.

He twisted the dial to the exact midway point, then went back to his book.

The sounds of splashing in the bathroom ended. After a few minutes, Edwin emerged, dressed in dry clothes, his hair wet around his face. He said, "Does it have to be so bright?" and lay down with his arms across his face.

"No," Brandon said, "It can be dimmer. Or brighter. It's a variable switch."

"Ed, how're you feeling?" Kay asked.

Edwin made a "Mmgh" noise.

"He's fine," Seth said. "If you're staying, sit down."

"He needs some water." She picked up one of the glasses that stood on a little tray with cups and teabags and sugar packets, and she went into the bathroom – Brandon watched her step over the towels – and filled it from the tap.

"Ed, here," she said.

Edwin still had his arms over his face. "My head hurts."

Kay rummaged in her handbag. "Take a couple of paracetamol."

"Thanks," Edwin mumbled. He swallowed two of the pills. "My clothes are all wet … Mum's gonna ground me *forever.*"

"We'll wring the water out and shove them on the radiator overnight." She sat down next to him, on his bed, and put an arm around him.

"You'll feel better once you've had something to eat, Ed." Seth pulled a colourful flyer from a drawer and waved it in the air. "Pizza menu. What do you all want?"

Brandon didn't mind, and Edwin just leant floppily on the wall, but Kay and Seth decided on a *Four Seasons* and a *Mexicano*, and Seth phoned. Edwin didn't move much, which seemed to be making Kay anxious. Brandon tried to reassure her. "He drank two of the test tubes, and four of the Sins, and the drink he had when we got to the pub."

"I think that was just a Coke," Kay said.

"And vodka," Edwin said, without opening his eyes. "Coke and vodka."

"It was over the course of approximately six hours and forty minutes," Brandon said. "And then he was sick. So there's only an extremely small chance that he'll die from alcohol poisoning."

She didn't look as reassured as he'd hoped.

When the pizzas arrived, Seth sent Brandon and Kay to get them. On the way down the stairs, Kay said, "You really think Ed's all right?"

Brandon considered. "He hasn't been sick again."

"Yeah." A man was waiting in the lobby with their pizzas; Kay paid. "Maybe Seth's right, and he'll perk up once he's had something to eat."

Brandon had never drunk alcohol in his life, and never would. It was a dangerous thing. It sank into people's brains and took away the ability to work through even the simplest problems. Sometimes, they forgot the way home, or they forgot that they had a child.

"You all right?" Kay asked.

Brandon found that his fingers were digging hard into a pizza box. "Yes."

Back in the room, they all sat on the beds – Seth next to Brandon, Kay next to Edwin – and ate the pizzas. It was like the best squats, where everyone sat around and shared and talked and played games. Brandon especially enjoyed puzzles, with things to solve.

And he had a puzzle here, too. He had been with Seth for the majority of the day, and still couldn't pin him to a number. Kay was an eight, round and warm; Edwin was an eleven, uncomfortable with himself; but Seth was an n that could take on multiple values. Brandon watched him, trying to work him out.

"Are you all done with pizza?" Kay asked.

Brandon took the one slice that was left, then Kay picked up the boxes, stacking them neatly by the door. Edwin had propped one of the pillows against the wall and was leaning against it, gazing into mid-air.

"Ed?" Kay asked, "Do you want to lie down?"

"The room spins when I close my eyes."

Brandon watched her look at Seth, but Seth was intent on his laptop screen.

"I know you don't want to hear this, but I think we should call your mum and get you on a train home –"

"No! She'll be really mad at me."

"Seth, you've got his mum's number, right?"

Without looking up, Seth said, "Yes."

"What is it?" Kay had taken out her phone.

Grabbing her arm, Edwin said, "Kay, please, don't phone her, she'll be upset! Seth, don't give her the number."

Seth was typing on the laptop, but paused to say, "Ed. Relax."

"I really think –" Kay said.

"He'll be perfectly all right once he's slept it off. You can't seriously want to take him back home at this time of night."

"It's only nine, there'll still be trains."

Seth folded the laptop lid closed, and stood up. "Look, he just needs some sleep. You can take him back first thing in the morning, if that makes you happy."

Kay didn't look happy.

"I *am* all right," Edwin said.

"Can we have a word?" Seth asked her, quietly. "My room, not here."

"Yes, okay," she said, then she looked at Brandon. "Will you keep an eye on Ed? Come and get us if he seems any worse."

Chapter 14

Seth closed the door. "Look, forget about Edwin for a minute. I need to talk to you."

"Yeah. What the *hell* is going on? These nightmares – and you saw that mark on Edwin, right?"

Before he realised what she was doing, she reached up and pushed his hair aside, staring at his own forehead. He shoved her hand away. "Stop it. Sit down."

She stayed standing. "You didn't just make the Prince up for Hallowe'en, did you?"

He needed to know how much she'd already pieced together. "What makes you say that?"

"We're all dreaming about a forest. You and Ed have got marks on your foreheads – and I bet Hannah and Mark do too." She touched her hand to her own head. "But I haven't. And I know the Prince isn't new. At the Old Gate, there's that inscription: *nightmares dwell within*. That's been there since I joined the game."

She was more observant than he'd thought. As he opened his mouth, he realised he had no idea what to say.

"Everything the Prince says and does in the game ... that's not just you typing, is it?" she asked.

"No." There was no point lying to her now. "None of it is."

He watched her take that in: she backed off a step, staring at him.

"Look, Kay, I need you to do something for me." He held his laptop out to her. "Log in as Tristram. Talk to the Prince for me."

"No. God, no. Seth, you don't know what you're doing –"

"Yes, I do."

"Then you know how dangerous it is. You need to stop it."

"I need to control it. And I've been through all the logs, it talks to you more than anyone else."

She'd gone pale.

"So come on, I'm just asking you to type a few –"

"No. No. I'm not having anything to do with this." She turned, reaching for the door handle.

He caught hold of her arm. "Kay."

"Get off."

He let go. He fought down fear, and realised what he needed to say to make her agree. "The Prince has shown a lot of interest in Edwin – so if you won't do it, I'll get him to instead."

"No!"

"I mean it."

"I know you do."

"I'm just asking you to type a few words," he said, as calmly as he could.

Folding her arms, she said, "Tell me exactly what's going on. Why couldn't Cyrric control it?"

"I ..." He'd been trying not to think about that. "Look, Cyrric is an idiot. He's not *me*."

She didn't break eye contact or back away. "So you've got it all under control, have you?"

"Of course I have."

"Then why are you having nightmares?"

That question snatched the breath from him. Her eyes narrowed: she'd meant it to hurt. And, worse, she'd seen that it had. "We need to get control of the Prince in the game, that's all, then everything in real life will ... fall into place."

"Really?" There was a distinct edge of sarcasm in her voice.

"Yes."

"And what about that?" She pointed at his forehead.

"It doesn't matter." He hurried on, in case he'd not managed to get sufficient conviction into the words. "Look, Ed's upset about his medallion, about the dreams. Help me get this fixed for him."

She glanced away from him for the first time, biting her lip.

"Just log in, okay." He gestured to the laptop. "Type the name, see if it'll talk to you."

She hesitated, then sat down on the bed and picked up the laptop. Sitting next to her, he watched as she logged in.

"Come on," he said, when she didn't type anything, "It's just letters on a screen."

"Then why don't you do it?" she asked.

"It won't talk to me."

For a moment, she just gazed at the keyboard. Then she typed, "Prince of Nightmares?"

"Hello, Kay." Then, *"Hello, Seth."*

She shivered. "Why won't you talk to Seth?"

There was a low, rumbling noise in the room. Laughter. It took him a moment to gather his thoughts, pull himself fiercely back into control.

There were more words on the screen: *"He can speak to me in the forest."*

No. He wasn't ready, not yet. He needed to be sure that the Prince would obey him.

Kay glanced uncertainly at him, then kept typing. "Why's the forest so important?"

"Ask Seth."

She looked at him, eyebrows raised expectantly.

"We're not talking about that," he said, and the words came out hoarsely.

The next thing she typed was, "What's Seth so afraid of?"

"I'm not –"

More words appeared on the screen. *"He's afraid of me."*

"Why?" she asked, out loud.

"Because he's mine."

That rumbling sound echoed around the room. The screen of the laptop went suddenly black. Kay looked at it, then at him. She pressed the "on" switch; nothing happened. He snatched it from her. There was the smell of smoke and mud in the air, and freezing rain on his face, and dark trees lurking very close by, a shadow falling across him ...

Then he was back in the room again, his knuckles white where he gripped the laptop.

Kay put her hand on his arm. For an unguarded second, he was grateful. He wanted, almost overwhelmingly, to reach out and hold onto her.

"Seth –"

He pulled his arm away. "Are you going to help me, or not?"

"I'll help you destroy it." She was quiet, but certain. "Nothing else."

"Then I'll do this without you." He stood up. "It's late. I'll see you at breakfast."

She got between him and the door. "Seth, listen to me. You ... you don't know what you're playing with."

"And you do?"

"No. Maybe. I –"

"Either you're on my side, or you're not," he said.

"I'm not going to help you."

"Then have the fucking good sense to keep out of my way."

She didn't move.

He took a step closer, his face inches from hers. "I mean it, Katherine."

"What're you going to do, hit me?"

He kept his eyes locked on hers, waiting for her to flinch and look away. She didn't.

"Listen to me," she said. "I know what I'm talking about. This is dangerous – for you, for everyone else. Please, just end the whole thing, destroy the demon in the game and forget it all. Please."

"I'll sleep on it, all right? We can talk in the morning."

She didn't look at all convinced – but she finally pulled the door open, and left. He stood watching her until she was back in her own room, then he knocked on the door of 203.

Brandon opened it. "Edwin was crying."

"No I wasn't!"

"You were," Brandon said, sounding puzzled, and sat back on his bed, picking up his textbook again.

Edwin was sitting up, one arm over his face, looking shaky and miserable.

"Drink some more water," Seth said. "It'll help."

"What were you talking to Kay about?"

"About the Prince."

Edwin looked away.

"Did you bring your medallion?" Seth asked.

"Yeah."

100

"Can I see it?"

There was a long pause. "Okay. It's in my rucksack."

Seth found it under a rather battered volume of Poe's short stories. Holding it up to the light, he looked at it closely. It was an exact match for the item in the game – he didn't need the printouts to see that. The details were carefully etched: the wolf's fur, the jaw line, the hint of teeth. On the back, *R.R.* had been scratched into the metal.

"Any idea what these letters mean?" he asked Edwin.

"No."

Brandon glanced over, clearly listening, though he wasn't saying anything. Seth handed him the medallion. Brandon held it by the chain, looked at it curiously, then gave it back to him.

"We could ask Kay if she understands it," he said.

"No," Seth said, hastily. "She's gone to bed – we don't want to disturb her. Ed, this belonged to your dad, right?"

"Mm."

"What's his name?"

"I don't know." Edwin took a gulp of water. "Mum won't talk about him. She hasn't seen him since before I was born."

Perhaps its origins weren't important. Perhaps the Prince had simply latched onto some real-world object which was significant for Edwin. "You used to wear it every day. Why?"

"Dunno. It made me feel safe. But now ..."

Seth unspooled the chain of the medallion and said, "Put it on."

Edwin shook his head, too hard; he winced, screwing his eyes shut.

Time for a trump card. "Come on. You're not scared of it, are you?"

"No."

"Okay, then." He put one hand on Edwin's shoulder, pulling him round slightly. "Hold your hair out the way for me."

Edwin bunched his hair, still damp, in his hands. Seth slid the medallion around his neck. Edwin flinched at his touch.

"See? It's fine," Seth said.

Edwin lifted the thin chain away from his skin, then let it fall again. He mumbled, "I guess."

"There you go, then," he said, standing. "Now, I suggest we all get some sleep."

The buzz of alcohol had worn off and he felt an empty exhaustion. But back in his room, he opened up the laptop again, and tapped the power switch. Still nothing. He plugged it into the mains, in case it was a battery problem. Nothing.

In the en-suite, he stared into the mirror. The mark on his forehead was a little redder today. He looked more tired than he wanted to. He looked scared – and that had probably been far too obvious to Kay.

He'd do this alone, if he had to. Clearly, she wasn't going to help him; he'd have to make sure she couldn't do anything to get in his way. He suspected she knew something that she wasn't talking about – she'd been too ready to believe that the demon was real.

As he was undressing for bed, the laptop whirred into life. A faint grey image of trees stretched from the bottom to the top of the screen.

It stayed there even when he held down the off switch. After closing the lid, he shoved the laptop into his bag for good measure. He wasn't ready to go back, not yet. This was nothing to do with fear: he wasn't *afraid* to walk into the forest. He just needed to have everything else in place. This time, he had to know that he could control the Prince.

He was tired. As soon as he lay down and pulled the duvet around himself, he felt the cloudy fog of alcohol and the exhaustion of too many late nights catching up with him. When he closed his eyes, he saw the trees. Branches black against the night sky, moonlight turning everything monochrome.

There was a voice whispering across the borders of sleep. *"Seth. Seth. Seth."*

The forest was closer than it had been in years.

And he stopped running away. He turned to face it. He wanted answers; this was where he'd get them. These were dreams. Nothing more. They couldn't harm him.

He was in the forest, more suddenly and more deeply than he'd been prepared for. He choked back fear. It was dark. The trees pressed in – close, solid shadows.

"Seth."

There was something wrong. He grasped for it, fumbling for a thought which wouldn't quite form.

"Welcome back, Seth."

This was a dream. It was just a dream.

"Welcome home, Seth."

If it was just a dream, how could it hurt? The pain wasn't sharp, but it was everywhere. This was *his* dream, though. He was in control. As firmly as he could, he said, "I want you to obey me."

"Kneel to me, Seth." The words came with the seduction of a dark invitation and the power of a command.

"No," he said. "That's not going to happen."

The trees were moving around him, shifting in the night, curling closer. There was a black mist in the air, visible despite the dark. He began to back away.

The ground rose up and, dizzily, he found himself lying on it, still feeling as though he was falling. As he grasped for something to hold onto, his hands slid through air and mud.

"Bring me a gift, Seth."

"What do you want?"

The dream shifted. He saw a face; pale, tear-streaked. Limp black hair, a thin chain around the throat. Edwin.

He got to his feet. The trees were still close around him. There was rain in the air, cold on his face and his arms. His body ached with something close to fear or loneliness, rather than pain.

"Bring me my offering, Seth."

It was hard to talk, but he pushed the words out. "And then? You'll do what I want?"

The Prince laughed again, and the sound shook the forest. He fell against a tree, and the black smoke was in his face. He couldn't see.

Enough. He knew what he needed to know. He was going to wake up now.

He was going to wake up.

Now.

He couldn't breathe properly. The ground was shifting: the trees brushed against him, sharp against his skin. He pushed his way through them, blindly stumbling forwards until he ended up falling.

It was never this hard to get back. He could pull himself straight out of nightmares, he could wake up whenever he wanted.

The laugh was very close now. His arms and legs were heavy, weighted down. He was pressed against the ground, and he couldn't move.

103

"I missed you, Seth."

He closed his eyes. He'd ignore it all. This was a dream, it was all in his head. Nothing could really hurt him here. He was only dreaming a sensation of pain, just like he only dreamed the things he heard and saw.

"Seth." The tone had changed, colder now, mocking. And the dream was changing too; the air smelt of smoke, there was an unearthly fire racing through the forest ...

"You want Edwin? Fine, I'll bring him to you." He tried all the usual tricks to wake up; visualising his room, thinking the word *awake*. But nothing worked.

"All right. Let me go," he said, tightly.

New nightmares flickered on the edges of his sight: a white-washed room; an almost-deserted playground; a group of teenagers armed with stones ...

"Let me go! Please!"

He was staring up into the dark, breathing hard, a headache pressing around his eyes. And he was awake.

Chapter 15

The room swirled around Edwin, spinning him down into sleep.

He was in the forest again. It was darker than before, and colder. The trees were very close, and bark scabbed from them. There was mud beneath his feet, and brambles snaking near his ankles.

A tiny part of him knew that he was asleep, and fought to wake up. But the wind was blowing cold in his face, snatching his breath, snatching his thoughts. The idea of "awake" – the idea of any other world – slid away.

A wolf's howl, long and haunting, tore through the air. Edwin began to run, felt that he must run, though the forest was even blacker now and he couldn't see the trees. The howl came again. He was being hunted. He kept running, through the slippery mud. The trees reached out, branches scratching him. Something snatched his ankles and he fell, screaming for help. "Kay!" He was being pulled down, and down.

He woke up with a dry mouth. His head was pounding. The nightmare was slow to fade; he could almost smell the forest, the cold earthy air. Had he actually been yelling for Kay? He really hoped he'd only dreamt that. Sitting up, he looked across the room at the shadowy lump that was Brandon – thankfully asleep.

Edwin stumbled out of bed and into the bathroom. He slid his hand along the wall, a panicky feeling gripping him until he found the light switch.

He got a glass of water. His neck hurt. The medallion had twisted round in the night, the wolf's head digging into his skin. He could feel a slight dent there, but no blood.

He hadn't wanted to wear it. But he couldn't let Seth think he was scared. And it hadn't seemed so bad with Seth and Brandon there, with his head still fuzzy and the edges of everything softened. But now he felt ill, and when he peered in the mirror he could see that his eyes were red and his face was blotchy and the weird bruise on his forehead was bigger than before.

There was no way he could go back to sleep with the medallion around his neck. He slid the chain around till the fastening was in front of him.

The clasp was stuck.

He tried again, and again, and again, even though it jabbed into his thumb. It wouldn't open. He tried to snap the chain, wrapping it around his finger and yanking hard. It left a ring of tiny ovals. It didn't break.

Now his eyes stung, and the back of his throat ached. His head was still hurting. If he could just go home – if he could just see Mum, give her a hug –

The room had gone all blurry. He rubbed the tears away with his sleeve, and realised that he'd fallen asleep in his clothes. More tears were welling up.

He pressed the clasp again. It was definitely stuck. Perhaps it had rusted, because he'd gone to bed with his hair still damp. He looked in the mirror to see it more easily. And the hairs on his neck prickled. What if there was something in the bathroom? Something lurking behind him, something he'd see if he spun round fast enough ...

Very slowly and deliberately, he turned. He thought he saw a wisp of black smoke; he blinked, and it was gone.

After backing out of the bathroom, he tried to yank the medallion over his head. He couldn't get it past his chin. If he went home, he could get some pliers and cut it off. But his phone told him it was only four-fifteen. Even if he could find out where to get a taxi, there wouldn't be any trains yet.

Seth was only next door. He could go and wake him up, and tell him about the medallion: Seth might know what to do. But Seth would also see that he'd been crying.

He lay back down for a while, hugging the duvet. Every time he closed his eyes, he saw the trees loom towards him. He kept wanting to touch the medallion chain – but he forced himself not to, trying to believe that he *wanted* to wear it, that he'd chosen not to take it off.

108

Even when he tried not to move at all, his head still hurt, a tight clenched feeling behind his eyes and under his scalp. There was a bruise on his hip, and grazes on his knees that he didn't remember getting.

It was still pitch dark outside. Edwin looked at the time again. Nearly five. It wouldn't be so much longer till there were trains, and it wasn't too far to the station.

Quietly, he got up, shoved his phone into his pocket and turned the light switch a tiny bit so he could scribble a note. He pulled his shoes on, and put the light back out. As he stumbled across the room, he knocked a chair against the wall, but Brandon didn't stir.

He closed the door as quietly as he could, and put on his coat in the corridor. The whole place was totally silent. He stood outside Seth's room for a minute ... but then he tiptoed down the corridor, down the stairs, out of the front door of the hotel.

It was colder than he'd expected outside, and very quiet, the world grey and misty. It didn't feel quite real. He pinched himself just to be sure that he was awake.

He wasn't a hundred percent sure where the station was. Last night was a confused haze in his mind, a patchwork of moments: falling into the fountain; throwing up; Seth pushing him up the steps into the hotel; Kay telling him to drink some water.

His phone was still out of data, but he could manage without a map. He decided to go back towards the main square. At least, he thought he was going towards it, but he found himself in unfamiliar streets of tall Victorian houses and a few shut-up shops. He was shivering now, and walked faster to get warm. It would be all right. All he needed to do was turn back and retrace his steps, then at least he could find the hotel again.

Except he couldn't. It was like being in a maze, and he wasn't so sure where he was now or what direction he should be going in. His head hurt, and he felt sick and dizzy and wanted to lie down.

He stumbled along another street, and found himself at a wide main road, *Castle Boulevard*. On the other side of the road was the canal. Okay. He could do this. The canal went near the station, they'd driven over it in the taxi. All he had to do was follow it. Easy. And then he'd be on a train, warm, heading back home, and everything would be okay.

He walked along fast, hands in his coat pockets. It was so dark still that the water looked black. There was litter scattered along the path, crisp packets and chocolate wrappers floating in scummy puddles. His knee was hurting now with every step, but he kept going. He walked under a bridge where rainwater had pooled across the path. As he picked his way through, he held his arms out for balance.

The underside of the bridge was covered with artistic graffiti; the bright paint was dark in the gloom. One piece caught his eye. Trees, high, towering ones, stretching up the concrete, curling above him. He stared at them for a minute, then his legs went out from under him, and he was suddenly on his knees in a cold puddle.

He got to his feet, knees hurting more, palms smarting where they'd smacked into the concrete. Water dripped down his coat and trousers. There was smoke in the air in front of him, and a choking smell. Up ahead, there was a sound – a bark. No, a howl. He wouldn't, couldn't, go any further. He backed away, scrambling out from under the bridge.

There was black mist in the air, seeping towards him. He began to run, because he *knew* that something was after him, the same thing that had been hunting him in the nightmare. But this was no dream: the concrete was too hard beneath his feet, and the air was too cold on his skin, and his head hurt too much.

He kept on running, away from the canal, back across the main road. Eventually he had to stop, doubled over, hands on his knees. His head was pounding: he closed his eyes for a moment.

Where was he? There weren't any signposts for the station. He went up to a bus stop, but the timetable said there wouldn't be any buses for a couple of hours yet. He sat there anyway, on the bench under the scratched shelter. He should've just stayed in the hotel. Now he was lost, and freezing, and everything hurt. His wrists smarted in the cold air – there were reddish scrapes where Seth had yanked his hands out of the handcuffs.

Maybe he could call Seth, and ask how to get to the station from here. Seth might think he was an idiot, but that didn't matter now. He just wanted to be somewhere warm and safe. He pulled out his mobile and fumbled through the menu for Seth's name, his fingers numb.

There was something wrong with his phone: the call wasn't connecting, even though he had loads of minutes left for the month.

He talked anyway, hoping that the message would somehow get to Seth.

"Seth? Seth, I got lost. I was trying to get to the station but I couldn't, and I'm not sure where I am, I'm at a bus stop somewhere but there aren't any buses yet. I saw, I saw this black mist ... If you get this, can you ring me back? Please? Please?"

Chapter 16

Kay got dressed as quickly as she could, and opened the door. Seth hadn't budged, though he'd finished buttoning his shirt. His hair was sticking up, and he looked like he'd barely slept.

"And you didn't get any message?" she asked, "Just the call?"

"It didn't connect properly. Just showed his number. It only rang once – wouldn't have heard it if I wasn't already awake."

"You tried calling him back?" She hurried down the corridor after him.

"Of course I did! He didn't pick up."

Edwin's bedcovers were in a heap on the floor. His rucksack and coat were gone, though his clothes from the previous day were still hanging on the radiator.

"Brandon, did he seem okay?" she asked.

"I heard him crying in the night."

Seth rubbed his hands over his face, and muttered "Fuck it."

"Did you upset him somehow?" Kay asked him. "Seth? Did you?"

"He put the medallion on Edwin," Brandon said, as though telling her about the weather.

"What? Why?"

Seth didn't answer, just walked over to the window and pulled the curtain aside, his back to her.

"Seth, why the hell would you do that? You know he was terrified of it."

"Just go back to bed. I'll sort this out."

"No fucking way." She saw something in his hand – a piece of paper. "What's that?"

"Nothing."

She grabbed for his arm. He held her off easily. But Brandon leant over, snatching the paper.

"It's a note from Edwin," he said, holding it out to her.

To Kay, I've gone for a train. There was black mist. I think there was. I don't know now if I only dreamed it. Please will you text me when you read this? I'm sorry I got drunk. Edwin.

"What the hell have you done?" she asked. Seth wouldn't meet her eyes. She tried Edwin's number; there was no answer.

Seth, abruptly, headed for the door.

"Wait," she said, "I'm coming with you."

"Fine. Whatever. Brandon, stay here, phone me if he comes back."

As soon as they were outside the hotel, she grabbed Seth's arm. "Tell me what's going on."

"Nothing!"

"The black mist? Ed going off like that?"

"Look, it could be worse. All right? It could be worse. We should just be glad it isn't." There were heavy shadows under his eyes.

She didn't say anything for several long moments, fighting the panicked feeling in her stomach. Yes, it could be worse. Edwin could be hurt. Unconscious. Even dead.

They kept walking. They called his name. As they got nearer the canal, they were walking into fog, unable to see more than a dozen or so paces ahead of them.

"Fuck it," Seth said.

"I'll try phoning him again." She did, twice. Still no answer.

They looked at one another in silence. Seth glanced away from her, over her shoulder, as though he'd seen something.

She turned.

There was nothing, just the buildings either side of the street, the pavement, the fog obscuring anything more than a few feet away.

Then she saw a thin trail of black through the whiteness.

Seth was staring fixedly at it.

"What the *hell* did you do?" Kay got in front of him. "Did you offer Ed to the Prince? Just like Benedict in the game?"

He glanced away from her.

"Oh God, Seth –"

"Let's just find him, all right?"

She nodded. As they walked forwards, the black mist drifted away. It stayed a few paces ahead of them, leading them down the street.

And then it was gone.

They looked around; there was no-one in sight.

"Ed?" Kay called.

Seth's phone was ringing. He snapped it open. "Edwin! Where the fuck are you? Find a street sign." Pause. "I don't care." Pause. "Lenton Avenue? Stay there. Don't move."

He pulled up a map on his phone. "This way. He's fine."

They ran down the road, round a corner, down another road. The sun was just rising, a red glow past the buildings. She saw a huddled figure on a bench in a bus shelter.

Seth got there first, grabbing Edwin by the shoulders. "What the fuck were you thinking?"

Edwin was shivering hard, staring at Seth and then at her. He'd obviously been crying, his eyes red, his face unhealthily pale in the grey light. His teeth were chattering.

"You should be glad that *I* caught up with you, rather than something much nastier."

"I'm s-sorry." Edwin pulled away from Seth to hide his face behind his arms.

Seth clenched a fist.

"Seth!" She grabbed his arm. "No! Calm *down!*"

For a moment she thought he was going to hit her, instead – and then he turned away abruptly, strode several yards down the street, and stood there, facing away from them, hands in his pockets.

Kay put her arms around Edwin, and let him cry onto her shoulder. "Hey, Ed, come on, you're okay, right?"

"No!" His teeth were chattering, and he choked the words out through tears. "My head hurts. And my stomach and I feel sick still."

"I know," she said, and hugged him a little tighter. "It's a hangover. You'll feel better soon."

"And – and – Seth –"

"He's not going to hurt you, I promise."

Back at the hotel, she made Edwin a mug of weak, sugary tea. Then she beckoned Seth into the corridor and whispered, "If you so much as

115

touch Ed again, I'm not only calling his mother, I'm calling the police too. I mean it."

Just for a moment, she saw his jaw clench in anger – then he shrugged and said, tiredly, "I wasn't going to hit him."

She was still furious, on Edwin's behalf, but she forced that down to ask, "Are *you* okay?"

He blinked. "Yeah. Yes. Of course."

"You sure?"

He met her eyes this time. "Katherine, if you've got something to say, then say it."

"All right, then," she said. "Something happened, didn't it?"

"Edwin had a nightmare, that's all. And a fit of utter stupidity."

She wasn't buying that. "And what about you? Did you have a nightmare too?"

"None of your fucking business." The sudden glare startled her.

"Look, I'm trying to help."

"Yeah?" He turned on her, arms crossed defensively. "Well, Katherine, you had your chance to help, yesterday."

"I told you, I'm not going to –"

"Yes, you made that very clear." He was glaring at her. "I don't need you. So fuck off."

It would've been easy to just storm away. But she didn't. "Seth, I'm still your friend."

"No," he said. "No. You're not."

Chapter 17

Mark woke up too early. The bed was hard, and the room was stiflingly warm. He remembered he was at the in-laws'. Hannah was already up and dressed, gazing out of the window. She turned, and he wasn't quite quick enough to close his eyes.

"We need to have a talk," she said. "I mean, what're we going to tell Mum? What're we going to *do*?"

Mark parted himself, reluctantly, from the bedclothes, picked up his jeans, and pulled a clean T-shirt from his bag. "Yes, all right, okay. I'm having a shower first."

He headed into the bathroom, wishing he'd not had to sacrifice his morning to Hannah's parents. Normally, Sunday was the highlight of his week: Hannah would take the kids off to church, and he'd get a decent lie in, followed by a bacon butty in front of the telly. It was the one part of his life that his eighteen-year-old self might have recognised.

Once he got the temperamental shower dial to provide nice warm water – rather than a scalding or freezing jet – he began to unwind. He even found himself appreciating, momentarily, staying at the in-laws'. The bathroom here hadn't become a repository for bath toys and mountains of laundry. It was spotlessly clean and he made a more concentrated effort than usual to leave it that way: if he took long enough, Hannah might go downstairs for breakfast.

He went back to the bedroom, rubbing his hair vigorously with a towel. She was still there, with a token of mercy – a mug of tea.

"Look, I'm sorry I didn't tell you," he said, and took the tea.

"What else have you been keeping from me?" she asked, quietly.

Where could he even begin? The unpaid bills? The two credit cards he'd never got round to mentioning to her?

"Love," he said. "It'll be okay. I'm going to get a new job."

"It's not just –" She broke off, began again. "I want to know what's happening."

"You *do* know. You know exactly what's happening." They'd been through this yesterday, on the drive back from Nottingham to Leicester. "I'm leaving work in a week. I'll move into something else."

She started making the bed. He moved to help, taking the corner of a sheet, but she waved him away, saying, "I can manage."

"Okay, okay."

"What really upset me is that you told *Seth* about quitting, and not me."

"Because I knew you'd react like this!"

"You hardly even know him!"

They glared at each other across the bed.

"Actually, we talk quite a lot online, all right?" he said. "Anyway, it wasn't like I just decided to quit and then told Seth about it. He ... he was encouraging me to find something better."

"Oh. I see."

"What? What's that supposed to mean?"

"Nothing." She grabbed the pillows, shook them and thumped them down.

"No, what do you mean?"

"Well, he's got a Cambridge degree – I'm sure *he* can just waltz from one job straight into another whenever he damn well feels like it."

"He works for himself," Mark said, though he had a pretty hazy idea of what Seth actually did to make money. Lycopolis was still in beta, so none of them paid to play it. Maybe Seth ran other games too.

Tucking the sheets in, Hannah said, "So what the hell does he know about job hunting? And how could you just quit without something lined up? I'm not saying I don't believe in you…"

But that was exactly what she was saying. They both knew his Third in Computer Science was hardly in high demand. But he had been perfectly all right at his job – and he could be doing something much better.

"It's going to be fine," he said. "Stop getting upset."

"I don't want to be kept in the dark." She straightened the quilt. "I don't deserve that, and neither do the kids."

He couldn't help feeling resentful. She was making him sound like a failure. Even if he had quit hastily, it wasn't the end of the world, and she didn't have to pretend that it was. "It'll be all right. I've got lots of applications out. Some good leads."

"Right. Okay." She was pulling her hair into a ponytail. "Let's just pack the kids into the car and head home. And for goodness sake, don't say anything about this to Mum."

Mark drove all the way back to Swindon. He refused to feel bad that Hannah had ended up driving last night. She had insisted, even though he'd only had a couple of drinks.

"I think we'll give church a miss today," she said, once they were home.

Great. He wasn't going to get *any* of his Sunday to himself. "The kids like going."

"I know. But we'll be late by now, anyway, and I'm knackered. I didn't sleep well."

Mark wasn't going to let her guilt-trip him. "I'll be in the living room," he said, and headed for the computer.

He managed five minutes of quiet before the kids bounced in.

"Mum says we can watch cartoons!" Denny said.

"Daddy." Megan tried to climb onto his lap. "Daddy, will you play the princess dress-up game with me?"

"Not now," he said, trying not to let irritation show. "Go and watch the television. Look, it's ... that yellow talking sponge thing. You like that, right?"

"But Daddy –"

"Go on. Be a good girl, and I'll take you both to buy sweets later."

He put his headphones on to drown out the telly and the kids' chatter. He pulled up his music folder, found some of the stuff he'd listened to in his teens: Nirvana, Guns N' Roses.

One more week. Five more days. Then, on Friday afternoon, he'd drive home from the office one last time. He'd crawl along with the traffic, curse the lights, turn up the radio, slow down near the school, one last time. When it came to it, perhaps he wouldn't be able to drive the whole route. Perhaps he'd find himself taking a left where he should take a right, heading out of Swindon, driving and driving until he escaped everything – the whispered rows with Hannah, the unpaid bills, the mistakes of the past.

He glanced round at the kids. Denny was sitting with his elbow on the arm of the sofa, face cupped by a small hand. Megan was lying on the carpet, giggling at the yellow sponge on the screen. He tried to make himself love them. He tried to think how awful it would be to abandon them, how much he'd miss them. But all he felt was a cold, hard sense of duty.

It didn't matter whether or not he felt anything. He was their father. He couldn't just leave them. He had to stick it out. He'd find a way, somehow. There'd be enough money to pay the mortgage, enough for Christmas. He couldn't just run away – he wasn't a kid now, and he couldn't abandon Hannah like he'd abandoned Lucy.

Back then, fifteen years ago now, he'd left everything: Lucy, his A-levels, his friends. But the day his life had changed had been just like any other – until he found Lucy waiting on the doorstep when he got home from college. He reached out to hug her. She let him, then said, "I'm pregnant."

At first, he couldn't believe it, couldn't take it in. He asked, "Are you sure?" and when she said yes, of course she was bloody sure, he said, "I mean, really sure? Really? Oh, God."

In the years since, he'd tried and tried to put it all out of his mind. It had just been a brief teenage relationship, born of boredom. It had only lasted six months. He never kept a photo of her. He never went back to her house for the stuff he'd left there – a few tapes, the three dog-eared volumes of *Lord of the Rings,* a handful of miniatures, painstakingly painted.

In some parallel universe, there was a different Mark, one who'd given up everything at seventeen, ditched college, stayed with his girlfriend and brought up a kid that neither of them had wanted. That would've been hell, surely. He'd be looking after a teenager by now. And it didn't seem long, really, since he'd been that age himself.

He skipped through a few tracks. Did teenagers still listen to Nirvana? He'd have to ask Edwin or Kay. Would they have heard of Kurt Cobain? Probably not. They wouldn't even remember September 11th: Kay would've been no older than Megan, and Edwin wouldn't have been born.

Mark felt suddenly horrifically old. He logged into Messenger and Lycopolis, needing to remind himself that he still had most of his life ahead of him, that he was on top of all the latest gadgets and trends and pop culture references. He read xkcd. He knew where to find The Pirate Bay's proxies. He'd joined Facebook and Twitter – and Instagram and WhatsApp – long before they were mainstream.

There weren't many people in Lycopolis. It was only just after noon: most of them were probably still in bed, or still in Nottingham.

A Messenger window popped up, from Kay. "Hi, Mark."

"Hi," he typed. "Home already?"

"Yep. We all got a pretty early start. Is Hannah around?"

When he removed his headphones for a few seconds, he heard the vacuum cleaner whirring. "I think she's cleaning."

"Oh. Have you seen the forums?"

"Nope." He headed straight there, and found a new post in Seth's "Announcements" forum. The title was "Admin Change".

Kay (Tristram) is no longer my Assistant, so if you've got any administrative problems, bring them straight to me. If you want an invite for a friend, let me know. You'll have to show them the ropes yourself.
Seth.

"You stepped down?" Mark asked her.

"No. Didn't know anything about it till he posted that."

That surprised him. And bothered him. Time and time again, he'd watched Kay talk newbies through their first bewildering hours in the game. And he liked her; she was uncomplicatedly kind. Anyway, hadn't Seth and Kay been friends – or even a bit more? They'd been exchanging glances across the table in the pub, and standing close together at the bar.

"What happened?" he asked.

"Bit of an argument."

"Do you want me to get Hannah?"

"No, don't worry. I'll talk to her later."

Mark tried to find something comforting to type. "Well, it's Seth's loss. And ours. You did a great job."

He got a smiling emoticon in return. "Thanks."

121

He flicked through the forums – none of the new messages had any impact on Roderic – and found himself gazing at the Lycopolis logo at the top of the page. The wolf.

He'd always liked wolves. When he was Denny's age, he'd loved cheering on the baddy, the naughty one. In his teens, wolves had become rebels, outsiders. Sometimes charmers, sometimes predators. He'd never thought to ask Seth how he'd chosen the game's name. What did wolves mean to *him*?

"Dad. Daaaad!" A voice broke in, too shrill and instant to be drowned out by the sludgy tones of Nirvana's *Lake of Fire*.

Mark pulled off the headphones. "What?"

"Can we have a snack?" Denny asked.

"Yeah, go for it."

They looked at him. Megan stopped pirouetting on the carpet and said, "We can't reach the box, Daddy."

"Oh, yeah. Right." He stood up, reluctantly. Where was Hannah? She normally legislated on snacks. "What do you want, then? Crisps?"

"Yes, please, salt and vinegar," Denny said.

"I want the pink ones!" Megan said.

In the kitchen, he lifted the box down from the top of the cupboard.

A movement in the den caught his eye. Hannah was in there, rummaging through the junk drawer, several envelopes already in her hand.

Shit.

He'd pretend he hadn't seen her. He'd wait till she said something to him about it. By then, he would have a solution. Or at least a plausible lie, to buy him some time.

He grabbed two bags of crisps, walked into the living room and tossed them to the kids.

"Thanks, Dad!"

"I'm going for a walk," he said. "Tell Mum I won't be back for lunch."

Chapter 18

Seth's flat was far too quiet after the buzz of Nottingham. He headed across the river and into the City, past St Paul's to Arti's wine bar: it was rather too hipster for his liking, but busy enough to feel companionable.

After a couple of glasses of good wine, and an afternoon lurking silently in Lycopolis, watching the Chatroom's reaction to Kay's sudden fall from grace, he was feeling calmer.

He hadn't expected to care. That was what had shaken him so much. Dragged from sleep, dragged from that nightmare into a cold and unnerving reality. He couldn't simply let the Prince take Edwin, not yet, not like that – not when Edwin's mother knew exactly who her son was with.

But he'd reacted badly. Edwin had gone home in tears, and while Seth didn't feel particularly sympathetic, he had to admit that this had been a strategic mistake. He'd wanted to force Edwin and Kay apart, and reel Edwin a little closer to him; he'd failed, quite spectacularly.

In Lycopolis, Benedict and Tristram were both in the Keep – along with, surprisingly, Matilda. Still invisible, he watched them for a while; Benedict was scared and failing to hide it, Tristram was a fierce ball of concern and anger and knightly righteousness, Matilda was storming around swearing vengeance on demon-kind.

Paging through the logs from a couple of hours ago, he found that Benedict had, once again, been confronted by the demon.

He moved Cyrric into the private set of rooms in the Court, then glanced up from the screen, at his fellow customers – all young; all laughing, drinking, chattering. No-one was paying any attention to him, hunched over a laptop in the corner. He typed, "When you told me you wanted Edwin, what exactly did you mean?"

He didn't expect an answer, so when one came, he found himself snatching his hands away from the keyboard. Luckily, nobody in the bar seemed to have noticed.

"Bring him to the forest."

He didn't want to go through with this. Despite himself, he'd started to like Edwin.

"What else can I give you?" he asked. "Instead?"

"Nothing."

Sometimes you didn't get the answer you wanted. Then there was a choice between striding on forwards and cowering away. He wasn't going to give in to weakness. He was going to do what he always did, and ignore everything but the goal he had in mind. "Leave him alone, for a couple of weeks. If you scare him, I'll never be able to persuade him."

There was no response.

"Well?"

"You'll bring him."

Was that an answer, or an order? He scowled at the screen, and poured another glass of wine. The Chatroom had quietened down now. He'd not jumped in at any point; he had no need to justify himself to them.

He'd expected Kay to make more fuss. He'd been prepared for a Messenger box to pop up from her, hurt and self-righteous. He was ready to be coolly cutting in response.

But, though she'd been online for most of the afternoon, she'd not said a word to him. He checked the forums again. She'd finally responded to his post.

It was fun while it lasted! Obviously I've not got the extra commands at my disposal now, but if anyone wants a hand, just let me know. I'll carry on unofficially. ;-)

He read it through a couple of times, trying to work out what feelings the words masked. The final sentence annoyed him: beneath the gloss of cheeriness and goodwill, there was a streak of defiance that he'd seen in her too many times already.

At the bar, he got olives and nuts; he wasn't particularly hungry, but he supposed he needed something to soak up the wine. The guy who served him looked bored and possibly stoned. "That's everything, yeah?"

"Yes, ta."

He really had expected Kay to talk to him by now. Even if she wasn't going to gripe about the assistant post, he'd thought she might ask if he was okay. He wanted to throw her concern back in her face; wanted to remind her, again, that they weren't friends, that there was nothing between them.

But she hadn't said so much as "Hi" to him.

In Lycopolis, he switched his status to visible, said "Evening, all," to the Chatroom. A handful of people greeted him in response. No-one asked about Kay. They probably didn't want to risk getting on the wrong side of him.

He couldn't remember when he'd last felt this exhausted; too many sleepless nights, too many mornings of waking before dawn. There were times when he had to remind himself that it was really worth it: once he had the Prince's power at his disposal, he would never be afraid again. No-one would be able to hurt him – and everyone who'd opposed him in the past would pay.

But Edwin looked up to him, like a little brother might: there was something lost and hurt there, a streak which ran deeper and darker than all the irritating Goth pretensions.

It didn't matter: Edwin was what the Prince demanded. No point regretting that.

He finished his wine, then opened up a Messenger window.

"Ed, how're you feeling?"

"Kinda sick."

Sympathy was easy enough to fake. "You eaten anything?"

"No."

"You'll feel better if you do."

"Mm." A pause. "I'm really sorry about this morning."

"Don't worry about it." Time for a little damage limitation. "I'm not cross with you."

"Really?"

"Really. You just gave us quite a scare. But I guess it wasn't the greatest weekend for you. Sorry about that."

"It's okay. I shouldn't have had so many of the Sins and stuff." Edwin sent a sad emoticon, perhaps forgetting that he generally eschewed them for a lack of Goth-ness.

"Anyway," Seth typed. "Doing anything next weekend?"

"Nope."

"Come up to London. I'll show you around a bit. And we'll get that bullying thing sorted out."

"What, seriously? Just me? Not all the others too?"

"Just you."

"Seriously?"

"Yes." This was going to get rapidly irritating. "Ed, don't be so incredulous. I like you, okay? You're good fun."

"Thanks!" Then, "I'm not sure if Mum will agree. She keeps going on at me today, she reckons I look ill."

"You could always imply that a group of us are getting together again for the weekend. Make her feel like you'd be the only one missing out." He kept to himself the fact that no fourteen-year-old's mother was going to feel comfortable sending him off alone to meet up with a near-stranger.

"Yeah, okay. That's a good idea. Thanks, Seth!"

The heavy mist outside had turned to rain, pattering against the window next to him. He finished the olives. They were good: meaty, nicely flavoured.

In Lycopolis, the Chatroom was still unusually quiet. He roamed around, invisibly, watching the scene in the Knights' keep developing – Brandon had joined them too now, as Sir Wilhelm. They were in Tristram's chamber, the doors locked and barred.

He thought about sending a spy along. Thought about hurling a few special effects into their scene; playing the Prince's role, sending black smoke drifting into the room. The idea was simultaneously tempting and very uncomfortable. It would mean striding carelessly over a line which he wasn't sure he could risk crossing.

So he sat and watched, hands idle on the table. The bar was starting to empty now, people drifting away, heading home, their weekends finished. Tomorrow, they'd join the commuter cattle on the packed morning tubes back into the City, submerge themselves in work, and surge back out again like a wave in the evening.

He could never live like that.

The game beeped softly, and he looked back down at the screen.

A coil of black smoke was seeping under Tristram's door.

Seth felt like his stomach had been given a sharp tug towards his back. In the game, Tristram was ushering Benedict away from the door – drawing a sword, Wilhelm and Matilda flanking him. The mist curled in front of them, drifted on towards Benedict, until Tristram stood directly in its path. Then it balled in the air and spiralled, before vanishing up into the ceiling.

He shut the laptop down, slid it into his bag, and headed out into the London night. He didn't have an umbrella, but the rain was thin and insubstantial. The cold air was waking him up, clearing his head. He walked home, rather than taking the tube.

The flat still felt too silent. He took out his phone and put on a podcast – *Moderate Fantasy Violence* – just to have some background noise. His journal was lying on his desk; he must have left it out when he went off to Nottingham.

He turned to the list at the front, and added a new name.

Katherine Blake.

Soon, very soon, no-one would be able to get in his way. No-one would dare threaten him. And every single name on the list would be crossed out, one by one. What price was he willing to pay for that?

Whatever it took. Nothing was too much.

And what he'd been asked for was little enough.

There was no point wishing it was something else: some kid he didn't know and didn't care about; a piece of society's flotsam, dragged off the streets and given to the forest. Perhaps that was the point: he'd ended up caring about Edwin. A sacrifice had to be meaningful. It had to be something you were sorry to lose.

Or was there more to this? Edwin's medallion had been an exact match for the game one. There had to be a reason why the Prince had created it. Edwin had mentioned that his father had originally owned it; did that mean anything?

No-one was untraceable, not online. He pulled up a browser window on the computer and opened Facebook. Of course, Edwin didn't have his mother listed as a friend. But Seth found a comment to Edwin from a Sue Mitchell: *'I'll be round on Sunday afternoon. Bringing a chocolate cake for my favourite nephew!'* She'd ended it with a smiley face.

Sue's page didn't list any siblings, but it had her school history right back to nursery. Plus photos.

Seth headed to the most promising album, which dated from July: "Edwin's fourteenth."

There were photos of Edwin – looking sulky – along with Sue, and with another woman who Seth assumed must be his mother, though she wasn't tagged. She was thin, a bit paler than Sue, with mousy brown hair and an alarmed smile.

He downloaded a photo of her.

There was no way of knowing whether Sue was the older or younger sister. He didn't have a date of birth for Edwin's mother, or even a first name. He searched through the logs of every conversation he'd ever had with Edwin for the words "mum" and "mother".

A throwaway line in a conversation three months ago told him that she'd been eighteen when Edwin was born. And he did have Edwin's date of birth. That pinned her to one of two possible school years. It seemed safe enough to assume that she'd been to the same secondary school as Sue. He made a list of names and started sending out messages, with the photo attached.

I wonder if you know this woman, Ms Mitchell? She might have been in your year at school. I'm a lawyer acting on behalf of her family, and I'm trying to track down a man who she may have been in a relationship with when she was about 17 – do you know his name?

Any help you can provide would be most appreciated.

After an hour, he'd had a few "No idea, sorry" replies, and a couple of justifiably sceptical ones – but then a longer message came in.

Oh my God, yes!! Lucy was in the year above me at school. She got pregnant when she was in Year 12. The guy she was with ditched her and ran off – everyone was talking about it for weeks! I suppose you're after him for the maintenance or something? His name was Mark Webster.

He stared at the screen.

Mark Webster.

Surely not?

He opened up the Lycopolis registration database, and looked down the list. *Webster, Hannah. Webster, Mark.*

He took a deep breath and let it out slowly.

The chances were incredibly small. Thirty-five people played Lycopolis: it wasn't like stumbling across a lost relative on Facebook or Twitter. But the pieces all fitted together. He grabbed his journal and jotted everything down. Mark was about the right age. He would probably have been exactly the sort of teenage boy to give his girlfriend a wolf medallion. And it had letters on the back.

Seth found the item description in the database. Yes: *R.R.* Mark's character – Roderic Revelry. Yesterday afternoon, Mark and Hannah had mentioned live action role-playing; perhaps Mark had stuck with the same character since his teens.

So, Mark was the father that Edwin wanted so much.

But how did *Mark* feel? He presumably didn't know anything about his son – the message from Lucy's classmate made it clear that he'd taken off in a hurry. He'd probably kept it secret for years.

One email was all it would take. A few lines to Edwin, or to Mark, to change their lives.

But, interesting as it would be to see how they'd react, he wouldn't send that message just yet. He wasn't going to waste such a powerful card by playing it too soon.

He'd wait.

Did the Prince know who Edwin's father was? Had the Prince's power been infused in Lycopolis from the start, drawing Edwin and Mark to the game? He felt faintly sick. Yes, he'd constructed Lycopolis for the Prince of Nightmares, had woven it from his own dreams, from the stories he'd written in the journal. But he hadn't expected the Prince to be … involved. Not without an invitation. Not before the summoning.

Perhaps the Prince hadn't demanded Edwin just because *Seth* cared about him. If he sacrificed Edwin to the Prince, Mark would lose the son he'd never known. Kay would lose a friend, the kid she'd tried and failed to protect.

It would be a last resort. If there was another way to control the Prince – any other way – he'd take it. But if not, Edwin was, surely, a small price to pay.

Chapter 19

"You sure that's enough?" Robert asked, counting out ten-dollar bills. Two hundred and thirty, two forty, two fifty.

"Course it is," Carl said, handing the laptop over. "Enjoy."

"Thanks." Robert slid it into his backpack.

"Can you do a shift on Saturday?"

"Sure." It'd be a good excuse to get out of the church picnic.

He headed out of the bookstore, the laptop heavy against his back. Over the weekend, his parents had moved his desktop from his bedroom to the family room, after some sermon about the evils of pornography, violent games and movie piracy. He knew better than to object.

As he walked, he sent his mother a text. *Got an extra credit class, home late.* He never felt guilty about lying. He tried to. Last night, he'd lain awake, turning over his thoughts, searching for some nugget of regret or shame. In church, he grasped at the prayers for forgiveness, but they just washed over him now.

He headed past McDonald's, straight to the coffee shop at the end of the row. While he stood in line, he dug a few crumpled dollar bills from his pocket.

"You've got wi-fi, right?" he asked the girl behind the counter.

"We sure do! There's no password, just go right ahead and connect. You enjoy your coffee now."

"Thanks." He wasn't really buying coffee, though – he was buying some freedom. Three dollars was a bargain, for that. He found a quiet corner of the coffee shop, near a power outlet; Carl had warned that the battery wasn't great. He put his backpack carefully on the floor and pulled the laptop out. It was chunky and solid – a bit dated, perhaps, but he liked its rugged, slightly battered look. Most vitally, it gave him a lifeline: a place he could escape to, if only for a few snatched hours.

There were several new posts on the Lycopolis forums, including some photos from Nottingham. He wished he'd been able to be there. He did have the money. But he also had school, and his job at the bookstore, and parents who'd barely let him out of the state, let alone out of the country.

Under the textbooks in the bottom of his wardrobe, though, his passport was waiting.

He scrolled through the photos; Hannah had captioned them with everyone's character names and their real ones. The first was *"Kay (Tristram) and Edwin (Benedict)."* He knew Kay was a girl in real life, but it still somehow took him by surprise. She had her hair in a braid, and she wore lipstick. Although she was smiling, Edwin was staring stony-faced at the camera. His hair was black, almost to his shoulders, and he was wearing a black T-shirt with some band logo on the front. Robert had seen a whole group of Goths the one time he went to Austin. They'd seemed nice enough.

"Mark (Roderic)" was a bigger guy than Robert had imagined, holding a beer. If he ever made it to England, he wanted to try their beer. Over there, he'd be old enough to drink already.

The next photo was *"Brandon (Wilhelm)"* staring down at a book. He was sitting on a wooden chair with carved arms and a high, curved and pointed back. A row of shelves next to him held dusty bottles, like a creepy drugstore from a horror film.

There was a shot of Edwin standing on the bench, hands through metal rings that were fixed in the wall. He looked like he was trying not to laugh.

Another shot of Kay came next: she was smiling at something off-camera, a coloured drink in her hand. They were all good photos – deftly composed, neatly focused. The only picture of *"Hannah (Matilda)"* was a little bit blurred. He liked Hannah instantly; there was something reassuring about her, motherly. There was a small silver cross just visible around her neck.

There were no photos of Seth. Robert didn't waste long wondering why. He was keen to get back into Lycopolis. For an hour or two, he could be Heidi, and forget about his real life.

132

A couple of people greeted him when he logged in, but the Chatroom was mostly busy with talk about the weekend. Edwin and Mark were discussing the Seven Deadly Sins, which confused Robert until he realised that these were the names of some cocktails.

What would his father think, if he knew that Robert had online friends who were Goths and atheists? Robert imagined printing out the photos, thrusting them at his parents, saying, *Look, these are my friends, these are the people who care about me and who accept me, just as I am.* It was another ten months till he could escape to college. He was going to head as far out of state as possible. Out of America, if he could. He'd pack and leave; he'd write to say he wanted nothing more to do with them or their church.

In the Chatroom, people were talking about a forum post, something to do with Kay. Robert clicked on the link, read the post and Kay's response: it was so unexpected that he didn't feel shocked, just confused. Why would Seth get rid of her?

He broke with his usual policy of not getting involved, and asked the Chatroom, "What happened?"

There were a few "dunnos," but he got a private message from Mark, asking, "Did you think there was anything between them? I'd had the impression they were going out, or close to it."

Robert's first response was bemusement: why would Mark expect him to have any idea? But, of course, Mark thought he was a girl, and one the same age as Kay – it was getting harder and harder to keep up the pretence. Mark must assume they talked about boys or something.

"I don't know," he typed, cautiously, "She's not said much to me about him."

There was never going to be a good time to explain. He'd stuck with "Heidi" in the Chatroom and on the forums for too long, and he'd let their assumptions stand unchallenged. He felt like he was lying, and for some reason, that bothered him, even though telling outright lies to his parents didn't. But he could hardly just log in and say, "Oh yeah, forgot to mention, I'm actually a guy."

When Kay appeared, the Chatroom filled up with greetings and commiserations. A couple of the other Knight players were offering to get together a petition to have her reinstated.

"Seriously, it's fine," she told them.

Then Robert got a message: "Got time to role-play? Sir T wants to talk to Heidi. Some Big Plans coming up..."

"Sure thing. Come to the University."

* * *

"I'll be brief," Tristram said.

Heidi lifted a stack of papers from a chair and set them on the already precarious heap on her desk.

"I need your help." He didn't sit down.

"Go ahead."

He hesitated, as if gathering his thoughts. "You know my squire was ... was given to Matilda, by that demon."

"Yes," she said. "I gather you have him back, though?"

He looked surprised for a moment, then sighed. "If only supplies could travel as fast as gossip. Yes. I have him back and – this, I hope you have not heard – I've granted Matilda the protection of the Keep."

"No, I had not heard that. In fact, I'd be less surprised if you told me you'd shoved her head on a pole outside your gates."

"A good number of my men feel the same way." Lowering his voice, he asked, "Are we safe to speak in confidence here?"

She nodded.

"We need to stop this demon. It's growing more powerful and more dangerous."

He told her about it in brief and unemotional words – which conjured up vivid images in her mind. How the demon had caused the ground to shake, how Tristram had seen true fear in Matilda's eyes, how Benedict had been given a medallion which could not be unfastened.

There was so much she did not know; so much to learn. "This medallion is extremely significant. It's the one physical artefact we have. Might I examine it?"

He frowned. "I wish Benedict had never been involved in any of this."

It was not often that she heard concern in his voice. "What is it you wish me to do?"

"Stop this demon. Destroy it."

She looked at him. He was serious. "Sir Tristram – I don't have that kind of ability. No-one does. What Lord Cyrric did in the Temple of Shadows was something entirely new."

"There must be demon lore. Old stories, folk tales, I don't care. Some way to do it. Heidi, surely you have come across *something* in your studies."

Slowly, she nodded. "The library at Kystanton has archives. And there have always been rumours of – unusual practices – there."

"Then we're going to Kystanton."

Heidi blinked. "You and me?"

"Matilda too, and Wilhelm," he said.

"You're not going to like what I'm about to suggest..."

Tristram made an impatient gesture.

"...we should take Benedict," she said.

"No. Out of the question."

But the medallion might be a gift from the demon, imbued with magic. Heidi had to look at it, and perhaps show it to other scholars. And if it really was inseparable from the boy, then she could hardly take it to Kystanton without also taking him.

She knew this argument would not win Tristram round, though. So she said, "He'll be safer with us than left behind here."

"Damn it," he said, then shook his head a couple of times. "You're right. We'll take him. We go tomorrow night, by the Old Gate."

She grimaced. "That's hardly the easiest route..."

"You have a better idea?"

"No." At least with two knights and Matilda, the wild animals would be less of a danger.

"At twilight, before the patrols begin," he said. "Meet us there."

They shook hands, and Tristram strode out, leaving Heidi with her papers and her thoughts.

It was perhaps half an hour later when she heard the whisper.

"Heidi. Heidi. Heidi."

She lifted her gaze from her book. The door was locked. The furniture was unmoved. The window was closed.

"Heidi. Heidi."

Closing the book, she spoke aloud to the empty room. "If you want to speak to me, then speak."

"You would not destroy me." The voice had an odd quality. She focused on that, trying to isolate what was strange about it. A hoarseness, as though it had not spoken for a very long time. A slight echo. Some distortion, as if it came through a sheet of glass to her.

"I am not taking sides," she said, hands folded calmly in her lap. "I am an academic. I came into this to observe, not to take part."

"I have so much to give you. Knowledge, greater than any mortal's..."

She felt, and tried to rationalise, a tug at her heart, a quickening of her pulse; that same brightening she had always experienced when some new and deeper knowledge beckoned. This demon could take her into mysteries that no-one had ever explained. There were volumes to be written that no hand had dared attempt.

"I said, I'm not taking sides. It's Sir Tristram who talks of destruction. Not me."

"Good." The word was breathed around the room. She caught a glimpse of smoke, a thin trail of black around the window frame – and then it was gone, and she almost doubted the evidence of her own eyes.

Firmly, she reminded herself that she needed to keep her wits about her.

The room was somehow a little colder and almost dull: heaps of flat papers, cheap, practical furniture. Shelves of dusty books that never quite lived up to her hopes.

Her thoughts turned to tomorrow night, and the days to follow. She would go with Tristram, of course, but she was in no way subject to his command. If she chose to do a little research of her own whilst in Kystanton, he needn't know.

* * *

Two new words on the screen caught Robert's attention so suddenly that he knocked the mug with his hand. Cold coffee spilled across his wrist.

Hello, Robert.

No-one in Lycopolis knew his name. He'd been very careful about that, right from the start. How in the world could Seth have found out?

I know you're there, Robert.

He folded his arms, forcing himself not to touch the keyboard. Had Seth somehow worked out who he was from his registration details? But he'd set up a new email address for Lycopolis, there was nothing that had his name attached.

Robert. Robert. Robert.

His hand shook on the touchpad as he closed the Lycopolis window. He looked around the coffee shop, grounded himself back in reality. Tinny music. Men in suits. Staff chatting behind the counter.

If Seth was going to play stupid games, then Robert just had to man up and tell him to quit it. He logged into Messenger, where he used "Heidi" as his handle, just like in Lycopolis.

"How did you know my name?" he asked Seth.

"Hmm? I don't."

"But you called me Robert, just now."

There was a short pause. "In the game?"

"Yes!" Robert blew air out through pursed lips, feeling quite justifiably irritated.

This time, it was three full minutes, according to Messenger, before Seth replied. "Ah. Yes."

"So how the hell did you know my name?" He felt a brief twist of something hotter than anger when he typed *hell*.

"Like I said, I don't – or, rather, didn't. That wasn't me. Anyway, your name's Robert? I thought you were a girl?"

Robert could feel a prickle right up the back of his neck and over his scalp. "I'm not, but that doesn't matter. If it wasn't you just now, then who was it?"

"You won't want to hear it."

"I do. Shoot." His head was already full of muddled ideas: maybe Kay had been pushed out of the assistant position because Seth wanted her playing the Prince instead; maybe there'd been someone else behind the game all along and Seth was just a figurehead.

"Bear with me a minute," came from Seth. "This might sound like a tangent, but it's not. When the Prince was talking to Heidi, how did she feel about that?"

"She was excited. Curious. Keen to know more. Knowledge is what matters most to her."

"How about to *you*?"

"Huh? You lost me," he typed, which wasn't quite true. His stomach felt tight, and he could feel his heart beating a bit harder and faster than usual.

"You're after knowledge, aren't you? Truth."

Robert stalled, played dumb. "I don't know what you mean."

"Look, even though I should've realised you were playing cross-gender, it's never been much of a secret that you're a Bible Belt kid trying atheism on for size."

"It's more than that! Look, I can't even talk about this stuff to anyone. My parents would have a fit. I'm just trying to work out what's *real*."

"So ... knowledge and truth?"

For a long moment, Robert looked at the screen without typing anything. He glanced at his watch. It was almost six. He should get home.

He closed the laptop and shoved it into his backpack. The front of his head ached oddly, as though he'd bruised it somehow. He headed into the coffee shop's bathroom to look at his forehead in the mirror. There was a mark. He touched it with a finger. The flesh was slightly raised, a little warm to the touch, tender.

Much later, when he lay awake in the dark, thinking about knowledge and truth and what was real and what was just a bunch of stories, he still couldn't reason everything away.

It was unsettling. But, beneath that, there was something else. If he'd been brave enough to listen earlier, perhaps Seth would have told him everything. Maybe there was something real. Something to fill that emptiness inside him, to replace the hollow where he'd once believed in God.

When he slept, eventually, he found his way into the forest, and he kept walking, deeper and deeper into the trees.

Chapter 20

Tristram's lantern barely pierced the fog. They were all on horseback, following the rough path leading away from the Old Gate. It was a cold evening, rain starting to fall; a stroke of luck – Cyrric's guards would stay holed up in a tavern, neglecting their patrols.

They rode in silence for a while, the horses' hooves and the howl of the wind the only sounds. The path was already becoming rougher.

For a cold, uneventful half-hour, the rain gradually worsened. Suddenly, a streak of lightning split the sky. Thunder roared from the mountains. Tristram's lantern swung sharply, then was snuffed out by the wind. Benedict's horse reared. Tristram saw the movement, turned hard, reached out and grabbed its reins, bringing it back under control.

"Keep a firm grip," he said to Benedict. "Don't get jittery or you'll unnerve her too."

It was poor advice. He could hardly expect the boy not to be frightened, riding out into the wilderness in heavy fog, with Matilda alongside them. The rain was pouring down now. He wished there'd been some other route – but this was their one decent chance. The five of them were the city's hope of salvation.

It was almost impossible to hear anything over the rain and the beat of hooves. They rode on through the night, the wind biting through clothes, animal howls rising out of the wilderness as the path grew rockier. Dawn was casting a grey light as they reached Kystanton. Heidi and Benedict were both pale, exhausted; Matilda hid her tiredness better, but he saw it in the way she dismounted, slowly and unsteadily.

The guard on the gate was a scruffy boy no older than Ben. Tristram asked him for directions to the nearest boarding house, and they rode there.

A stable-hand took the horses from them; Tristram passed him a handful of coins. A girl, barely ten years old, led them shyly through the tavern – deserted at this hour – and up a staircase.

"There's room for five here," she said, heaving a door open. "You can pay Ma this evening."

It was clean and warm, which was all he could expect. Tristram nodded, and said, "See we're not disturbed, will you? We've been riding all night."

The girl nodded, gave Matilda a timid glance, then ran off.

They were all too tired to do more than shed an outer layer of clothing and find somewhere amongst the straw to spread a blanket. Tristram stayed close to Benedict. "You look troubled."

Benedict hesitated. "What if it comes after us?"

"Have you heard its voice again?"

Benedict shook his head – but his hand went to the medallion around his neck.

"We're going to destroy this demon, Ben. We're going to set everything to rights."

* * *

Kay wished she could be that confident in real life.

But what could she do? She was trying to pull the storyline back round in the game and get as many of the characters as possible away from the city. She'd planned it all. But with her assistant powers, she'd have been able to do more: generate invite codes and create new characters to help.

She and Seth had been friends, just a few weeks ago. They'd chatted almost every evening for months. And now he'd sacked her, without even bothering to email first. He'd left her to find out from the forums, like everyone else.

When she went into the corridor kitchen, she found Brandon lying full length on the table, gazing at the ceiling.

"You all right?" she asked him.

"Yes."

She poured milk into a pan. "Want cocoa?"

140

"Okay." He sat up, on the table. She found a couple of clean mugs and made cocoa for them both.

She wanted to talk to him about the weekend, about Seth, about the demon. But she didn't know what to say. It seemed wrong to drag Brandon, or anyone, into this. Besides, if she talked openly about what she knew – the reality of what was happening – would he even understand?

Sitting on the table next to him, she drank her cocoa silently. Perhaps she'd done all that she could, for one night. She'd pushed the story her way in the game. Tristram would destroy the demon. This had all started in the game: surely it could be ended there too.

She tried, very hard, to believe that.

"Are you upset?" Brandon asked. "About not being Seth's assistant any more."

Cupping her hands around her mug, she said, "Yeah, a bit."

"You didn't sound upset on the forums."

"No. I ... didn't want to." She'd written three drafts of that post before she'd managed to strike a suitable nonchalant tone. "It wouldn't have helped."

Maybe she should've let everyone get up in arms about it. She was still tempted to. A few words from her would set the Chatroom ablaze. They'd rally round her. And faced with sufficient unpopularity, Seth might actually start to listen. He might change the storyline. Might.

"Brandon, I know it's an odd question – but have you had any dreams about a forest?"

He shook his head. "No. I don't dream like that."

"What do you dream about?"

"Numbers."

She blinked. "Really?"

"Yes." He didn't sound annoyed, nor at all embarrassed.

"Well ... the rest of us have been dreaming about a forest. The *same* forest. Me and Hannah and Edwin at least, and I'm pretty sure Seth is too."

"A real forest?"

"Sorry?" she said.

"Is it a real place?"

"No, it's –" She stopped. Because there was no reason why it couldn't be. "I don't know. Perhaps."

And, for some reason, that thought was especially chilling. What was it the Prince had said about the forest? *It's where Seth met me.* Could the twisted trees and gripping mud of her nightmares be real? And if they were, if this forest was an actual place, was Seth planning to go back there?

"I've got some things I need to do," she said to Brandon, and headed back to her room. She shut the door, and leant against the wall.

She needed to keep everyone safe. She closed her eyes, screwing them so tightly shut that she saw flashes of sickly red. If only she could've fixed it through the game alone – but that didn't seem like it was going to work.

There was one thing she could do. One thing she'd sworn never to do again.

Pulling on her coat, she headed out into the cold afternoon. The sky was already dark. She walked across the river, and turned right – it would be quieter than trying to push through the High Street. But the pavements were crowded with pedestrians, and Holywell Street was full of cyclists. At last she reached Broad Canvas, where she picked her way down the narrow stairs, and searched for what she needed – coloured skeins of thread, needles. She added buttons, some lengths of ribbon. There wasn't much in the way of fabric, but that didn't matter; she could cut up some clothes.

It would have to do.

Back in her room, she upturned the bag over her bed, letting the ribbons and threads spill out. She looked at them. Her arms felt heavy. It seemed like an effort just to take her coat off and hang it over her chair.

Three years ago, after she'd hidden that terrible doll, and sat there, too numb to cry, she'd promised herself that she'd never try anything like that again, never.

But there was nothing else she could do. Seth had taken her assistant powers away. She couldn't compete in Lycopolis. She couldn't twist the game away from him and protect them all.

There wasn't much she could use: no hair from any of them, nothing signed by their own hands. She went over to the computer and opened up her Messenger logs. They went back for months. She copied hours of conversations; one file for each of them: Edwin, Hannah, Mark. There was hardly anything for Brandon, of course – but a couple of times, they'd talked on Messenger while playing Lycopolis.

She shrank the font size and printed it all out, covering sheets of paper in dense black text.

Heidi was more of a problem. She didn't even know Heidi's real name, and all their conversations had been in Lycopolis, often in the Chatroom. She pieced together as much as she could.

And then there was Seth. She'd come back to him.

Carefully, she took the first page of printout: Edwin's. She tore it into thin strips, which she screwed up into tight balls. Then she got started on the doll. She cut the limbs and torso from an old T-shirt, stuffed it with the paper balls, and sewed it together. She made clothes from a black sock, hair from black thread.

It was hardly a work of art. But it didn't need to be.

She moved on to the next, fastening pieces of cloth with tiny stitches. Her fingers were starting to cramp. She paused, flexed her hand, then kept going.

Two down.

She worked steadily through the evening, forgetting about dinner until her stomach growled. She grabbed a sandwich and got back to work.

What did Heidi look like, in real life? She had no idea – and there was no easy way to find out; she couldn't just ask for a photo, without any explanation. She made the doll look a bit like the character Heidi, with pale skin and blonde hair.

There were five little dolls lying on her bed now.

She signed her name, over and over, on a piece of paper, and made a doll for herself. Six. Carefully, she stuck her needle into the notice-board next to her desk.

The worst that could happen was that there was nothing real here at all, just make-believe.

No, that was far from the *worst*, and she knew it. But it would be okay. She'd made each doll with love, with care, thinking only how she wanted, more than anything, to keep each person safe.

She wasn't sure she could do that for Seth.

Chapter 21

Oxford Street was packed with people. The shops and buildings were so huge that Edwin felt like he'd shrunk. The pavement was crowded, everyone surging in different directions; men in hoodies and men in suits, groups of girls teetering on high heels, groups of teenagers with rucksacks and cameras. And Seth was already moving.

Edwin followed, hastily, keeping his eyes on Seth's coat – long and black and sort of sweeping, it'd have made a good Goth coat. He almost got run into by a woman with a pushchair, and mumbled "sorry" at her.

Once they got to a quieter bit of pavement, he managed to catch up with Seth properly. Most of the shops were familiar names, but they were stretched-out versions of the ones back home – H&M took up three enormous windows.

"Never been to Oxford Street, then?" Seth asked, as they stood waiting to cross the street.

"Nah, Mum's not really keen on shopping." The green man lit up, and they walked across in a scrum of people. "I don't go shopping with her any more, of course, well, only for school uniform and stuff like that."

"Of course. Anyway, there's a shop just along here I think you'll –"

"Oh cool!" Edwin could see it now, the name, *Metal Militia,* in a spiky font above the door.

It was just a small shop but it was packed with clothes. He started leafing through a rack of T-shirts. There was one which had *DEATH* printed across the front in silver. He pulled it out and held it in front of himself.

"It'd look good on you," Seth said.

Edwin reckoned so too. Except he only had £12, and it cost £15. He kept hold of it anyway, though, while he looked at the others. He considered and rejected a lurid Iron Maiden T-shirt, then contemplated one with a wolf emblazoned across the front. A couple of months ago, he'd have wanted that.

Leaving the T-shirts, he flicked through a rack of belts: black leather with silver studs and sinister buckles. One belt was a chain, chunky links of metal that hung heavily in his hands. He looked at the price tag. Never mind.

Seth came over and took it from him. "I'll get it for you. Found some T-shirts you like?"

Edwin couldn't just let Seth spend money on him. It didn't feel right. "You don't need to –"

"Ed, if a few belts and T-shirts will cheer you up a bit, grab some. I've got plenty of cash."

"But ... you can't pay for things for me."

"Of course I can. I *want* to, okay?"

"Um, I kinda like this." Edwin held up the *DEATH* one.

Seth took it from him. "Is that all you want? Go on, get another."

They went to an Italian place for lunch. Seth seemed to know the waiter, who looked at Edwin, raised an eyebrow, and murmured something to Seth that Edwin couldn't hear. Seth laughed, shook his head, and said, "No. He's ... a friend."

Edwin still had to suppress the very un-Goth urge to grin whenever Seth said that.

There were a few other people in the restaurant, all older than them; a grey-haired couple and a group of women about his mum's age, all in flouncy jackets and skirts and tall boots.

"Right, Ed. What do you want to eat?"

The menu was in Italian, so he said, "Um, lasagne."

Seth picked up the wine list, ran a finger down it. "Now, this seems like as good a chance as any to get you into red wine."

"I don't really drink wine. Well, white, sometimes." Not that Mum usually let him. Plus, he'd pretty much decided last weekend that alcohol just wasn't worth the hangover.

Seth raised his eyebrows at him across the table. "Come on, Ed, you're a Goth, you're going to have to start drinking red at some point."

"Well, what about vodka and Coke? That's *black*."

"Black isn't necessarily the pinnacle of Goth. I'll get you a glass of Chianti."

"Oh, cool, like Hannibal Lecter?"

"Yeah. Cannibalism's optional, though. Even for Goths."

The waiter brought wine for them both, in tall glasses filled half-way – not like the little round ones Mum had at home. To Edwin's surprise, he liked it. The lasagne was great too. Mum hardly ever made lasagne, and when she did, she never put enough cheese on it. He dug down through the pasta and meat: as usual, he was hungry.

In between mouthfuls he said, "This is really good."

"Yep. It's one of my favourite places." Seth was eating something which had an unpronounceable name, but seemed to be pasta in a thick tomatoey sauce, with chunks of sausage.

"D'you come here a lot then?" Edwin asked, tearing a piece of garlic bread in half.

"Not infrequently."

"On your own?"

Smiling, Seth shook his head. "Usually with girls."

Edwin laughed, sort of embarrassed. "Oh. Right, yeah. You've, um, got a girlfriend?"

"Nope. Too much hassle."

Edwin continued with his lasagne, trying, and failing, to imagine himself in the sort of life where he took girls to restaurants.

"Seth," he said, "Can I ask you something?"

"Sure."

"Have you ever been in love?"

Seth frowned, just slightly. "I'm not convinced there's really any such thing as love. Lust, maybe, or even infatuation, but not love."

"But when it's ... I dunno, something more?"

Seth leant back in his chair, wine in hand. "It makes people vulnerable. Why're you asking?"

"It's just something I think about. Sometimes."

"Want a bit of advice?"

147

He nodded, and tried to mirror Seth, who was sort of slouched – easily, casually. He couldn't quite make it work.

"Forget about love. It's just a form of weakness. Look, Ed, whether it's romantic or familial or platonic love ... it's all the same. It's all going to end up with you worrying about other people's feelings when you should be concentrating on yourself."

Edwin finished his lasagne. "That's sort of ..."

"Bleak? Yeah. Welcome to the real world." For a second or two, there was something a bit mocking in Seth's smile. "Love is overrated. You're better off getting high, or drunk."

"So why do you bring girls here, then?"

Seth grinned. "I didn't say *sex* was overrated."

Seth had the most awesome flat that Edwin had ever seen. It was in a swish block right by the Thames. The living room was huge. There was a window from floor to ceiling on the far side – looking right out over the river – and a sofa facing it, and a wide-screen television on the wall opposite, with a couple of armchairs in front of it.

It was Seth's computer, though, which really grabbed Edwin's attention. "Oh cool, you've got two monitors! How can you do that?"

"With two graphics cards. Grab a seat, Ed. Do you want a coffee?"

"Um, no thanks." He sat down on the computer chair. Seth's desk was super tidy, bare except for a couple of pens. Maybe he should take a photo to show Mum, then he'd have *proof* that Seth was a good influence.

Pulling a chair over, Seth said, "Open up a browser window. We'll sort out this bullying crap. Who's the ringleader?"

That was easy. "Darren Miller. But what are we going to –"

"I'll show you."

And for the next hour, Seth taught him how to find out all sorts of things about Darren Miller online. They used Google for a lot of it, though Seth had some bits of software that sped things up. Once they'd got Darren's email address, they could find him on Facebook and Instagram and all sorts of other sites.

"It's amazing how much people put online," Seth said, "Photos, phone numbers, home addresses."

For a moment, Edwin wondered how much *he* had put on the internet ... how much Seth, or anyone else, might be able to find out about him. But then they came across a forum post by Darren's mum.

"I didn't know Darren had a little sister," Edwin said. On the screen, there was a picture of Darren, looking as bulky and nasty as ever, holding a toddler in his arms. If there hadn't been a caption beneath the photo ("Darren holding Stacey, he's so good with her!") – Edwin would've reckoned that Darren was about to steal her or something.

Seth took over, bringing up a list of all Darren's mum's posts on the forum. They read that she was worried about how Darren was getting on at school, concerned he "doesn't mix very well" with the other kids, and that she thought the Maths teacher was picking on him.

Edwin had never seen it that way at all – Darren was always clowning around in class, laughing off anything the teachers said. "Maybe we shouldn't read this, it's sort of private, isn't it?"

"Ed, she's posted it online for the world to see."

That was true, but ... "Well, she doesn't use his name or anything. Maybe she wanted to keep it anonymous."

"Nothing's anonymous online unless you're very careful and very clever. Anyway. We've got enough. Home address, family details, photos. We know he's a mummy's boy. And that he's a miserable failure at school."

"He's not, though," Edwin said, still trying to put together in his head the Darren Miller who shoved him around on the bus every day and the Darren Miller whose mum worried about him being victimised by teachers. "He's really popular. And I'm getting sick of all the crap he puts me through."

"Well, we're about to fix all that. With one email."

It took them ages to write it, though. Seth helped a lot, offering suggestions, leaning over Edwin to type in a new sentence or change a word. Eventually, Seth nodded, and said, "I think we're done."

Edwin read through the email again.

Darren Miller,

You don't know me, but I know you, rather well. I've been watching you, Darren. Watching every single step you take. Watching you on the bus, at school, trying to make yourself out to be someone.

I've been watching you with your precious little sister (you won't be around to protect her forever, you know). Watching you when you're all alone. I've seen you cry.

I know about you, Darren. Beneath that thin surface, that bravado and bullying swagger, I know who you are. You're afraid you'll never amount to anything, never pass an exam, never get a girl. Never have a real friend.

I don't like you, Darren. I don't like stupid, pathetic little cowards. I've been watching you, Darren, for a long time. So have my friends, quite a pack of them.

You might want to start keeping a low profile, Darren. Just a hint.

You'll hear from me again.

Edwin felt the skin along the back of his neck prickle as he read it. His forehead hurt a bit; he touched his fingers there, remembered that bruise, that weird mark.

"Well?" Seth asked, "Happy with it?"

"I dunno, I guess so." But the nastiness of it made him hesitate. "He does deserve it, doesn't he?"

Seth put a hand on his shoulder. "Ed, this bastard has been making you miserable for weeks. Of course he fucking deserves it." There was a warm anger in his voice – on Edwin's behalf.

"Yeah." Every single day. Every bus journey. He'd had to put up with Darren all term. "And no-one can trace it, can they? No-one will know it was us?"

"Like I said, if you want to be anonymous online, you need to be very careful and very clever." Seth still had his hand on Edwin's shoulder. "And Ed ..."

"You're both?" Edwin finished for him.

"Precisely. Now. We need to finish the email. We need an alias, a name."

"Like what?"

"Up to you, Ed. Something chilling, something evocative. What name would scare *you*?"

There was one obvious answer. Edwin looked at the screen. It'd fit. He didn't want to say it out loud. He looked at Seth.

Seth raised an eyebrow, as if he knew exactly what Edwin had thought of, as if he was telling him, *go on, then.*

Edwin reached for the keyboard, and typed it.

The Prince of Nightmares

"Send it," Seth said.

Edwin moved the cursor to the *Send* button. And then he hesitated again. It wasn't just the email that made him uncomfortable now – it was the name they were sending it in, it was what they'd evoked.

"Go on," Seth said, impatiently.

Edwin clicked the mouse. And then the email was sent, gone, irretrievable. It was just words, after all, only words.

It had all been words when they'd summoned the Prince of Nightmares. He thought about the medallion, tucked under his T-shirt, the clasp that wouldn't unfasten.

"Ed? You all right?"

He made himself smile, even though smiling wasn't very Goth. "Yeah."

"Stuff on your mind?"

He shrugged, mumbled, "I guess."

There was a pause, then Seth asked, "You ever been high?"

Till last weekend, he'd never even been drunk. Not that he wanted to admit that to Seth, because he'd just look like a loser. "I don't do drugs. I know some Goths do, but ... I don't."

"Okay, I respect that," Seth said.

But Edwin wondered what it *would* it be like to get high. Was it anything like being drunk? In Nottingham, before he'd got to the point where his legs were wobbly, it'd felt good. He'd been warm and happy, and almost brave enough to look Kay in the eyes.

"So, films, then," Seth said, and held out a bunch of DVDs. "Take your pick."

Chapter 22

Rather predictably, Edwin chose *The Crow*. Seth put it on, indifferent; he was more interested in watching Edwin. Did he look like Mark? Perhaps there was an echo in the shape of his face, but he didn't have Mark's build. There was something waif-like about him: the straggly hair, the slightly-too-big clothes – long sleeves trailing over his hands.

They spent the rest of the afternoon and evening slouched on the sofa, moving on from *The Crow* to the Tom Cruise version of *Interview with the Vampire*. When Seth started making a Spanish omelette, Edwin came through into the kitchen and watched, fascinated. "You can cook!"

"Yep." Seth nudged him out of the way to get into the fridge. "It impresses girls."

"Do you want me to help?"

"I'm nearly done on the omelette, but you can do the fruit for the sangria." Seth gave him a couple of oranges and a knife.

"Wow, this is sharp."

"Yes – try not to dismember yourself."

They ate, drank, listened to music. Later, when the jug of sangria was almost empty, Edwin leant back on the sofa and said, "Seth?"

"Mm-hm?"

"Is this being drunk? Everything's kind of soft around the edges."

"Yeah, that's pretty much it," Seth said.

"I don't feel sick or anything."

"I wasn't going to let you drink so much you threw up. Feels good, right? Relaxing?"

"Yeah ... Seth?"

"Mm-hm?"

"What's it like to be high?"

Seth stretched one arm along the back of the sofa. "It's something you have to experience to understand."

"I don't want to take drugs."

"But you want to know what it's like to be high."

Edwin mumbled, "I just ... I just wondered."

"Why?"

"Well, they make you forget, right? I mean, for a bit. You know." Edwin was still looking away, one hand fiddling with the collar of his T-shirt. For a moment, Seth thought it was just a nervous tic – but then he saw the thin chain there.

He leant in closer, reached out to slide a finger round the chain, drawing Mark's medallion out from Edwin's shirt. "Didn't think you'd still be wearing it."

"Mm."

"You've had it on all week?"

"Yeah."

"You don't sound too happy about that."

Edwin was still staring at the carpet. "I dunno."

"Ed, what's up?"

"I couldn't take it off. I ... it's *stuck*. The clasp. I tried and tried, I couldn't undo it."

Seth hadn't expected that. He fought to hide a jolt of fear. Of course, Edwin could just be mistaken. But if the medallion really wouldn't unclasp, it was behaving exactly like the item in the game. This was proof, or the nearest thing to proof he was going to get, that the Prince of Nightmares could manipulate something *real*, something more than bits and bytes.

"I – I figured that I'd wear it anyway," Edwin said, "I mean, I wanted to. I wasn't scared."

Seth looked at the chain, a neat line across Edwin's skin. A week ago, he'd put the medallion around Edwin's neck. And somehow, he was sure that only he could unfasten it.

"Ed," he said, "Are you still having nightmares?"

Edwin didn't answer at first, his shoulders hunching up. Then, quietly, he said, "Yeah."

"About the forest?"

"Yeah. And, and something else as well. But it's always dark. I can't see properly."

"What else?"

"It's stupid."

"Tell me."

"My dad, I dreamt about my dad." The words came out in a rush. "I couldn't see his face, he had his back to me, I ... I tried to shout, I couldn't."

Seth leant forwards. "Where were you?"

"In the forest." Tears were brimming behind his lashes. "Seth, I wish it would just all stop."

"Hey, calm down. Let me have a look at that medallion." He made himself reach out, taking the wolf's head in his hand. It was just a piece of metal, nothing obviously strange about it. "Let me see if I can unfasten it."

"You can't, it's seriously *stuck*, I've tried and tried and tried."

He just pushed Edwin's head forwards, and opened the clasp, easily. He let the medallion fall into Edwin's lap.

The shock on his face almost made Seth laugh.

"But it *was* stuck!" Edwin said. "It was! Seriously. I wasn't messing around."

"Yes, I know. I believe you."

"How come you could undo it?"

"Because I fastened it on you, perhaps."

Edwin held the medallion out, his hand shaking. "Why – why would that make a difference?"

Seth shrugged. And took the medallion.

"You keep it." Edwin ran his hand over his neck. "For now, yeah? You'll look after it?"

"If you like." Seth said. "You want something to take your mind off all this?"

"What?"

"You asked about getting high. Up for trying something?"

"No, no drugs."

"That's okay. I haven't got any." He had plenty of stock in the top kitchen cupboards ... but he also had something more interesting in mind.

155

"Then what –"

Holding up a hand to shush him, Seth said, "Ever played the Choking Game?"

Edwin shook his head.

"We used to do it at school." Seth hadn't invented it – but he'd always led it. In the dorm, often in the dark, with a couple of mattresses yanked off the beds and spread on the floor. During the summer term, they'd played it out in the woods, too deep in the trees for the eyes of authority to ever see. It quickly became known as just "The Game."

"I dunno what it is," Edwin said. He gripped his hands together, fingers twisted.

"Well," Seth said, "It's basically like holding your breath."

"How, um, how does it work, then?"

"Stand up."

Edwin didn't, just leant away from him, shaking his head. Perhaps Seth had pushed him a little too soon, but he was getting impatient. "Come on, Ed, stand up."

"Um, tell me how it works first."

"Okay." Seth leant forwards, looking down at him. "This is what we do. You stand up. You breathe fast, hyperventilate. Then I put my hands on the sides of your neck, like this."

He only touched Edwin lightly, but Edwin still flinched away, a shiver rippling through him. Seth raised his eyebrows. Reddening, Edwin glanced down at the floor.

"I won't hurt you," Seth said, softly.

"I, I know. But how does it work? You'd ..." Edwin made a throttling gesture with his hands.

"That cuts off the flow of oxygen to your brain, just for a moment. You'll black out for a few seconds, and when you come round, you get a natural high from the restored oxygen."

Edwin was chewing his lower lip, still leaning away. Seth just moved in closer. "Well?"

"I dunno."

If it had just been about giving Edwin a quick thrill, he'd have let it go. But it was more than that. He needed this too. Softly, he said, "Ed, it won't make much sense till you try it. Come on. You trust me, don't you?"

156

Silence, then, "It really won't hurt or anything?"

"No. Ed, you'll enjoy it."

Edwin didn't say anything, but he got up, his arms wrapped around himself. Taking hold of his shoulders, Seth turned him so he had his back to the sofa.

"Now," Seth said, crouching a little, his eyes almost level with Edwin's. "Breathe shallow and fast."

Edwin hesitated, then did it, shoulders rising and falling under Seth's hands.

"Faster than that."

He could hear Edwin's breathing, eager and nervous. He felt a surge of adrenaline, the sharp tang of power.

It took a couple of minutes before Edwin's eyes focused on nothing. Seth pressed hard against the sides of his neck. He remembered exactly how much pressure to apply: not quite enough to bruise. Silently, he counted to five. Edwin staggered, knees buckling.

Seth shoved him backwards. He sprawled limply onto the sofa, eyes closed. For a few sweet seconds, Seth just watched him. His cheeks were flushed pink, his mouth open. One of his arms was twitching.

Seth could've knelt on the sofa and pinned him there, with a hand around his neck. Could've sent a sobering jolt of fear through him. Could've hurt him, a little, or a lot.

But he stood and waited as Edwin came round, twitching back into consciousness with gasps of laughter. His head was tilted back, his body shaking helplessly.

Seth leant over him. "Told you you'd enjoy it."

Edwin's face was flushed, his eyes still refocusing. He struggled for breath, through laughter, then moved his head slightly from side to side and said, "Woah."

Seth felt a bit giddy himself. "So? You liked it?"

"Wow." Edwin was breathless, and still grinning. "Yeah ... that was ..." He shook his head a little, as if to clear it, blinked a few times.

"Different?"

"Yeah. Wow."

Seth swept a finger along Edwin's forehead to pull a lock of hair out of his face. He didn't blanch now, still not quite back with it. "Maybe you'll believe me, next time?"

"Yeah, well, it just …" Edwin trailed off.

"I generally know what I'm doing, Ed."

For a minute or two, Edwin just stared at the window, still breathing a little faster than normal. Then, not managing to hide eagerness, he said, "Can we do it again?"

Chapter 23

Robert fumbled in his wallet for a five-dollar bill.

"You okay, honey?" The girl pointed at his head. "You've got a bruise."

"Oh, it's nothing." He took his change, and his coffee. "Thanks."

Once he was safely in his corner of the shop, he touched his forehead. Was the mark more prominent now? It didn't scare him. It fascinated him. For years, for longer than he could remember, he'd wanted some sort of sign. Something real and tangible, something to tell him that his faith – his parents' faith – wasn't all dust and false hopes.

There'd never been anything.

After all those years of disappointment, he longed for this to be something tangible. In the game, Heidi had been marked – and so had four others. In real life, Robert had the same mark – and he guessed the others did too.

In the game, they'd seen power, true power.

He flicked the laptop on and logged into Lycopolis. Benedict, Tristram and Wilhelm were online, and a new character, "Remegius, Demonologist."

Excitement rippled through him. He felt *alive* for the first time in days.

He logged into Messenger.

"Hey," he typed to Seth, "Is Remegius yours?"

"Yep. Come to the university. Bring Ben, he wants to tag along."

* * *

A student in shabby robes met Heidi at the gates, glancing around nervously before he beckoned them in. Heidi introduced herself, adding, "And this is Benedict."

The student nodded. "I'd rather keep my name out of it." He walked quickly across a courtyard and shone his lantern on a wooden trapdoor which Heidi would never have found in the dark.

"So –" she began.

"Remegius knows you're coming. Don't mention this to anyone. I wasn't here, all right?"

Before Heidi had the chance to ask anything else, he'd scuttled off. Stooping, she lifted the trapdoor.

"I think we should've told Sir Tristram," Benedict said.

"We don't want to waste time." She led the way down the stone steps, raising the lantern. A room came into view: an antechamber, furnished with a wooden bench and a desk. There was a door on the far side.

As she hesitated, wondering whether to knock, it swung open. A tall man stood framed in the doorway. There were streaks of silver in his long black hair, and Heidi guessed he was forty or forty-five. He wore dark robes, woven with an intricate, twining pattern.

"Heidi of the Plains." She held out her hand.

Remegius didn't take it. He gave Benedict a long look, then turned back to her. His hands were in the folds of his robes. She caught a glint of metal; he had a weapon concealed there, perhaps a knife.

She took a step back.

"What do you want?" His voice was low.

"I am a scholar from Lycopolis," she said. "I'm seeking information which I believe this university once held. It has taken me several days to track it to you."

He smiled, as though pleased that her search had been arduous.

"I am hoping you might be able, and willing, to help."

When he pulled his hand from his robes, saw that he had not a knife but a mirror. He held it up towards her, staring into the back of it. She gazed at her own reflection, and was struck by how white she looked, how drawn and tired her face seemed.

After a long moment, Remegius gave a nod and turned to Benedict.

Heidi angled the lantern towards them.

160

"I don't need the light." Remegius peered intently at the mirror, then pointed at the bench and said, "Take a seat."

He clearly wasn't going to invite them any further than his antechamber. This was hardly a surprise: of course he would be reclusive and paranoid, if he truly did have the information that she needed.

She longed to ask him a dozen questions about the mirror: what was it made from, how did it operate? What did he see through it – their intentions? Their histories? But she forced herself to remain focused. She sat on the bench and tugged Benedict's sleeve so that he did the same.

"I received your letter, Heidi." Remegius held it up. "The details in it are scant. Understandably so. As you perhaps surmised, the University does not look favourably upon discussions about controlling demons."

"It is a case of destroying." She should make at least a token commitment to Tristram's wishes. "Not controlling."

"The difference is academic, for now. We can discuss details later. Let me be upfront: I am keen to help you, very keen. You have stumbled into an area that I have been researching since I was no older than the boy there." As he leant towards Benedict, the candlelight illuminated his face from below, like a ghoulish mask. "What's your name, child?"

"Benedict." He was very pale. Heidi wondered whether she'd been right to bring him.

To her, Remegius said, "You must give me all the details that you have. Particularly regarding the summoning of this demon, and its manifestations since then."

"I was present at the summoning, and took copious notes." She drew her notebook from her bag.

Remegius snatched it from her hand. "Excellent. I will keep this and cross-reference it with my library." Curiosity must have shown on her face, because he added, "My books – and other materials – were gathered at great risk and cost. Not only to myself."

She wasn't sure how to reply.

"I will have questions for you, once I have reviewed these notes."

"I shall be happy to answer them," she said. "To the best of my knowledge and ability."

"Good. Now, I assume the boy has prepared no such notes?"

161

"No," she said.

Remegius took up a quill, dipping it into a pot of black ink. "Benedict, tell me everything you can remember about the night the demon was summoned."

Benedict glanced at her, as if waiting for permission. She nodded for him to go ahead.

Hesitantly, he explained how he'd crept in after the others and crouched at the back of the temple. As he talked about the slave girl bound to the altar, he shivered; he told them that he'd looked away when Cyrric brought the knife down.

Heidi found new reflections coming to mind as she listened. That night, she'd entered the Temple of Shadows as an observer, feeling no sense of responsibility or concern over what took place. But she had become as caught up in it as any of them.

"What happened after the slave girl was sacrificed?" Remegius asked.

Benedict went on, quietly, talking of Matilda, and the medallion.

"Let me see that." Remegius ran a finger around the thin chain. "You cannot remove it?"

"No, it won't unfasten. And it seems to hook into my skin." There was a long silence. "Is there any way ... can you get it off me?"

"Oh, given time, of course. Now, I must speak with Heidi." Remegius pointed towards the staircase.

Heidi said, "I'm not sure he should walk back alone, at this hour."

"There are patrols. It is not that late."

They watched him leave. Remegius sat down at his desk, and turned the pages of Heidi's notebook for several minutes. She waited, hands folded in her lap.

"The position seems clear enough," he said.

She raised a quizzical eyebrow.

"One." He held up a finger. "A demon has been summoned, but not bound to any master."

She nodded.

"And, two." Another finger. "That demon has a strong affinity to the city of Lycopolis – indeed, is known in myth as its patron."

"Yes."

Leaning across the desk towards her, he said, "There is one point on which I remain unclear. Do you really wish to destroy this demon – or do you in fact seek to control it?"

"It would be a shame to waste any opportunity for new learning."

"Quite." Looking down at the notes again, he said, "Six people were present at the summoning. Cyrric, who led it, yourself, Benedict, Matilda, Roderic ... and Tristram. And you were all marked?"

When she touched her hand to her forehead, she felt the slight heat still there. "All except Tristram. He was the only one who did not kneel."

"Yes. In case you have not yet gathered, the Prince of Nightmares draws power in this world from those present at his summoning. At, if you will, his *birth* in this realm."

"How? Draws power how?"

"Why do you think he has the name *The Prince of Nightmares*?"

"He ... draws on our fear, you mean?"

"Yes, but more basic than that." His grey eyes were locked onto hers in the candlelight. "Nightmares, Heidi. Where do they come from?"

"Well – from the mind, the imagination."

"Precisely! All things are created twice. Take, for instance, a building. The architect must *conceive* the plan before a single brick is laid. Our ability to imagine, to create a picture within our mind, makes us human."

"And that's what the demon needs? Our imaginations?"

"Yes. Yes." He stood again, and came to sit next to her on the bench. The smell of books – musty, comforting – clung to him. "But your first answer also holds. This demon does not, after all, call himself the 'Prince of Dreams' or 'Prince of the Imagination'."

"I see," she said. Her mouth was dry.

"It needs greed and fear and anger. Tell me, Heidi, have you ever been truly angry with anyone?"

She shook her head.

"If you had, you would know that anger means having a very clear picture of just how much you would like somebody to suffer." It was impossible to miss the bitterness in his voice.

Slowly, she said, "The demon appears to be getting stronger."

"Yes. It was incompetently summoned and loosed upon the world." His voice was quiet and matter-of-fact. "It is an ancient, clever and

163

powerful force, and – left unchecked – it could cause great harm to all of you."

There was silence for several minutes.

"We must bind it properly," Remegius said. "To do that, we will have to re-create the initial ceremony. I shall lead it, so we do not need Cyrric. But the rest of those who knelt – you, Benedict, Matilda, Roderic – must all be there."

Two problems presented themselves. She tackled the easier one first. "Roderic is not with us."

"Send for him," Remegius said. "Judging from what you have written in these notes, he would respond to an offer of money."

She nodded. And raised the second problem. "Tristram is not going to like this."

Remegius held her gaze in the dim light. "My dear Heidi. Tristram does not need to know."

* * *

Robert's coffee was cold. He finished it anyway. The empty chatter in the coffee shop, overlaid with the whirr of the machines, was suddenly irritating. Even the blonde girl at the counter looked plain. The whole world felt drab and meaningless.

Before, Seth had talked about power, true power. Robert brought up the Messenger window, and made himself type it. "How much of this is ... real?"

"How much of it do you *want* to be real?"

He leant forwards, hiding the screen – even though there was no-one near enough to see it. "I want there to be *something*. Some power, something greater."

"How about I tell you that more of this is real than you could dream?"

Last night, he'd dreamt of that forest again, the trees bending aside for him last night to make a path. He'd dreamt of walking on a carpet of leaves, following a sound that wrapped around his wrists and dragged him forwards. There'd been nothing frightening about it – only compelling.

"But it's a game," he typed. "How can any of it be real?"

"Looked in a mirror recently?"

His hand crept up to touch his forehead. It took him a moment before he could type, "I don't know what to do."

"Come to England."

He blinked at the words. "What?"

"Book a flight. The weekend after next."

The blood beat hard in his ears. "But then what?"

"We'll make it real, all of it."

He had no idea what to believe any more. But Heidi, even when she was scared, stayed on the path of knowledge.

"Rob, I'm just asking you to trust me enough to come to England."

"I need some time to think about it."

It was all he *could* think about, as he packed up the laptop, wrapped it in a sweater and shoved it into his backpack. On the bus home, he stared out of the window and thought about the forest, those black trees beckoning him in.

He skipped his homework. He couldn't make himself care. It seemed so pointless.

Lying awake in the dark, he touched his hand to his forehead. It still smarted. And that, somehow, made all of it seem true: pain couldn't be explained away.

At two a.m., he gave up trying to sleep. He switched his laptop on, pulled his bank card from his wallet, and booked a flight.

Chapter 24

Hannah stood in the queue in W.H. Smith's, and counted thirteen people in front of her, all clutching overflowing baskets. Hers contained an assortment of Christmas cards: cartoonish ones for Denny and Megan's classmates, religious ones for church friends, tactfully neutral ones for everyone else. Years ago, she'd always made her own cards, a glass of mulled wine to hand, listening to carols on the radio. But now, she didn't have the time or the energy or the space to do anything creative.

The queue shuffled forwards. Hannah's phone beeped. Juggling her shopping bags, she put down the basket and hooked her phone out of her coat pocket, tugging it free from the hole in the lining.

The text was from Mark. *When you home? Megan was sick at nursery & I had to collect her.*

Was it bad that her first impulse was to pretend her phone was on the blink again? She could wander the shops a while longer, disappear off for a leisurely lunch – it was already almost noon.

People were moving in front of her. She struggled along, pushing the basket with her foot. She began a reply: *How sick? Did you* – then an impatient voice broke in. "Next please. NEXT please."

Abandoning the message, she slid the phone away and hoisted her basket onto the till. The girl – perfect hair, polished nails – swiped everything through. "Thank-you-have-a-nice-day. Next please. NEXT please."

She finished the text on the bus. *How sick? Did you take her temperature? I'll be home in fifteen minutes.*

The bus jolted along, the windows steaming up. She was glad to get off, even though it meant struggling all the way up the street with her bags. As she shoved open the front door, Mark appeared from the living room.

"I didn't think you'd be shopping all morning," he said.

She set the bags down in the hall, at the bottom of the stairs. He made it sound like she'd been on some indulgent girly trip, rather than standing in queues, trying to decide who they could quietly and not-too-guiltily cut from the present list.

"Well, I had a lot to get. I did tell you yesterday, before you went out." She'd managed to bite her tongue last night, when he'd said he was going to the pub. She'd tried very hard to be understanding, telling herself that he just needed some time to adjust, that, surely, he'd be getting down to job hunting soon.

"I haven't even had a coffee yet," he said.

She looked at him – in a wrinkled shirt, which smelt of beer and sweat. He hadn't bothered shaving, either. "Did you go out like that?"

"For fuck's sake, what does it matter? I thought collecting Megan was a bit more important than having a shower. Anyway, there was nothing clean to wear."

No, there wasn't; Hannah had left a note propped against the kettle. *Gone to the shops. Could you put some laundry on? Everything's sorted into lights and darks. The powder's under the sink.*

But this wasn't the time to get into another fight about the housework. "Is Megan okay?"

"I've tucked her up under a blanket on the sofa. She's watching cartoons." Turning towards the kitchen, he said, "I need a coffee."

Hannah peeked into the living room. Megan was happily engrossed, gazing at the television.

"Did you take her temperature?" she asked, as Mark walked off.

"No, look, I just got her settled, you do whatever else you like." He banged the kitchen door behind him.

She walked into the living room, more calmly than she'd thought she could manage. Kneeling next to Megan, she said, "How're you feeling, sweetheart?"

"I was sick."

"I know, Daddy told me." She reached out and touched the back of her hand to Megan's forehead. "You don't feel hot."

"Can I have Coca-Cola?"

167

"Well..." She usually insisted that fizzy drinks were for parties and Sunday lunch only.

"Daddy said I could." Megan looked up at her, lower lip starting to wobble.

"Of course you can, then. Did Daddy give you any medicine?"

Megan shook her head.

"Silly Daddy," Hannah said, and managed to smile.

"Silly Daddy!" Megan echoed, cheerfully.

Mark had vanished upstairs, and Hannah could hear the shower running. She got a chair from the kitchen, wobbled on top of it to get the first aid box from the top of the cupboard in the hall. With the can of Coke as a bribe, she persuaded Megan to swallow a spoonful of Calpol. She laid the strip thermometer across Megan's forehead, smoothing away a strand of hair. It confirmed her guess: no temperature.

"Am I very poorly?" Megan asked.

"No, love, you've probably just got a stomach bug." Hannah wrapped the blankets around Megan again, and turned the volume down on the television. She boiled an egg, buttered two slices of toast, added a smidge of Marmite, and sliced them into soldiers. She kept hoping that her anger with Mark would fade. Life would, surely, go on. She could cook and clean and take care of Megan and Denny, and lose herself in it all – she'd forget about next week, next month, Christmas.

It didn't work. A hard, growing lump of worry lodged in her stomach and stole her appetite and her energy. She stared at the cartoons and took nothing in. After Megan finished her egg and toast, she dozed off; Hannah re-tucked the blanket around her, then switched on the computer.

Before she'd even logged into Lycopolis, a Messenger window appeared, from Seth. "Got a minute?"

"Just about," she typed, feeling suddenly irritable. She didn't want a conversation; she wanted to sink into Lycopolis and forget about real life for a few minutes. Since Nottingham, she'd barely exchanged two words with Seth.

"I wanted to apologise."

She blinked at the screen – but yes, that definitely was what he'd written. In the four months that she'd known him, she'd never seen him apologise for anything, to anyone.

His next message said, "I knew Mark was unhappy at work. I thought I was doing the right thing in encouraging him to do something about that. I certainly didn't mean to cause any difficulties or hardship for either of you."

She'd blamed Seth; she'd told herself that he'd somehow talked – goaded, pushed – Mark into leaving. But the choice had been Mark's, Mark's alone. "It's okay," she typed. "He'd probably have done the same whatever you said."

"Probably. I don't know whether he mentioned it, but I told him I'd keep an eye out for any leads. I know a few people in the IT world."

"Thanks. That's kind of you."

"It's no trouble. Anyway, I shouldn't keep you ... Mark mentioned your daughter's ill?"

Hannah glanced over at Megan; still dozing in front of the cartoons. "Just a stomach bug. She's sleeping at the moment."

"Ah, glad she's all right. Actually, if you do have a few minutes, could I ask you about something?"

"Go ahead."

"I'm planning a new scene for tomorrow night: Heidi's going to be there, and it would be very handy to have Matilda and Roderic too. Can you both make it? It won't be before nine."

"Probably." The kids would be fast asleep – and it wasn't like she and Mark had anything better to do. But she was reluctant to commit without knowing a little more. "What's it for, exactly?"

"Remegius is going to bind the Prince properly."

"I see. Well, in that case, I'd prefer to stay out of it." After what Kay had said in Nottingham, she'd begun to think again about those odd nightmares, and the small round bruise on her forehead. Early that morning, she'd lain awake while the sun came through the gap in the curtains, illuminating a similar red sore on Mark. It was unsettling.

She expected irritation from Seth, but all he said was, "Really? Why?"

"It's dragged on a bit long, don't you think?" she typed.

169

"Well, yes, that's why we're ending it here. I'd just like to do so in style – rather than letting the whole thing drop."

After several minutes, she managed to compose her thoughts into a message that hopefully didn't make her look crazy. "Kay said a few things in Nottingham – she's really quite concerned. She mentioned nightmares."

"Yeah. I know. Look, can I tell you something in confidence?"

Curious, she typed, "Of course."

"Kay's having a bit of a rough time at the moment. Settling into Oxford, being away from home. That's one of the reasons why I took the assistant position away from her, actually; I didn't want to put her under any pressure in the game."

"Oh? I'd gathered you two had a falling out."

"Yeah, well, that too." He added an unhappy emoticon. "She's taking the game very much to heart."

Hannah hesitated. "Yes."

"I'm a bit worried about her. I gave her parents a ring last week – you know she had a year out during sixth form, don't you?"

"Vaguely – I never really asked her about it."

"Me neither; it's hardly my business. But her mum mentioned it, said there'd been some family stuff going on – Kay's kid brother got hit by a car, nothing too serious, but Kay was really shaken up by it. Started going to church for a bit."

"Plenty of people go to church, you know." She felt defensive – and guilty. It was a fortnight now since she and the kids had been; things were so hectic at the moment.

"Yes, of course, but she was taking her brother too. As though she thought the accident was to do with something ... evil."

Hannah tried to remember what exactly Kay had said in Nottingham. It had, perhaps, verged on paranoia.

The next words from Seth were, "All I'm saying is, it seems like Kay might be a bit fragile at the moment, and this isn't the first time she's been struggling. I don't want anything upsetting her."

"No. Poor Kay – do you know if there's anything I can do? Should I give her a ring?"

"Probably better not. She and Brandon are out at an Oxford Union thing tomorrow night, I gather, so that would be a good time to put all this Prince of Nightmares stuff to rest. Can I count on you and Mark to help?"

"Yes. Yes, of course, we'll be there."

Chapter 25

History was the one lesson where Edwin had a good seat: right at the back, next to a window. He drew on the inside cover of his exercise book while Mr Davis droned on at the front of the room. It was Tuesday and for two days, he'd ridden to school on a Darren-free bus. For two days, no-one had tripped him up in the corridor, or flicked chewing gum into his hair. Everyone left him alone, with no Darren around.

Mr Davis went on and on. Edwin kept doodling. It wasn't like Mr Davis was saying anything he didn't already know.

"Turn to page sixty-two, and answer questions one to five," Mr Davis said. There was a collective groan, and a rustle of thirty textbooks. Only half an hour till lunch – and there'd be no Darren hanging around outside the classroom, waiting for him.

He heard the door creak open, but didn't bother looking up until Mr Davis said "Class!" and clapped his hands.

The Head was standing at the front of the room, but everyone kept on chatting.

"Year Ten, quiet, please!" Mr Davis sounded annoyed.

"Thank you," said the Head. "Boys and girls, I am sorry to interrupt when you are so deeply engrossed in your work."

Edwin went back to doodling, already tired of the sarcasm. He'd sketched a wolf's head – it wasn't brilliant, but you could tell what it was meant to be. He began to draw in its body.

The Head went on. "You may have noticed that your classmate Darren Miller has been absent from school this week."

Edwin's heart started beating twice as loudly as usual. The classroom was horribly quiet.

"I'm afraid that Darren is in hospital."

A rising murmur passed from desk to desk. Edwin's face was burning hot.

"Darren was attacked late on Sunday night by what we believe was a dangerous dog."

The wolf he'd drawn stared up at him from the page.

"I do not wish to alarm any of you." The Head planted his hands on Mr Davis's desk. "The doctors have assured Darren's mother that his injuries are not serious, and he should be back at school within a week or two."

"Sir?" One of Darren's groupies raised a hand, "Did he get bitten, Sir?"

"Is he going to have scars?" asked a girl on the far side of the room.

The Head's tone was the kind that killed any discussion dead. "I do not have any further details."

Edwin felt sick. He closed his eyes. The Head was still talking, something about reporting dangerous dogs to the council. Edwin barely heard it. Somehow, he had caused this. He'd sent that email, and used the Prince's name, but he hadn't meant it, hadn't imagined anything like this could happen. All he'd wanted was to scare Darren. He'd only meant to make him understand what it felt like to be bullied.

The Head left. The murmur and chatter swirled around Edwin. The words in his textbook blurred. He shoved everything into his rucksack, picked up his coat and scrambled over the jackets and bags and scarves and feet to get to the front of the room.

Mr Davis looked at him. "Edwin?"

"I ... I feel really ill, Sir, can I go to sick bay?"

He must've looked pretty bad, because Mr Davis just said, "Yes, yes. Go."

Edwin ran down the corridor and out into the empty yard, rucksack over one shoulder, coat clutched under his arm. He headed straight out through the gates.

He didn't stop running till he got to the park nearby. Then he sat down on a bench, his breath coming in gasps. There was no-one around. The air was freezing, and the sky was dark grey. After putting his coat on, he covered his face with his hands, pressing his palms against his closed eyes. He kept imagining that wolf attacking Darren, sharp claws tearing through cloth, tearing skin.

174

He'd sent an email, that was all. It was just words, only words. But now Darren was lying in a hospital bed.

He grabbed his phone from his trouser pocket, scrolled through the contacts to *Seth*.

"Ed. What's up?"

"Something awful's happened." He could hardly get the words out. "Darren, the email, he was attacked, oh God."

Seth's voice was calm. "Okay, Ed. Slow down. Take a couple of deep breaths."

He did. They just brought the sobs closer.

"Ed?"

"I'm ... I'm trying." A gust of wind caught him right in the face, stinging his eyes.

"Start again. Tell me what's happened. Darren's been attacked?"

"By a ... they're saying it was a dog but I just know ..." He stopped, and tried to make himself calm down. He wasn't going to cry, not while he was talking to Seth.

"You think it's a wolf," Seth said.

"Y-yeah. We signed it, we signed it 'The Prince of Nightmares', we used the name and now, and now ..."

"Hey, it's all right. Is Darren badly hurt?"

"I dunno. He's in hospital. The Head said he'd be okay." The wind was blowing harder now, scattering skeleton leaves across the grass. Edwin's hair trailed over his eyes.

"Well, then. He's probably not hurt much. Come on, he's been bullying you all term."

Edwin pushed his hair out of his face. "I know, but–"

"Ed, he deserved it."

Maybe he *had* wanted it. He wouldn't have said so, not even to Seth. But deep down, he hadn't just wanted Darren to be scared. He'd wanted Darren out of his life. He'd wanted Darren *gone*.

"Where are you?" Seth said, "I'm guessing not in school?"

"No, I got out, I said I felt sick. I *did* feel sick." His face and hands were stinging with cold. He put his right hand into his jacket and kept the mobile clutched against his ear with the left. "I'm in a park."

"You need to go back."

"I can't. I can't!"

"Yes, you can and you have to, Ed. They're going to notice that you're missing. People will put two and two together. If you run off just after hearing about Darren getting hurt, it's going to look odd."

He mumbled, "I guess."

"Go back to school."

"Mm. Yeah." Now, he didn't feel like crying or throwing up any more. He just felt cold and empty and scared.

"It'll be all right."

"I thought this was all over. I wasn't having nightmares, not since the weekend, everything was okay. And now, and now ..."

"Ed, stop. Just go back to school and get through today. Call me this evening if you want."

There was a piercing howl in the trees: no, he'd imagined it. He left the park, though, and hurried back to school. It was lunch time now, but the yard was deserted – everyone was crammed into the dining hall and the computer rooms.

In the library, he hid in a corner with *The Catcher in the Rye*. He didn't want to read Edgar Allan Poe today. Holden Caulfield's voice drew him in and blocked out the world. He only looked up when the librarian said, "Edwin, my dear, the bell's rung for registration."

In Maths, he tried not to look at Darren's empty desk, two rows in front of him. Maybe Darren was lying in the hospital right now and thinking that at least he'd got out of Maths.

Finally, it was three fifteen. Edwin stared out of the bus window the whole way home. No-one bothered him. No-one spoke to him, or sat next to him.

As he pushed the front door open, Mum called, from the kitchen, "How was school?"

He put his bag down in the hall and went and gave her a hug, burying his face in her shoulder.

"Sweetheart, what's wrong?" she asked.

"Nothing." His chest ached. He couldn't tell her anything. She'd think he was insane – and if she believed him, about the demon and the wolf, the nightmares, the mark on his forehead, then she'd be horrified at what he'd done.

"Are you sure? You don't look too well."

"Just tired." He picked up his rucksack on his way upstairs.

176

For several minutes, he just lay on his bed, shoes still on, arms folded across the pillow with his face pressed down on them. He'd left the medallion at Seth's, hoping he'd never see it again and that he'd escaped all the weird stuff. And now it had all come back.

He wanted his dad. He wanted someone who he could talk to, someone who'd put everything right.

Much later, when Edwin logged into Messenger, a box popped up from Seth. "Wondered where you'd got to."

"Didn't feel like playing earlier."

"We've got a new scene coming up. Bring Ben along."

He couldn't just say he'd rather not. "What's it about?"

"Heidi and Remegius are going to sort things out. Control the Prince."

That was what he wanted. That was what he'd been talking to Kay about, after Nottingham. If they could sort things out in the game, then everything in the real world would be okay too. Except now, he wished he could switch the computer off and curl up in a ball under his duvet, and pretend that none of it was happening.

"We can't do it without you, Ed."

* * *

"Shouldn't we wait for Sir Tristram? And Sir Wilhelm?" Benedict asked, as Heidi hurried him out of the boarding house.

She shook her head.

In the street, Matilda was waiting, her arms folded. "We're doing this, then? What about *him*?" She jerked a thumb at Benedict. He managed not to flinch.

"Him too, all of us," Heidi said, impatiently. "Is Roderic here?"

Matilda grunted, and pointed towards a shadowed doorway. Roderic emerged. There was a clink as Heidi handed a small cloth bag to him.

Now, Benedict was *very* sure that this was a bad idea. Heidi and Matilda didn't like Roderic, but they'd sent for him from Lycopolis. "I'm not coming, not without Sir Tristram."

177

All three of them stared at him. Matilda said something to Heidi that he couldn't hear. Heidi hesitated, then nodded.

Benedict left it a second too late to run. He'd barely made it across the street before an arm caught him around the neck. He kicked, and then a knife point jabbed his chin.

"Apparently, we need you alive," Matilda said, "But I can get creative."

A shiver seized him.

"Benedict," Heidi said, "Just come with us. This won't take long, we'll have it finished before Tristram and Wilhelm are back. Then we can all go home."

Somewhere in the shadows, at the edge of his mind, a voice whispered about strength, power and knighthood.

"All right," he said, managing to get the words out despite Matilda's arm around his neck. "I'll come."

The streets were quiet. Heidi led the way to Remegius's underground room. It was just as cold as last time, but now there was a different quality to the shadows: they were darker and heavier than those above ground.

Heidi knocked on the inner door, three times quickly, then a pause, then another three times.

It opened. Holding up a candle, Remegius swept a glance across them. "Enter."

The room was much bigger than Benedict had expected – easily twenty feet across. Each wall was lined with shelves, holding books, bottles, all sorts of odd artefacts that he couldn't make out in the dusky light. Deep channels were cut in the stone floor. Benedict followed them with his eyes: they were a series of circles, inside one another. A line sliced through from the centre to outside the widest circle.

"No-one else knows?" Remegius asked.

Heidi shook her head. "Tristram and Wilhelm won't be back for hours."

"Good. Stand around the outermost circle, evenly spaced."

Heidi moved first, then Matilda, then Roderic. But Benedict stayed where he was. He couldn't shake the memory of that poor girl, her blood running dark against the altar in the Temple of Shadows.

"Benedict." Remegius came over to him and gripped him with cold, firm hands, then guided him onto one of the inner circles.

"Are you all here willingly?" Remegius waited as, one at a time, they nodded. "And Benedict?"

Benedict stared at the floor, and saw blood. Closed his eyes, and saw blood.

"You, boy, are you here willingly?"

The whispers came from the shadows. Power. Glory. Knighthood. Dreams made real. Nightmares ended. And they had to bind the demon properly, or they were all in danger; Heidi had explained it to him.

"Yes," he said.

"Good. Then we begin." There was a pause, a heavy silence hanging in the cold air.

Remegius snuffed out his candle, and they were plunged into darkness.

"Kneel, all of you," Remegius said.

Benedict heard the others moving. As he knelt on the stone floor, the cold seeped into his knees. There was a strong smell in the air, like a bitter incense.

"And *listen*," Remegius said.

In the dark, the voice was louder. The words came clearly. *"You'll be a knight, Benedict. You will triumph over your enemies. You will win every battle."*

That was what he wanted. Wasn't it? He was finding it hard to think: the voice was quiet, but overpowering. *"You'll be victorious. Triumphant. People will fear you..."*

Just the idea of it made him feel stronger. No-one would ever hook an arm round his throat again, no-one would press a knife to his chin, or kick him, or punch him, or laugh at him.

"... you'll be the greatest ..."

Despite the voice filling his mind, something else was tugging at him. Sir Tristram didn't want anything like this: he wanted the demon destroyed.

"YOU will be the greatest, Benedict."

Sir Tristram hadn't been able to protect him from Matilda. Or from the Prince.

Above the whispers came Remegius's voice, sharp and certain. "We are ready."

Something shifted in the air. A breeze swept the room, tugging images through Benedict's mind: a knife coming down; blood on stone; black mist; the wolf on his medallion.

His head sagged towards the floor. He slumped forwards, dizzy, the stone pressing hard against the side of his face. There was a low hiss, a choking smell in the air, like damp wood burning. He coughed hard, smoke in his mouth. A candle flame flickered above him, but then the blackness closed in.

Remegius, sounding very far away, said, "Stand, the rest of you, stand!"

And Heidi, faintly, said "You didn't tell me, we should not have ... Remegius, what have we done?"

The whispers no longer spoke of glory and knighthood. They breathed fear and darkness, eternal darkness.

The last words Benedict heard were from Remegius. "We have succeeded."

Chapter 26

Remegius stood. The demon's voice swept through the dark, and made everything else into a shadow. They were sweet words, words he'd waited for years to hear:

"What do you ask of me?"

He could feel its presence before him in the circles, something more palpable than air. He heard Matilda shift and mutter sharply, heard Heidi shush her.

Very quietly, he said, "I ask that you serve me, and no other."

"And as payment?"

He was unwilling to offer any. But he had endured years of dashed hopes, rumours and stories, wild guesses and clutching at air.

"The boy," he said, the words a mere breath. "You can keep the boy."

"Agreed."

Thick coils of black smoke wrapped around Benedict's body. The others stared, but stayed on their knees.

"I am sorry," Remegius said, aloud. "The demon has taken him. There was nothing I could do."

"And is it ... done?" Heidi asked. "The Prince is bound?"

"Yes," he said, calmly, despite the excitement that beat fast inside. "You may stand."

Matilda was up first, gesturing at Benedict. "Dead?"

"Unconscious," Remegius said. "Do not touch him, or step into the inner circle."

"Tristram isn't going to be at all bloody happy about this," Matilda said.

"Indeed. Ensure that he does not know." Raising his voice, he said, "Keep Tristram from this place. You understand? The demon will serve you all, but only as long as it has the boy. That is the price it demanded."

None of them uttered a word of protest. Roderic was already edging away.

Remegius held the door open. Heidi, pale, seemed in a hurry to leave. He caught her arm as she passed him. "My dear, you wanted this."

"Yes," she said, quietly. "Yes, I did."

Matilda lingered till last, frowning down at Benedict. Then she shrugged to herself, and walked out.

As soon as she had gone, Remegius closed and bolted the door. Stepping into the smoke, he crouched beside Benedict. The metal chain hung limply round the boy's neck. It unclasped at a touch.

He stood, and weighed the medallion in his hand.

* * *

Seth paced the room, seized with energy. Edwin's medallion was spooled on the coffee table; it had been there since Saturday night. Several minutes went by before he could get up the courage to touch it. Eventually, impatient with himself, he snatched it up. It was cold in his hand. He held the two ends of the chain and clasped them together in the air, then unclasped them again. The wolf's head glinted in the light.

The obvious thing to do was to put it on. He could speculate all he wanted about the exact relationship between the medallion and the Prince, about whether the medallion really did have some effect. The only way to prove anything was to wear it.

The wolf's red eye gazed up at him. Sitting on the sofa, he shifted the medallion from palm to palm.

He wasn't going to get scared and back out now. He fastened the chain around his neck. It hung down on his chest.

Nothing happened.

He could hear his own breath in the silence of the room, too loud and too fast.

Nothing happened.

He got up, closed the curtains to hide the grey skies, switched off the lamp and returned to the sofa to sit in darkness.

And still, nothing happened.

All his attention was on trying to pinpoint anything which felt different. Was there some thicker quality to the air, and an odd scent that he couldn't name? Did he feel as though someone was watching? Was the room a little colder? Could he hear something very faint, like a low laugh?

Maybe. Or, more likely, he was just imagining it all.

He leant forwards, fists clenched tight, the medallion swinging loose in front of him. "Come on. Come on, *come on*. Speak to me."

Nothing. Nothing at all.

This was idiotic. He stood up, reached for the light and almost fell over the coffee table.

"Fuck!" He rubbed his shin.

Did he hear something? Did he hear a laugh, so very faint? No. No, he'd just imagined it.

This was real. This was all real, but he had no proof, nothing solid: just the nightmares, and a few unexplained bruises on foreheads. Edwin had told him a garbled story about Darren Miller being attacked by a wolf. Or a dog. Or, for all Seth knew, nothing at all.

It was late. He'd sleep, and think through everything in the morning. The medallion was a waste of time: he reached up to take it off.

It wouldn't unfasten.

The chain was cold against his neck, cold against the steady thump of hot blood.

Methodically, he tried it again. He twisted the chain around until the clasp was under his chin, so that he could peer down at it, and watch it fail to move when he pressed it. Of course, he could take wire cutters to it, snap it apart. But he didn't want to do that, couldn't risk destroying whatever power it had.

Sleep came faster than he'd expected. The forest was more vivid than it had ever been. The air smelt of damp earth. He walked forwards, and his body obeyed him. The trees bent before him at his command, bowing to create a path into the forest.

183

The nightmares were his. He was in control. As he walked, he came to a clearing among the trees. He waited, and concentrated.

They came into the dream. Mark first. Then Hannah. Then Brandon. Then Robert, blurry and indistinct. None of them moved; they just stood there, like actors waiting for the curtain to go up.

He looked around the clearing, impatiently. He pictured Edwin – long black hair; eager, frightened eyes; a too-long T-shirt. He was treading a careful line. If he let himself become too conscious, too deliberate, he'd tear the fabric of the dream and wake up. And if he was too passive, the nightmare would be back in control.

But he stayed in the dream.

Edwin was there now, lying in the leaves and the mud, his hair tangled around his face.

That wasn't how Seth had imagined it. He could change the dream. But perhaps this was how it was supposed to be, how it *had* to be.

The figures began to move. They knelt. Seth did not. He gazed at the forest, and up at the dream sky, dark and starless. There was light around him, obscuring the others; a blueish light that sank into him.

And he started to walk. The trees moved for him: he ruled this forest now. He walked through the forest, and there was power in his hands, and he knew that he could do anything. The forest was his. The world was his: everyone who'd ever stood against him. All his.

Seth woke, laughing, in the soft glow of dawn. He showered, letting the water cascade over his head, over his face, down his neck, over the medallion which hung warm against his skin.

He got dressed: an old pair of jeans, a plain T-shirt, his college sweater, maroon and grey. In the mirror, the shadows under his eyes were lighter than before, and the mark on his forehead was so faint that he could almost convince himself he'd only imagined it. He tucked the medallion under his clothes.

For a change, he was hungry. Normally he woke up wanting nothing but coffee and the stark safety of daylight. In the kitchen, he mixed porridge oats with a teaspoon of brown sugar and a pinch of grated nutmeg and cinnamon, and added milk. Cooking absorbed him, with its blend of creativity and meticulousness. In his third year at Cambridge, when the nightmares had struck up again, he'd mixed milk and oats in the middle of the night, hunched in a dressing gown, kitchen lights blazing bright.

The porridge had reached just the right consistency, no longer sloppy and not yet stodgy. He sat in the living room to eat, gazing out across London. The Thames sparkled in the cold November light. Today was the day that everything changed.

But as he finished breakfast, his thoughts turned back to the previous night. Benedict had been taken by the Prince. He'd been the sacrifice demanded. And in the dream, Edwin had been unconscious, maybe dead.

In Lycopolis, he typed, "Talk to me."

There was no response. He kept his eyes on the screen, leaning forwards. The medallion's chain tugged slightly across the back of his neck.

And then a word came.

"Hello."

"You'll do what I want, now?"

He waited.

"Yes."

From the bottom drawer of his desk, he took a small bag of dice. It was a relic of school days, of war games played with troops of plastic soldiers on the common-room carpet.

He pushed the keyboard forwards to clear a space on the desk and tipped a few dice from the bag. As he cupped his hands around them, he thought of victory, extraordinary luck. He let them fall.

Each showed a six.

Next, they came up threes – then all ones.

This was a message; he was being told something. In the game, in the dreams, he'd needed the others. It had only been with their imagination – their fear – that any of this had worked.

Who could he trust? Robert was his first choice, but Robert wouldn't be in the UK until the weekend. Kay was obviously ruled out. Brandon was too close to Kay, and impossible to predict. Hannah was still suspicious of him.

In Messenger, he typed, "Mark – do you have any dice?"

"Yeah. Just normal dice?"

"Yes. Get them. Think of the number six. Roll them."

"What for?"

"Just humour me, okay?"

"Okaaaay..."

There was a long silence. Seth stared at the screen, and thought of luck, a string of perfect sixes.

"Shit! Wow! I don't know what to say."

Seth smiled – then winced at the low throb of a headache. He'd had too many late nights recently. "Want in on this?"

"God, Seth. What the hell?"

It took him half an hour of patient explanation. Even then, Mark kept saying, "I'm not sure. It's weird. Creepy."

"Powerful."

"But you're really doing this? You're controlling it?"

"Yep." An idea had come to him: a real test of the Prince's powers. "Mark, ever been to a casino?"

"No. And I know what you're getting at. But, fuck, I mean, are you sure it would work?"

"Absolutely."

"I've never gambled."

"You play Roderic," Seth pointed out.

"Well, yes, but that's only in games. I've never gambled for *money*."

"Time to take it to the next level, then? Look, we can't lose."

There was a pause. "Well, if that's really true, then we'd basically be cheating."

"Life owes you some lucky breaks," he typed. "See it as redressing a balance. Righting a wrong."

He waited, the headache tight behind his eyes. If Mark didn't agree, he could just go alone. But he wasn't convinced that would work. Mark needed money; Seth didn't. Mark was afraid; Seth wasn't. And the Prince fed on that need, that fear.

Remegius had known that. Perhaps Seth had known it for years, but it had only been through Remegius that he'd managed put it into words.

"Look, Seth, I'll be honest with you. I don't really have any money to gamble with."

The risk mattered, the *need* to win: he wasn't going to lend Mark anything. "Come on. It's completely safe, you saw what happened with the dice."

186

"I guess I could manage a grand."

"By tonight?"

"Yeah, but I can't get away tonight – we've got to go to Denny's parents' evening. Tomorrow, maybe."

He'd have to wait a day. But what difference did a day make, a day out of an eternity? "Right. Come to London. King's Cross, 8pm tomorrow. Wear a suit. And remember, you're doing this for Hannah and your kids."

"Yeah. Look, if we pull this off – I'll really owe you one."

Seth got up and went into the kitchen for a glass of water, tried to massage away the tension around his temples. Ignoring the headache, he picked up his journal, turning to those first few pages, to the start of his list.

Michael Harrington (my father)

Victoria Harrington (my mother)

Richard Harrington (my big brother)

Soon, very soon now, he'd be able to strike out every single name.

Chapter 27

Night had fallen suddenly: Kay came out of the Balfour Library and found herself in darkness. With her essay notes finished, her mind was all too free to wander as she walked down Parks Road, skirting the centre of town and heading onto the High Street.

It felt like she was being watched. Several times, she glanced back over her shoulder to see no-one there. She walked faster anyway. When she was finally back at her room, she felt unreasonably relieved; she drew the curtains to shut out the night.

As soon as she switched the computer on, a Messenger box popped up on her screen, the spiky font instantly recognisable as Edwin's. "Kay? Are you there?"

It was the first time he'd talked to her in days. "Yep, I'm here. How're things going?"

"Okay."

"You sure?"

"I don't know. Everything's weird at the moment."

The oppressed feeling was back again. She glanced around the room, and felt silly. Of course there was no-one there. "Ed, what's happened?"

"I did something. I didn't mean to. I really didn't. It was supposed to just be a joke."

Her heart thumped hard. "What did you do?"

"I didn't know anything would really happen. It was just words."

The whole of Lycopolis was *just words*. "What happened, Ed?"

"A guy at school got hurt. Darren. The Head told us yesterday."

He'd talked about Darren before: one of the boys who'd been bullying him. "Got hurt how?"

No response.

"Ed? Are you still there?"

"I don't want to talk about it any more."

"Can I ask just one more question? Was Seth involved in this?"

There was a long pause, followed by, "Yeah."

The rush of anger shook her. She found herself gripping the edge of her desk, fingertips pressed hard against the wood.

More words came. "I thought it was all going to stop, Seth said he was going to sort it all out. And now there's stuff happening in the game again too."

"What stuff?"

"This role-play last night. Benedict's hurt and I didn't want that to happen."

A file transfer request popped up: Edwin was sending her the log of the scene. She downloaded it and opened it up.

"Tristram can't know anything in-character," Edwin told her.

"That's fine," she typed. "Give me a minute to look at it."

Unease gripped at her stomach and her throat as she read. It was the story of another summoning – except, this time, Tristram hadn't been there to stand up to the Prince.

"Did Seth deliberately plan this for when me and Brandon weren't around?" she asked.

"I think so. We weren't supposed to tell you anything about it."

She took a deep breath, hoping it'd help her calm down. It didn't. "Right. I'll talk to him."

"Don't tell him I said any of this."

"Okay," she typed, then, "Ed, stay away from Seth."

"He's been really nice to me. I don't know why he did this role-play but he must've thought it was the best thing."

"Was he nice to you at the weekend?" she asked, carefully. She'd not heard anything about it until it was far too late to intervene.

"Yeah! Yeah, definitely."

"What did you get up to?" she asked.

"Just hanging out and stuff."

Before she could ask anything else, another message popped up from him. "I've got to go."

She picked up her phone, and called Seth.

No answer. She left a voicemail. "It's Kay. I need to talk to you. I'm worried about Ed."

When she scanned Messenger again, she saw that Hannah was online.

"Hi," Kay typed. "You don't have Ed's home number, do you? Or his mum's mobile?"

"No, sorry. Is something up?"

Kay sent her the log of her conversation with Edwin, adding, "You can see why I'm worried?"

"Was this all he said?"

"Yep."

"And Darren is someone at his school?"

"Someone who's been picking on him all term. I'm guessing whatever he and Seth did, it was some sort of revenge. A spell? I don't know."

"Are you okay?" Hannah asked.

The question surprised her. She had to think it through. "Yes. I guess so. I'm worried about Ed. And Seth. And all of us, really. With Hallowe'en, then Nottingham, and now this."

"Things are all right at college?"

"Yeah. Well, I've got essays to do, but I'm coping."

"It must be a pretty hectic time for you, though."

Why was Hannah suddenly worrying about her? "No, honestly, things are fine."

"That's good. Sorry if I sound like I'm prying. It's just that Seth said he's worried about you."

"What?"

"He told me you were taking all this game stuff very seriously."

"It *is* serious! Look, you know it is, you've had nightmares, you've got a mark on your forehead too, I bet."

The words were out there, and she couldn't take them back. Did they make her sound crazy – was that what Hannah thought? Could she be imagining everything?

"I'd better go," came from Hannah. "Look, don't worry yourself about the game. Make sure you take things easy, won't you?"

A cold anger churned in her stomach. Everyone was behaving as though there was something wrong with her. Dad had phoned up the previous day to check on her, to ask, fairly tactfully, if everything was okay, whether she wanted them to come and visit. In the morning, she'd found a card in her pigeon hole from Mum, reminding her to have a chat with the college nurse if things were getting too stressful.

There was no-one she could talk to. Her parents would just think it was a relapse, after almost two steady years – and they could never know the truth about what had happened back then. Hannah had been the only person who might have helped her, who might have believed her.

Her messenger logs with Seth went back to January: she printed each one, in tiny black letters. Then she took out the scraps of old T-shirts from her desk drawer. An hour later, she was still looking at them. She picked up her phone, and tried Seth's number again.

To her surprise, he answered this time. "What do you want?"

"Edwin told me what happened with Darren. Seth, this has gone way too far."

"Edwin lets his imagination run away with him."

"It's not only that. The game, last night. I saw the log."

"It's a game." He said it lazily, as if he didn't care whether or not she believed that any more.

"We both know it isn't. You have to stop this." Her voice was shaking. "Look, it's getting worse, it's becoming real."

"I know."

"Seth –"

"If you're thinking about interfering, don't waste your time."

"I'll – I'll do whatever I have to."

He laughed. "Which is what, precisely?"

She looked at the fabric and threads, and said nothing.

"Yeah," he said. "Exactly. You can't do a fucking thing. And Kay ... have the sense to stop pissing me off."

"Is that a threat?"

"Yes, actually. Yes, it is."

She hung up. For several minutes, she just stood there, looking at the phone in her hand.

And then she made the seventh doll.

It took her an hour, working carefully. This one had to be just right. She gave it blonde hair and a scrap of grey felt for a scarf. When it was done, she took the ball of string that she used for hanging laundry across the room. She cut several lengths from it.

Picking up the doll, she whispered, "Sorry."

She bound it with the string, tying its arms to its body, tying its feet together. She pulled the knots tight.

It was nothing like the time three years ago. This was *necessary*. She was doing it for the right reasons.

The other six dolls were safe, in a shoebox locked in her bottom desk drawer. She didn't have a separate box for this one – in the end, she used her pen-pot, leaving pencils and biros scattered across her desk.

She tied string around the pot, too. For protection. For containment.

As she closed her eyes, tight, she hoped that this would be enough.

Chapter 28

"Let's move." Seth gestured left, strode off, cutting through a line of commuters. Mark dodged briefcases and umbrellas and caught up with him.

"How's the family?" Seth asked.

"They're fine." Hannah was barely speaking to him. He'd not made much effort either; he'd been unable to think of anything but the casino. One minute, he'd tell himself not to get his hopes up; the next, he'd be daydreaming about what he'd do with the winnings. Obviously, he'd pay off the bills first, but then he'd sort out a really good Christmas for them all. He'd get something nice for Hannah. Clothes, maybe, something pretty, something lacy. Though that might seem a bit self-serving.

They walked along in silence, Seth barely glancing at the traffic before striding across roads, pushing impatiently around groups of tourists. Mark was all too aware of the cash in his wallet: five hundred pounds. It felt like he had a neon *mug me* sign over his head.

"Right," Seth said, once they were in a quieter street. He stopped to put a hand on Mark's arm. "We should figure out what we're playing for. How much do you want to win?"

There was no point being cagey about it. "Well, we need about four grand to cover the bills and, you know, Christmas and everything."

Seth looked at him, silent for a moment, before saying, "How much do you *want* to win?"

"I ... I don't know."

"Pick a number."

"Ten thousand, maybe? But I don't need that much. Maybe it's not fair to –"

"You want a better life for Hannah and your kids. It's not selfish to want to take care of your family."

Seth was right. Mark just wanted to be a good husband, a good dad, get everything back on track, forget about the past and move on with the future.

"How," he began, then faltered. "Seth, how exactly does this work?"

"Don't worry about it. Just focus on winning. You need to win. You're going to win. Think about that, and leave the rest to me."

Loosening his collar, Seth touched a thin chain that he was wearing. Mark wouldn't have pegged him as the jewellery type. Seth glanced at him, then drew the chain out from his shirt.

A horrid jolt of recognition sent Mark's thoughts right back to the past. The streetlamp overhead glittered on the silver metal, glinted from the little red eye.

"Where did you get that medallion?" He'd had one just like it. He'd given it to Lucy, fifteen years ago. It belonged to a different life.

"On eBay."

He followed Seth down the streets, trying to shake off the uncomfortable thought that the medallion was some sort of omen. When he'd given his to Lucy, everything had been going so well ... and then, just a couple of weeks later, she'd told him she was pregnant. He hadn't asked for it back, hadn't wanted it back.

A drop of rain splashed onto the sleeve of his jacket – he saw it, rather than felt it, through the thick material. Several more drops followed. They strode along faster, down a street lined with grand Victorian houses, past a sleek glass-fronted building. Seth stopped at a pair of wide oak-panelled doors, then gestured him through.

They stepped into a disconcertingly grand lobby. Mark felt instantly out of place. Everything was very clean, very neat, and definitely very expensive. The portraits on the walls all had heavy gold frames. A giant fish tank was set into a dividing wall, water bubbling in gentle streams to the surface. Slivers of bright orange and silver darted to and fro.

Once Seth had signed in at the reception desk, Mark followed him through doors flanked by twin eagles, wings half-unfolded, and into a wide corridor.

"It's a bit overstated here," Seth said. "All this baroque stuff. Still, it's a good place for a few games."

At the end of the corridor, the next set of doors stood open. Seth strode through. Mark's neck was hot under his tie and collar.

The room was long and wide, with roulette wheels over on the right and half a dozen mahogany tables on the left. Chandeliers above, and fake candles on the walls, gave the room a gold, warm glow.

"Ready to play?" Seth asked.

"Yep. Sure." He followed Seth to the far end of the room, where a red-waistcoated man sat behind a desk, presiding over fancy boxes filled with rows of chips. Seth handed over a thick stack of banknotes.

When Mark took out his wallet, he noticed for the first time how battered it was. He switched his five hundred pounds for a bunch of chips.

"Where do you want to start?" Seth asked.

The room was lively, but not crowded, a sea of suits broken by the occasional flash of a colourful dress. "Blackjack?" he suggested.

Seth led him over to a table, where they joined a couple of men who glanced them over before going straight back to discussing their anticipated Christmas bonuses. Bankers, Mark decided.

Leaning in close, Seth said, "You understand how it works, right? We're playing against the dealer, only his cards matter. He plays last."

"Yep. I know."

Smoothly, the dealer flicked cards out from the pack. Mark examined his: a nine and an eight. Normally he'd stick on seventeen. But, after all, he wouldn't need *much* luck to get a four or less. He tried to figure out the odds.

"Stick or twist, sir?" the dealer asked him, a touch impatiently.

Yesterday, he'd thrown those dice – and they'd all shown a six. He thought about the difference that just a few hundred quid would make. He gestured for another card.

It was a four.

His cards totalled twenty-one. Seth, next to him, stuck with nineteen. They both won.

The next round played out similarly. Seth and Mark won, and so did one of the bankers. Mark added more chips to his pile. The casino didn't intimidate him now. All that mattered was that he was winning. Later, he'd go home and tell Hannah that everything was okay, he'd sorted it all out.

A couple more rounds passed. His cards were perfect. Then, with stacks of chips teetering on the table in front of him, he turned over his first two cards to reveal nineteen.

It was a good result. It was probably a win. But he didn't have to settle for "probably." He gestured for another card.

The dealer blinked. Something in his expression said, *it's your money*. The younger of the two bankers laughed, not bothering to be discreet about it.

The card was a two. Mark set it down on the table, breathing through the head-rush of power. He could win however much he wanted. He could do anything.

"Lucky bugger," one of the bankers said.

Seth's cards came to twenty-one, too. The dealer had twenty. They took their winnings.

All Mark's chips were on the table now. Nine hundred and fifty pounds.

His next cards totalled twenty, straight off. He was about to call for another card just for the hell of it, just because he could, just to put the ace down with a flourish.

Seth murmured, "Don't."

Mark stuck with twenty. They both won. Standing, Seth scooped up his pile of chips.

"Good time to get out," the older banker said. "While your luck holds."

Mark couldn't stop grinning. He shoved his chips into his trouser pockets, counting them in. One thousand, four hundred and twenty-five pounds.

In the bar, Seth said, "Don't be too bloody obvious, all right?"

"Anyone can get lucky."

"We don't want to attract attention. And, look, don't push it so much."

Mark looked at him, sharply. "You said this was certain."

"It is! Just ... let's not overdo it. Now, what're you drinking?"

Mark eyed the bottles stacked behind the bar. It was hardly the sort of place that served a hearty selection of real ales. "Whatever you're having."

Seth ordered champagne, handed him a glass and gestured to a quiet table at the corner. The chairs were impressively comfortable, with leather seats and high wooden backs.

"Cheers," Seth said.

"Cheers." They clinked glasses. "How much did you win?"

"Don't know." Seth spread his chips on the table, ran a finger over them. "Bit over five grand."

"Hell." Mark shook his head a bit. Here he was, drinking champagne in a swanky casino in London. It didn't feel real. He'd walked off the train and through the cold city streets into a world of sparkle and light.

"What's on your mind?" Seth asked.

"This is all very ..." He lowered his voice. "It feels like a dream, but it's *real.* And what exactly are we playing with?"

"Power." Seth leant back in his chair, champagne flute slightly tilted in his hand.

"Yeah, but if we can do *this,* then ..."

Seth said nothing, just sipped his champagne. Mark looked down at his own glass and watched the play of golden light there, tiny bubbles fizzing to the surface like a promise of better things to come.

"Roulette next," Seth said. "It's faster."

After a couple of easy wins at roulette, Seth piled his chips onto an intersection between four numbers: twenty-two, twenty-three, twenty-five and twenty-six. Mark, figuring that it didn't matter what he played, moved to put his on the long row from three to thirty-six.

Seth caught his arm. "Don't bet *against* me."

"Oh, right, yeah, good point." Hastily, Mark moved the stack to the middle column. He felt a hot prickle of unease for the first time in half an hour. If he and Seth placed incompatible bets, who would the luck really favour?

The wheel spun, a whirl of dark resolving itself into reds and blacks, the ball skittering and finally landing on twenty-six.

"Let's move on," Seth said, quietly.

At the next table, Mark asked, as casually as he could, "So, what would happen, then? If you bet red and I bet black, or something?"

Pushing one of the lower-valued chips onto red, Seth said, "Try it."

Mark hesitated.

199

"Go on. Same value chip."

What the hell, it was only fifty quid. He thought about black. Thought about buying a few DVDs for the kids, and a big bunch of flowers for Hannah.

The wheel spun. The ball jittered as it lost momentum. Black. Red. He willed it on. Black. And finally, red.

The croupier raked Mark's chip away.

Again, they tried it; again, Seth won. Grinning, he took his chips and handed a couple back to Mark. "Here. Now, we bet together, right?"

"Yep." Mark's collar itched. His jacket was too snug. And he couldn't shake the thought that Seth had more control over this than he was admitting.

The wheel spun, and they both won chips. Mark totted his up. Two thousand, eight hundred and seventy-five pounds. It was enough to pay off most of the bills. He could get out now.

Seth tore his attention away from the table. "You okay?"

"Yeah. Just ... maybe we should stop. We've got enough, really." He could hear the lack of conviction in his voice. Still, he'd said it. He'd fought that rising tide of needing *more*.

"Losing your nerve?" Seth asked.

"No."

"Stay out for this round, anyway. I'm going for zero, and it'll look pretty bloody suspicious if we both do that and win."

Mark had barely looked at the other people around the table: he'd noticed them only as sleeves and hands placing bets. But now he glanced around. He whispered, "If zero comes up, they'll all lose. Everyone will lose except you."

Seth just shrugged.

It didn't matter. They could all afford it, those bankers and accountants and lawyers. Their suits and watches probably cost more than Mark's car.

Seth put down a thousand pounds on zero, and got couple of laughs. Someone next to Mark muttered, "Rich brat."

The wheel spun. The ball skittered, red black red black red black. And landed. Green. Zero.

There were groans as the chips were raked away. One man threw his hands in the air and stalked off. Seth took his thirty-five thousand pounds of chips. As he turned, Mark saw something so intense in his gaze that it made him catch his breath. This mattered to Seth, far more than Mark had realised.

Neither of them placed any bets for the next couple of rounds: they watched silently, then moved on to the third roulette table.

"Time to finish," Seth said. "How much do you have?"

"Two thousand, eight hundred and seventy-five. That's with the five hundred I had when we came in."

"Okay. Put it all on one number."

"*All?*"

"It's completely safe."

Only half an hour ago, Seth had been telling *him* not to push it. "Isn't it going to look a bit ... unlikely?"

"There's a one in thirty-five chance. It's hardly winning the lottery."

"Well, what number?"

"Doesn't matter." Seth was counting out a handful of his own chips.

"Are you going to play it too?"

"Not the same number. That *would* look fixed." He was speaking faster than usual. "I'll go for the row."

Mark started pulling chips from his pocket. "I can't even fit all these on one number."

"Change them with the croupier," Seth said, impatiently. "No, never mind. Here." He started switching his chips for Mark's. The ball bounced and fell without them.

"Go on," Seth said.

Mark hesitated, gazing at the board. It didn't matter which number he picked, but he couldn't help feeling that he should take his time choosing.

"Just put them down," Seth said. "Anywhere."

He went for eighteen. Seth stacked his own chips into the third of the board which covered thirteen to twenty-four.

The wheel began to spin. The croupier called, "No more bets."

Mark thought about winning, trying to grasp the idea of it. Thirty-five times two thousand eight hundred ... he was looking at about a hundred grand. They could pay off the mortgage. And Seth had put down a hell of a lot too, the whole thirty-five grand he'd just won betting on zero.

201

The wheel seemed to spin for longer than usual. The ball blurred around the edges of it, rising and falling in a smooth wave. The wheel began to slow, the reds and blacks separating out into fast bands of colour, the ball skittering over the twenty-eight, over the seven, heading for eighteen ...

And then it stopped.

On twenty-nine.

One number away.

Mark stared at the wheel. The safe, glitzy world had come to a jarring halt. Twenty-nine. How could it be twenty-nine?

He wanted to grab his chips back, say that it was all some mistake. But he couldn't do anything except stand there.

He should've had a hundred grand. Instead, he had nothing.

Abruptly, Seth pushed his way out of the crowd. Mark grabbed his arm. "What the fuck just happened?"

"I don't know." Seth shook him off, pressing his fingers to his forehead.

"We didn't win. We didn't *win*."

"Yes, well observed."

Why the hell had he gone along with this? He shouldn't have trusted Seth, he shouldn't have believed anything so stupid.

"How much more cash can you take out?" Seth asked.

"I'm *not* going to –"

"Keep your voice down."

Mark glanced around. They hadn't drawn much attention yet – the room was buzzing with chatter and laughter – but a couple of bored doormen were looking their way.

More quietly, he said, "I just lost nearly three fucking grand."

"Calm down, okay?"

Mark loosened his collar, rubbed sweaty palms on his suit trousers. He couldn't take it in. Three grand. Why the fuck had he let Seth talk him into carrying on? He'd been happy with what he had, he'd been ready to take it and leave.

Seth took a thick stack of notes from the cash point. "Come on, get your money."

It was too late to back out now. He'd already lost five hundred pounds. He had to at least win that back – which wouldn't be hard, not even with normal luck.

And he'd been so close. If that ball had moved just an inch further, he'd be holding a hundred thousand pounds right now.

He took out his final five hundred, then looked at Seth. "Maybe we were just plain lucky before."

"You know that wasn't luck. This is real, okay? This is very fucking real, and we're going to make it work."

"How? How?"

"We put everything down this time. All of it. We have to *need* this."

"And what if we lose again?"

"We won't."

"You were pretty bloody sure about that last time."

"We are *not* going to lose."

Once they were back at the roulette table, Mark said, "You go ahead. I'm sitting this one out."

"No. We need to do this together."

Mark shook his head.

"Come on. We just need one win. You've got to fucking *believe* this, okay?"

"I believed it right until that ball landed in twenty-nine."

"Look, it was bloody close. One number out. We'll get it this time."

Mark silently put his chips down on black. If he won, he'd double the five hundred pounds – and then he could put all the money back in the bank.

Seth emptied his pockets of chips and stacked everything onto six.

The wheel spun. The ball whizzed smoothly around before it began to slow, to jump, to rattle. Mark crossed his fingers. Thought of Hannah and how much he needed to win now: he couldn't go home empty-handed. Thought of the kids, and how he wanted to be a good father, how he'd really try this time.

The ball landed on twenty-five. Red.

Mark stared blankly ahead as the croupier took his last five hundred pounds. He felt numb. So that was it. Everything was over.

Seth was staring at the table.

"I want my money back," Mark said.

Turning towards him, Seth said, "It's gambling. Sometimes you lose."

"You told me this was safe." He didn't even try to keep his voice down. People were starting to look their way. He didn't care. "Seth, we're defaulting on the fucking mortgage. We *need* that money."

"Not my problem." Seth started to walk off.

"Yes it is!" Mark caught up with him, grabbed his arm to pull him around. "Look, I don't know what stupid game you're playing, what this was all about, but I can't lose that money."

"Like I said, not my problem." Seth yanked his arm away.

Mark's blood was pulsing hard, his head a whirl of thoughts; the kids, Hannah, the house, everything tumbling around him.

One of the doormen hurried over. "Gentlemen, if you wouldn't mind ..."

Seth stormed out. Running after him down the corridor, Mark yelled, "You told me we were going to *win*! You talked me into that last bet – so you can give me that money back."

In the lobby, the man at the reception desk glanced up. Mark grabbed at Seth again.

"Get off me." Seth's hands were bunched into fists now. "I mean it, get the fuck off."

"Look, it's a thousand pounds, bloody hell, it's probably pocket money to you, but we really need it –"

"Sirs, if you'd please separate." Another of the doormen had come over, along with a couple of men in plain black suits.

"Give me that thousand pounds!" The rest of the lobby was a blur now, a haze of golds and reds and mahogany, and all he cared about was Seth.

"No!"

He threw the first punch, but Seth was ready for it, dodged sideways, swung a fist and caught him on the jaw. His head rocked back, and the amber light splintered into white, sharp shards. He staggered.

The doormen closed in; Mark was manhandled down the steps, out into the rain. Seth was pushed after him, tie skewed, hair wild, shouting, "I don't fucking owe you anything!"

Chapter 29

Seth barely noticed the rain until he was out of it, hurrying down an escalator to the Underground. His coat was heavy with water. His hair was sticking to his face. The carriage was nearly full, but he still felt uncomfortably visible. He sat there, arms folded to stop his hands from shaking, fighting down a wave of fear with every unexpected jolt of the train, with every stranger who glanced his way.

Everything had gone *right*. They'd been on an insane, impossible winning streak. And then their luck had fizzled out – and Mark had managed to get every pair of eyes in the casino on them.

"Fucking stupid bastard," he muttered, and only realised he'd said it aloud when the woman sitting next to him edged away.

When he got off the tube, back into the cold rain and the grey night, he kept looking over his shoulder, kept checking the shadows. At home, he towelled his hair and pulled on dry clothes. Without the distraction of being cold and wet, fear gripped harder, hooking into every thought. Was the Prince simply weaker than he'd believed?

No. There had to be some reason why he'd failed, something that had dampened the Prince's power. Kay had been intent on stopping him. Was there any chance, however small, that he might have underestimated her? Could she have more knowledge and more power than he'd realised?

Anger rose up to replace fear. No-one played games with him. No-one. And if they were stupid enough to try ... he would win. He always won.

His mobile rang, obscenely loud in the silence of his flat. Mark's name showed on the screen.

"Fuck off," Seth said.

"Seth, wait, I need to talk to you."

"Yeah? I'm not in the mood to listen."

"Look ..." There was a pause, and Mark's next words sounded reluctant at best. "I owe you an apology."

"Yeah," Seth said, "You do."

"I lost my temper – I'm sorry – but you can see why, right?"

Seth didn't say anything, just waited. The fear was further away now.

"I really need that money. It's not just for me – Hannah, the kids ..."

"Like I said earlier: not my problem."

"But –"

He switched off his phone. He made a coffee, and stood in the kitchen to drink it, surrounded by shiny chrome and clean white light.

Tonight hadn't been pleasant. But at least he'd learnt that the Prince's power was real. He paced around the kitchen, leaving the half-empty mug of coffee on the counter. He *had* been certain. He had felt so sure.

Back in the living room, he turned on the computer and logged into Messenger. A window popped up almost straight away, from Robert: "Did you experiment with it, in real life, like you said?"

"Yes," Seth typed. "Not wholly successfully."

"But *something* happened?"

"Oh yes." Perhaps it was just his imagination, but Seth could almost sense the demon in the room now, just as Remegius had. It was an unpleasant sensation – like cold fingers closing around his wrists.

He looked around. The lights were all bright. The curtains were drawn.

The game meant something. Heidi's involvement mattered. And Robert was attuned to ritual, to the spiritual, to words and actions that could focus the human mind. He needed Robert's help.

"All set for Saturday?" he asked.

"I think so."

"When does your flight get in to Heathrow?"

"11.40 a.m. your time."

"I'll meet you there."

"You're sure? You don't mind? I don't want to put you to any trouble."

"It's no trouble." Even with every thought bending back to the casino, to the sudden, jarring loss – of luck, of money, of hope – he had to consider practicalities. "You've got my address, right? You'll probably need to fill it in on a form, before you go through border control."

"Yeah. I printed it out."

"What have you told your parents?"

"Nothing, yet."

"Good good. Leave a note. Say that you're with a friend. Don't let them think you've left the country."

"Okay."

Even though Robert was eighteen, Seth supposed his parents might be able to have him tracked down and returned. "Will they call the police?"

"No. I don't think so. They won't want to admit that I've run off. They think they're great. They think they'd never bring up *that* sort of kid."

Seth wondered how many years of simmering hate lay behind the words. He could use it all: Robert's broken ties to his family, his sense of betrayal, his fear.

After logging out of Messenger, he was about to close Lycopolis when a single word appeared.

"Hello."

His chest tightened. His shoulders tensed. He made himself reach out and touch the keyboard to type, "What happened? Why didn't we win?"

"Interference."

He had the sudden, overwhelming feeling that he was being watched. Not just watched – something worse. Stalked. He twisted round fast. The room was as empty and as neat as ever. The curtains were drawn, blocking out the night. The television was switched off. The coffee table was bare and perfectly aligned with the sofa. All the lights were unwaveringly bright.

So why was there a shadow moving on the ceiling?

He wanted to close his eyes. But he watched it, a sick dread clutching at his throat. It was sliding across the ceiling, sliding towards him.

"Stop it!" He hated himself for the note of panic in his voice.

There was a rustle behind him. He had to look round. The pages of his journal were turning, steadily, as though lifted by an invisible hand.

A thin wisp of smoke settled over it, then began to seep into the paper. Pencil marks began to appear, thin grey lines thickening and joining.

He watched them form a face. A girl, with her hair in plaits.

Kay.

"She stopped us? *How?*"

But the smoke faded. He snatched up the journal and slammed it closed. It was startlingly cold. He shoved it into the drawer, and locked it away.

There were several things he needed to do. Simple, practical things to concentrate on. First, he had to keep Edwin from talking about Darren and Mark from telling anyone about the casino. This was easily accomplished. He had a bombshell to drop on their lives: Mark's reaction to the medallion had confirmed what he already knew.

Ed,

I thought you had a right to see this message (below) from a woman who attended your mother's school. And yes, it is "our" Mark. I saw him earlier today and showed him the medallion. He recognised it.

I haven't said anything to him. I thought you should know first.

If you want to get in touch with him, here's his phone number and address.

Seth.

"Lucy was in the year above me at school. She got pregnant when she was in Year 12. The guy she was with ditched her and ran off – everyone was talking about it for weeks! I suppose you're after him for the maintenance or something? His name was Mark Webster."

He brought up the database of Lycopolis players and copied Mark's contact information into the email. Instead of giving Mark's mobile number, he used the landline one; if Edwin got hold of Hannah instead of Mark, well, that would just complicate things nicely.

With that taken care of, some of the tightness around his shoulder eased. Edwin and Mark would now be safely occupied.

Which left Kay. He should have realised that keeping Tristram out of things in the game wasn't going to stop her interfering.

He would go to Oxford, tomorrow. It'd be easy to find her. A couple of minutes' research on Magdalen College's website told him that Freshers lived in the Waynflete Building, across the River Cherwell. He zoomed in close on Google Maps. It would be easy enough to loiter in Sainsbury's next door, then follow another student in through the gates.

He would find out exactly what the hell she'd done. And he'd make her stop it, or undo it. He wasn't going to leave anything to chance now.

Sleep claimed him fast, like an arm around his throat. He tumbled into dreams, but not dreams of trees and mud. He was trapped in a maze of white-washed corridors that smelt of bleach. Tall faceless figures strode past with clipboards. None of them so much as glanced at him.

When he tried to find the way out, every turn took him back to the same door. He didn't want to open it, but he reached out and turned the handle anyway. It was at eye level, but this didn't strike him as odd.

In the room there was a doctor, sitting jauntily on the edge of a table.

He turned around and began to run, but the corridors towered high above him, and the faceless figures kept walking, and he still couldn't find the way out.

Long before it was light, he woke up, his hands tangled in the sheets.

After a long shower and two mugs of coffee, he still couldn't shake that dream. It had been years since he'd dreamt of hospitals – and years since he'd last set foot in one. Automatically, his hand went to where his journal should be, next to the computer. Of course, it wasn't there; he'd locked it in the desk yesterday.

He opened the drawer. The book was there, looking perfectly innocuous. He took it out and turned through the pages – past the earliest pencil drawings and the big cursive handwriting, on to the painstakingly neat diary entries. He'd been nearly ten.

At the top of the page, there was a title: "We Visited the Doctor." He remembered the layout of the room, the soft sinking feeling of the sofa. He could almost hear the relentless tick of the clock behind him.

The first line read: *Michael and Victoria have been taking me to the doctor.*

He couldn't remember when he'd started calling them by their first names. Perhaps it had been right after the camping trip, the same time he insisted on being called Seth.

They have taken me every week, and I go into a room with the doctor while they stay in the waiting room. I have not said anything about the Prince of Nightmares and I will not say anything because:

1. The doctor will not believe me

2. If the doctor does believe me, he will think I am crazy

3. It winds Michael up because he is paying for the doctor and I'm not saying anything

The doctor smiles too much. He asks lots of questions. He tries to get me to play. Sometimes he tells stories. Sometimes he guesses about things. I just don't listen. I pretend I can't hear any of it. Michael will give up soon. I don't let the doctor see anything on my face. I don't look bored or sad or cross. I don't look anything.

And I am NEVER scared.

Chapter 30

Kay had been staring at the same page for half an hour. The words kept blurring into one another. She couldn't concentrate. Pushing her chair back from the desk, she checked that all the dolls were still safe inside the bottom drawer. It was stupid; what did she expect – that they'd have vanished?

The strings were still tight around the seventh doll. She locked the drawer again, then went back to the book. She should at least finish the chapter.

Her door clicked open.

"Hey Brandon," she said, welcoming the distraction.

"I'm not Brandon."

She turned round, so shocked that it took her a moment to even recognise him.

Seth.

"Afternoon," he said, and closed the door.

"What – what're you doing here?"

"Came for a chat." His words were friendly. His tone wasn't.

Standing, she said, "Um, okay. So what's –"

"I am not fucking amused. What did you do?"

She managed a baffled expression. "Huh?"

"You know exactly what I'm talking about." He took a step towards her. "You're going to tell me what the hell you did, and you're going to *un*-do it."

Meeting his eyes, she said, "I'd like you to leave now."

"Katherine." He took another step forwards. "Tell me what you did, because I am not feeling very fucking patient."

"Get out of my room," she said. "Look, if you want to talk, we'll go down the bar and talk there –"

"No."

"Seth –"

He shoved her into the wall. If she screamed, someone in the corridor would hear. Brandon, hopefully. She snatched a breath.

"Stop it!" His hand pressed down hard over her mouth. She yelled anyway, but the sound was squashed back.

She kicked at his legs, but he didn't budge, just kept his hand on her mouth and leant against her to stop her getting her arms up to defend herself. He was more *solid* than she'd realised, and he was so close that she could smell him – musky aftershave, and the sharp tang of sweat.

"Look, just listen to me a minute," he said, sounding suddenly more calm and reasonable. "All right?"

Very cautiously, she nodded.

He took his hand away from her mouth.

"Get off me," she said.

"Okay." He shifted back, but was still much too close.

Taking deep breaths, she told herself it was going to all be all right: she just had to get around him, and run into the corridor.

"What did you do?" This time, he asked it quietly.

"Let's sit down," she said.

"I'm fine here."

If he backed off just a couple of paces, she could get out. "I want to sit down. Then – then I can tell you what happened."

He was leaning on her desk with his hands in his pockets.

"So you did do something?" he asked, and she heard the strain in his voice. He brought his arm up, made a flicking sort of gesture. Before she even saw what he was doing, she flinched.

There was a knife in his hand.

"Don't scream," he said.

Her heart was thumping hard, but her knees had stopped shaking.

"Or what?" she asked. "You'll stab me? There's cameras all over the halls." She had no idea if that was true. "And people will have seen you."

"Don't you fucking get it yet? As soon as I have the Prince – you think it's going to matter? You think anything's going to matter to me? No-one will be able to touch me."

212

Which was why she had to stop him. Whatever it took, whatever promises she had to break, she had to stop him.

"Tell me what you did, Katherine." He was so close now that she could feel his breath on her face.

She had one shot at this, and she had to get it right. It wasn't hard to sound convincingly scared. "Okay. I – I'll need to show you something."

"Go on, then."

"I ... you're going to need to move back a bit ..."

He took a step back, eyes fixed on hers. She dropped her gaze, deliberately.

"Um, a bit more. I need to get at the desk." She opened the bottom drawer, just enough to get her hand into it. Surprise was on her side now: she had at least a couple of seconds. She yanked her needle from the notice-board next to her. And then she tipped the pen-pot, took out the doll, held it with one hand and the needle with the other.

"What the fuck?" He stared at the doll, then back at her.

"Probably exactly what you think," she said. "Back off. Right now."

He didn't – but he didn't come any closer, either. "Is that supposed to be *me?*"

"Yes."

"For fuck's sake. You don't think I really believe that works, do you?"

"It works," she said, and gestured to the strings that bound the doll. "It stopped you, didn't it?"

"Untie it."

"No."

"I'm not asking a second time."

"If you try to hurt me –" she began.

"You'll do what, exactly? Shove a pin in that doll?"

As he stepped forwards, she brought her hands closer together, then stopped.

"Look at you," he said. "You can't do it, you don't have it in you."

"I'll do whatever I have to."

"Really? Because I'd say that making a doll and binding it is one thing. Stabbing a pin in it ... that's crossing a line."

213

This was completely different from before. She knew what she was doing. And maybe it was still wrong, maybe it was *evil*, but it was a lesser evil.

"Come on. You can't do it, so stop wasting my time." He made a sudden lunge, grabbing for the doll. She stabbed at it, but too late; the needle only scratched his hand. His fist caught her hard in the jaw, and she stumbled, pain lancing through her face, everything turning a yellowish grey for a few seconds.

He cut the strings off the doll and put it in his shirt pocket.

"That was a really bad idea, Katherine."

If she was fast, she could get to the door – scramble out in the corridor, screaming. She just needed to get him off-guard. She sagged against the wall, eyes half-shut, groaning.

"Do you think I'm that stupid?" he said. "Look at me. Look at me!"

He was still holding the knife. She opened her eyes properly.

"That's better. Now. I've got a problem, Katherine. I could just walk out of here with this little doll, but what's going to stop you making another one?"

Nothing at all. She could easily make another, and this time, she'd not take any chances. This time, it wouldn't just be strings.

"Well?" he said.

She tried to slide along the wall, away from him.

Grabbing a handful of her hair, he pulled it taut, making her yelp. He brought the knife up, and, before she had a chance to grab at his arm, or even scream, he cut off a lock of her hair.

And then he smiled.

It took a second for comprehension to kick in, over the thud of adrenaline. "You don't know how –"

"Maybe not. But if I make a doll, stuff it with your hair, then slice it in half, I'd imagine that would have *some* effect."

"Seth –"

"Stay out of this. Because I will hurt you. I'll kill you if I have to. So keep the hell out of my way."

Chapter 31

It was Thursday afternoon, which meant Robert didn't have a shift at the bookstore. Mom had started asking what he was doing after school every day, so instead of heading to the coffee shop, he went straight home.

He logged into Lycopolis. A week ago, he wouldn't have dared. But today, he lay on his bed, still wearing his baseball cap, the laptop resting on the pillow in front of him. Yeah, his father would be home soon. He didn't care.

A Messenger window popped up, from Seth. "Are you sorted out for your flight?"

"Yep."

Everything was ready – clothes, money, passport – in a backpack under his bed. And he couldn't wait to go; it was all he'd been thinking about for days. Except now, worries were starting to creep in. He kept going over it in his head, every night. He was leaving everything he knew: school, family, the church. That was, of course, what he wanted.

The bedroom door swung open.

Robert rolled off the bed and onto his feet, and stared at his father.

"What's this?" His father pointed at the laptop.

The words, rehearsed, came out strong. "I paid for it. With my wages."

His father reached for it. Robert snatched it first, slamming the lid shut – hiding the Messenger conversation.

"Give that to me, Robert. Right now."

"No!"

His mother was hovering anxiously in the doorway. "Robert, please. What's making you behave like this?"

"You're always treating me like I'm a kid! Look, I'm eighteen. If I want my own computer, what's the problem? And if I don't want to go to church any more, you can't make me."

His mother clasped her hands together, her lips moving silently.

That made the anger burn more fiercely. "Don't pray for me. Stop praying for me! I don't need your prayers."

"Yes you do, son. Your mother and I know that something is wrong. We heard you calling out in the night –"

During the dream? A jolt of fear hit him; what had he said? Why couldn't he remember?

Quietly, his mother said, "And the mark."

His father reached out, and pulled off Robert's baseball cap.

"Hey!"

"Alice, call the Pastor. Ask him to bring the elders –"

"What're you going to do?" The laptop was slipping in his hands. He clutched it to his chest, like a shield. "What do you expect *them* to do?"

He couldn't meet his father's eyes any more. He'd have been able to face anger or self-righteousness, or blind stupid conviction – but he couldn't look at his father and see that he was afraid.

"Pastor Lowrey will –" His father's voice faltered for a moment. "He will know what to do."

"You want them to exorcise me." Robert meant to spit the words out, unafraid – but his voice shook. "I'm not fucking possessed!"

"Do not use language like that under this roof."

"I'll call the police!" He hugged the laptop more tightly.

His mother was making the call: he could hear her murmuring.

"I'll call the police, I mean it!"

"Robert. Son. We'll help you. We'll rid you of this thing." His father reached for him.

"Don't touch me! Get the hell away from me!" He was too scared to think. Would they tie him down? Would they beat him?

Hastily, his father dropped his hand. "Robert, please, try to calm yourself."

He did. He really did. Making an effort to sound reasonable, even though it wouldn't make any difference, he said, "There's nothing wrong with me. I'm not possessed."

"Pastor Lowrey's coming straight over," his mother said.

216

"Didn't you hear me? I'm not possessed! This is stupid!"

His father reached for the laptop, trying to wrench it away from him. Robert clung onto it. "Then what's turned you from our obedient, God-fearing son into ... into *this*?"

"I don't believe in God any more."

His mother gave an audible gasp, and covered her mouth with her hand.

"Alice, don't upset yourself." His father was still trying to get his laptop. "It's the demon talking."

Faintly, she said, "Even the demons believe. They believe, and they tremble at His name."

"Shut up!" Robert said, and yanked the laptop free.

His father looked at him for a long moment, then stepped back, out of his room, and slammed the door. There was a scuffling outside: they were forcing something under the handle.

His father's voice came through. "Robert, I'm sorry. Pastor Lowrey will be here very soon and he'll ... he'll be able to help you, son."

Robert dragged his backpack out from under the bed and shoved his laptop and the power cord into it. It wasn't that much of a drop from the window. There was grass below. He lowered the backpack as much as he could, then let it go.

Desperate words formed in his mind, not quite consciously. *Help me, get me out of this. I don't care, whatever it takes, whatever you are, if any of what Seth says is real, then help me get away.*

He felt dizzy. His heart was thudding so hard he could feel his pulse in his ears. For a moment, he closed his eyes and saw a whirl of black, a streak of blood.

He opened the window and stared at the ground below. Climbing out didn't scare him, not nearly as much as the idea of what they might do to him, now they'd seen the mark on his forehead. He slid across the sill and wiped the sticky palms of his hands on his legs. Gripping tightly, he lowered himself down. He hung there, feet scrabbling for a solid grip against the wall of the house. Then he pushed hard, and fell backwards through the air.

He landed in a heap on the grass. All his bones felt like they'd been jarred. He gulped in a few breaths.

A howl split the air, long and piercing. He didn't know where it came from. With his backpack slung over one shoulder, he started to run. There was a yell and a gunshot somewhere nearby. Clambering over the fence, he fell into the neighbours' yard. His forehead stung.

He ran through back yards until he made it out into the street. He couldn't hear any footsteps or shouts now. He kept running though, to the bus stop. Miraculously, there was a bus just pulling up. He flung himself on, gasping hard.

"You okay, son?" the driver asked.

He nodded, then fumbled in his pocket for cash.

"Where to?"

"The depot." He could catch a bus to Houston there. And then he'd just stay at the airport – no-one would notice that he was there almost a day before his flight was due.

He fell onto a seat, sank low in it as the bus rattled through the streets. His throat hurt from struggling to breathe, and he felt sick. Something brushed against the bus window: he jumped, and almost hit his head on the seat in front.

It was just a plastic bag, caught in the wind.

His cell phone rang. When he took it out of his pocket, he saw "Home" on the screen. He switched it to silent and ignored the call.

A full ten minutes later, he'd calmed down enough to look at it again. He had a new voicemail. It was from his father.

"Robert, please listen to this. Please come home, come straight back home. We can help you. I know that you're confused and scared. But please just come home to us. Pastor Lowrey is here, and he's certain that he can drive out whatever's taken hold of you. Robert, believe me, we forgive you for everything you have said and done this evening. We do not hold you responsible. There's something evil in you, son."

There was a pause and indistinct words being exchanged. Robert made out a voice in the background saying, "Yes, tell him."

His father went on. "There are dark forces trying to stop us from helping you, Robert. The Pastor was confronted on his way to us, by an evil spirit. It took the form of a wolf."

The world lurched dizzily. Robert grabbed the seat in front of him with his free hand. So he had done it. He had called on some actual power. Something that had helped him. He fought a wave of nausea. It was true, everything Seth had hinted at. It was really true.

"Please, Robert, just come home, be strong. We'll help you fight this. God will give you strength. Pray with me Robert. Our Father –"

Robert shoved his phone back into his pocket. The dark world sped on: house windows and street lamps flickering in the night.

Finally they got to the depot. As he left the bus, Robert took care not to look at the driver – he hoped the guy wouldn't remember his face. There were teenagers hanging around in groups outside, smoking. In the scruffy waiting room, all the seats were taken – students, old folks, and a few kids who looked too young to be travelling alone at night.

Robert found a corner and slumped there on the floor. He pulled a book from his backpack – Nietzsche's *Beyond Good and Evil*. Opening it, he stared blankly at the words, keeping his head down.

The bus came. He sat at the back, cap yanked down to hide his face, pretending to sleep.

At the airport, he got a coffee and trekked to a distant corner of his terminal, then sat on a deserted plastic bench and hooked his laptop up to the wi-fi. He loaded Messenger, not really expecting anyone to be online. It was nine o'clock, which meant it was three a.m. and already Friday over in the UK.

Seth was there. Robert double-clicked his name. "Hey. Sorry I vanished earlier. Long story. I'm at Houston now."

"Impressively early. I doubt you need over twenty hours for check-in."

"I had to get away from home."

"What happened?"

He suddenly needed to tell Seth – especially about the wolf. "This is going to make me sound crazy."

"I'll draw my own conclusions about your sanity. What happened?"

Robert began to explain: how his parents had called Pastor Lowrey, how they'd shut him in his room, how they'd wanted to drive a demon out of him.

"I just wanted to get out of there, whatever the hell it took. I was hoping it'd somehow be all right, that I could just get to Houston."

"And clearly you did."

"Yeah." He hit the wrong keys when he tried to tell Seth the next bit, and had to start over. "I was praying, I guess. Not to God."

"It looks like you were answered."

"There was a noise – like an animal howling. I just kept running. But later, my father phoned, he left a message on my cell. He said Pastor Lowrey was attacked by an evil spirit."

He hadn't meant to type *evil.*

A couple of slow minutes dragged out before Seth asked, "Did this spirit, by any chance, look like a wolf?"

"Yes."

"It's happened here too, With Edwin. It's good news, Rob. It's proof."

Robert knew he should feel terrified or guilty, or probably both. He should run back to his parents, back to the sanctity of home. But instead, he was being pulled towards the truth. This thing, this *power*, was becoming more real every day.

His parents believed so fervently – they'd thought he was possessed. And all he'd done was finally take some responsibility for himself. He'd grown up. Even if he had once really believed in God, he didn't any more. It had been a comforting, childish fairy tale – that was all.

The intercom made him jump, but it was just a call for passengers to Paris. Robert told himself, firmly, that no-one was going to look for him at the airport.

"Have you got your mobile on you?" Seth asked.

It took Robert a moment to figure out that Seth meant *mobile phone.* "Yeah."

"Get rid of it. Don't make any calls, just switch it off and smash it with something if you can, or at least take the Sim card out and flush it down a toilet. They'll try to track you through it."

Robert hadn't thought of that. He was suddenly cold. "Okay. Will do."

In the restroom, he dealt with the cell phone, then splashed cold water on his face. He looked pale and there were tired creases under his eyes. He tried to forget his mother's tears and his father's shaking voice. But when he leant close to the mirror and stared at his forehead, he could make out the raised circle and the line that cut through it.

Chapter 32

"Why's Daddy sleeping on the sofa?"

Hannah finished pouring Megan's Coco Pops into the bowl. "Because Daddy got back from London very late last night and didn't want to wake Mummy."

"Oh," Megan said. "When's Daddy going to work?"

"He's *not* going to work," Denny said, rummaging through the cupboard. "Just like the rest of the week. He quit his job. He's unemployed. Mum, I can't find the peanut butter."

"Hang on," Hannah said, pouring milk onto Megan's Coco Pops.

"I *told* you we needed more."

"Denny, don't use that tone of voice with me, please."

"But I did tell you!"

Quite probably, he had. The last few days had been a blur of worry, interspersed with dark, broken nights.

"How about Marmite instead?" she asked, trying to sound cheerful.

He sighed loudly at her. She bit back the urge to snap at him. It wasn't like him to be so out of sorts. Maybe he was upset about Mark – had he overheard them arguing?

"Mummy, Denny's making a rude face!"

"Shut up!"

They made it to school without any punching or biting. Hannah left Denny in the playground and ushered Megan into nursery. She tried to calm down as she walked home. Would it have killed Mark to get up and help with breakfast? She was sure he'd been awake. No-one could've slept through Megan's tantrum about her socks.

She popped into the Co-op on the way for peanut butter, and the usual groceries – milk, bread, eggs, fruit. The card was declined; she had to hunt out enough cash from her handbag and her coat pockets to pay, apologetically. The checkout guy shrugged and said it happened all the time.

When she got back, Mark was slumped in his dressing gown, watching television.

"I thought you were going down to the job centre today," she said.

"I'll go tomorrow."

She opened her mouth, closed it again, and counted silently to ten. "Love, I don't think we've got much time to waste here. We did agree –"

"I'm tired, okay?"

She walked over and turned the television off.

"Hey!" He stood up, with that put-upon look which always grated on her. "I said I'll get it all sorted. Can't you just trust me?"

"No, I can't." There. She'd said it.

He stared at her.

"Look, could you at least phone the bank for me, about the joint account?" she asked. "I tried to pay by card at the Co-op just now, and it wouldn't go through."

"Oh. I just had to transfer a bit of money, just temporarily, that's all."

After nine years of marriage, she knew when he was lying. Something caught in her throat. "What for? What do you mean?"

He rubbed his hands over his face, and sat on the arm of the sofa. "Look, it's just – a temporary blip. Don't worry about it."

"No. What the hell's happened? What were you really doing in London?"

He glanced away from her, blew air out in a sigh. "Look, does it matter?"

"Yes! God, Mark, of course it matters! Is it another woman?"

"No!" He looked so shocked that she believed him.

"Then what?"

"It was a bad judgement call. I'm sorry, I'll sort it out."

She struggled to bring words out of the whirl of fears in her head. "We can't go on like this."

"Don't say that."

"It's true."

"Come on, it's just money."

"It's not just money." She folded her arms. "It's not about the money. It's about the lying."

He didn't say anything.

"And even now, you won't tell me what's going on?"

"I'm sorry, okay? I'm fucking sorry!"

She walked out of the room, and upstairs. He didn't follow her. She got a suitcase out of the wardrobe, very calmly. Even when it jammed against the door and she had to tug it free, she was patient: no slamming, no banging.

Methodically, she packed clothes for herself, then went into the bathroom and shovelled toiletries into a wash bag. It was only in Megan's room, folding little T-shirts in half, that she began to cry.

She kept going, wiping at the tears with the back of her hand, ticking off items in her head. Four pairs of pants. Four pairs of socks. Two T-shirts. Skirt. Leggings. Megan's favourite jumper and cardigan.

Denny's chest of drawers was a blur. She'd sanded down those drawers, had stencilled the dinosaurs on them. She dried the tears, fiercely. She couldn't turn up at her parents' looking a wreck. She needed to stay strong, for the kids. No, not for the kids. For herself. For once, she was going to have what *she* needed. A weekend to get her thoughts together, to work out a plan.

She zipped the suitcase and set it on the landing. Perhaps she should leave without a word to Mark, sit in a coffee shop until the end of school, then pick the kids up and take them to Leicester. She couldn't face another argument.

But it seemed wrong to go without saying goodbye. She'd tell Mark, then she'd head straight to school and get Denny and Megan. Otherwise she'd talk herself out of it.

She dialled from the phone on the landing. Dad, not Mum, answered; one small mercy, at least.

"I know this is a bit sudden, but could I possibly bring the kids up to yours today and stay the weekend?"

"Of course," he said, and, after a pause, "Is Mark coming too?"

"No. Just me."

"Oh, love," he said.

She managed to say, "I've got to go. I'll be round later." Then she hung up, quickly, and started to cry again. She went into the bathroom and washed her face. That mark was still visible on her forehead, and it felt hot.

In the living room, Mark was still sitting on the sofa, staring at the television. It wasn't on.

"Mark," she said.

He looked round.

"I'm going to pick up Denny and Megan and take them to my parents'. I think we all ... we just need a few days' space."

"Right," he said, quietly. "Okay."

She was almost disappointed, even angry. Wasn't he even going to try to talk her out of it?

"Bye," she said.

"Bye." He turned away.

At the school, she spoke to the lady in the school office and said it was a "family crisis." It wasn't a lie. This *was* a crisis – just not the sort with state-sanctioned rescuers. There were no blue lights, no sirens, no paramedics or police, no officials to swoop in and patch their lives back together again.

It was all up to her now.

As she bundled them into the car, Denny said, "Why are we going to Granny and Grandpa's? Where's Dad?"

"Dad needs some time to himself."

Neither of the kids said anything for a while, as she drove out of Swindon, onto the A420. Then Denny asked, "Are you and Dad getting a divorce?"

"No! Of course not. No."

"Who would we live with, if you did?"

"We won't. Denny, we're not going to discuss this."

Megan started to cry.

When they stopped at the Warwick North services, she took the kids straight to KFC. They cheered up at once. "It's like an adventure," she said. "We're going to stay with Granny and Grandpa for a few days, as a special treat for them."

"Can we feed the ducks?" Megan asked, picking at her fries.

Denny dunked another nugget in ketchup. "Will Grandpa let me help with his woodwork again?"

"I expect so," Hannah said.

Thankfully, only Dad was in when they arrived. While he got the kids settled down with colouring books, Hannah had five minutes peace to drink a mug of tea.

Then the front door clicked open, and her mother came into the kitchen with bags full of groceries.

"If I'd known you were coming, I'd have done my big shop yesterday," she said to Hannah. "Well, come and give me a hand."

Hannah took a couple of bags, and started unpacking.

"You know you'll always have our full support."

"Mum, it's nothing drastic." She straightened up, managed a smile. "I just needed a bit of space."

"Don't put the potatoes in the fridge, put them in the vegetable rack."

"Right. Sorry."

"Now, listen, do you need any money?"

"No. We're okay."

"Are you sure? Because I can get your father to transfer some over. He can do it on the web now, you know, he's getting very high-tech."

Dad poked his head through the kitchen door. "I've told Hannah that she and the kids can stay as long as they want, of course."

"Well, of course," her mother said. "You didn't need to *tell* her that."

Hannah said, "It's just for the weekend."

Her parents looked across her, at one another. Dad said, "I'll pop a bit of money in your account anyway, love. We were about to send you some towards Christmas."

"We can manage –"

"I'd like to," he said, mildly.

She mumbled, "Thanks."

Her mother handed her another bag. "I'm keeping the pasta in the top cupboard now. Not that one. Next to the tins."

Hannah put the pasta, carefully, in its new position, and decided that she would not waste a moment of her weekend thinking about Mark.

Chapter 33

Mark stared into a mug of coffee. How could it have come to this? Hannah would never leave. She was just having some crazy moment. It must be that time of the month. Or maybe she was broody. She wanted another baby. Something. Because she'd never leave him. She loved him. And she'd *promised*: for better, for worse, for richer, for poorer.

She would be at her parents' by now. Her mother had never liked him. Why should he be any better than they expected? No-one understood what it had been like for him, slogging through each hateful day in the office, surrounded by young guys who'd not yet had to pull out their first horrifying grey hairs.

His coffee was cold. Abandoning it, he put the radio on – he couldn't stand the house being so quiet. Maybe he should get the paperwork out and work through it all. Or maybe he'd just go to the pub and drown his thoughts in a pint glass. Surely that was what you did when your wife left you.

It was all Seth's fault. Seth had talked him into it – and Mark had been stupid enough to trust him. He'd liked Seth in Nottingham; Seth had seemed the sort of guy that Mark might've been, without Lucy and those screwed-up years. And Hannah would never understand. She'd been angry because he wouldn't tell her the truth – but how could he have explained?

She'd left thinking he'd done something idiotic and reckless. Which was better, surely, than her was knowing the truth – that he'd done something far worse.

There was a knock at the door, loud and fast. He jumped. Perhaps it was Hannah; she'd changed her mind ... but she had keys.

"Hey? Hello? Is anyone in?" The voice was muffled through the door.

Mark got up, ready to tell whoever it was to shove it. Salesman, charity collector, he didn't care.

He flung the door open. "What?"

For a confused moment, he didn't recognise the teenager standing there. He took in the black T-shirt, the black denim jacket, the limp black hair.

"Edwin," he said, bewildered. The kid's face was pale, though his cheeks were reddish, as if he'd been running. Half-a-dozen questions shoved up against one another: *What's he doing in Swindon? Shouldn't he be at school? How does he even know where we live?*

Edwin stammered, "Hi."

"Are you okay?" Mark asked. "Do you want to come in?"

"Yeah. Th-thanks."

Mark stepped back, ushering him into the hallway. He couldn't help feeling a bit pissed off. He had enough to deal with – too much. If Edwin was in some sort of trouble, surely someone else could help? "Look, you'd better have a seat."

But Edwin didn't sit down, just held onto the back of one of the armchairs in the living room, still wearing his coat.

"Hannah's not here," Mark said, and the words sounded more curt than he'd meant them to. "So if you were looking for her –"

"No. No, it's you I had to see."

"Why?"

Edwin hesitated, looked at him, and said, in a rush, "You're – you're my dad."

Mark stood there, unable to speak, unable to form a coherent thought. He managed to shake his head, numbly. *"What?"*

"Years ago, you gave my mum a medallion, a wolf medallion."

Seth had said he'd bought it online. He'd lied; he must have got it from Edwin. Mark couldn't cope with this, not today.

"You did – you did, right?" Edwin said, anxiously. "My mum's Lucy Mitchell ..."

Mark couldn't wrap his head around it. With Denny and Megan, he'd watched Hannah's stomach swell; he'd been there at the births, he'd let their tiny, perfect hands curl around his finger. But this ... this was a mistake, a long-ago mistake, appearing on his doorstep at the worst possible moment.

228

He bit back the first urgent question – *is Lucy okay?* "I don't know what the hell you're talking about."

"You do, you must – the medallion, it was yours ..."

"Well, let me see it." He knew Seth must still have it.

"I haven't got it, but it had 'R.R.' on the back, that's Roderic Revelry, right, your character? And I asked Mum, this morning, I asked her if my dad's name was Mark and she wouldn't say no ..."

Shit. Though, all credit to her, she'd clearly never told Edwin before. Fifteen years ago, she'd screamed at him to go – telling him she would decide what to do about the baby. Her body; her child. She'd promised, whatever happened, she'd keep his name out of it.

"Mark – *Dad* –"

Mark shook his head again. "No. No, look, this is some mistake, I'm not your dad."

"You are! You *are!* Seth knows too! I don't fucking care any more that you never sent me a birthday card, that you never checked Mum was okay. She's had therapy, she's on medication, and you never gave a shit, did you? But I've actually found you, finally, and now I know who I am."

"For fuck's sake! I don't want to be your dad!" He hated himself for saying it – but the words spilled out, coming straight from that dark core of fear, that awful secret he'd carried for so long.

"But all my life, I've wanted –"

"Look, this wasn't supposed to happen! I didn't want any of this! It's Lucy's fault, she was supposed to take care of it –"

"She did take care of me, she brought me up."

"No, I mean –" He realised what he was saying, and broke off.

"You mean she was supposed to have an abortion?"

Mark didn't answer.

"It – it doesn't matter, I'm still your son."

But he had Hannah and the kids, a family he was on the verge of fucking up. There was no way he could deal with this too.

"You're not my son. You're Lucy's son. I was seventeen – I didn't want a kid! You were a mistake."

He regretted the words as soon as he'd said them.

Edwin backed off towards the living room door. "I don't want you either, then!"

229

"Wait. Edwin – Ed – hold on." Mark grabbed his arm. "You're upset, I can see that."

For a moment, he thought Edwin was about to swing at him – but then he stepped back, and took a couple of shaky breaths.

"Ed, this is important – who else knows?"

"No-one, no-one except Seth."

Thank God. He kept hold of Edwin's arm, and struggled to find the right words. "Look, Ed, I'm sorry, but I can't be your dad. I've got Hannah now, I've got Denny and Megan. I think it would be best if they don't know about this, don't you?"

Edwin stared at him. "You don't give a fuck, do you? You don't care about me at all, you never did."

"That's not true," Mark said, weakly.

"Get off me!" Edwin scrambled down the hallway, yanking the front door open, running off down the street.

Mark leant on the doorframe. The cold air seeped through his sweater and T-shirt and chilled his skin. And then he locked the door, and sat in the living room with his head in his hands.

Chapter 34

Edwin's journey home was a blur. He had to change buses in Oxford and he thought about looking up directions to Magdalen College on Google Maps – but he didn't know how he'd find Kay's room or even whether she'd be in. He couldn't ring her, couldn't face trying to explain any of it on the phone.

So when the bus to Milton Keynes came, he got on, and huddled at the back where no-one could see him. He walked home from the bus station. The air was freezing and the sky had turned dark grey.

As he strode along, he kept his hands thrust deep into his coat pockets. He walked past all the red brick houses and the smashed-up bus shelter, past the row of shops. He barely heard the traffic, or the wind.

Mark's words were fixed in his mind. *You were a mistake.*

Life made more sense when he looked at it like that. He didn't fit in because he wasn't supposed to be here. He'd always secretly hoped that being weird made him special – the kid who didn't know who his dad was, the only Goth at his school. But it didn't make him special at all. It just showed he was never going to belong anywhere.

Forgetting to look first, he crossed the road. A car tooted, loudly, making him jump and hurry forward to the kerb. He didn't look round, just kept walking, as though the anger could pound out of him into the pavement. He wanted the concrete to crack. He wanted a rift to open in the earth and swallow him up.

You were a mistake.

It was hard to breathe, cold air rasping in his throat. He wasn't going to cry, not till he was home and in his room. Once he'd turned the corner onto his road, he ran to his house, and shut the front door behind him.

231

He bent over with his hands on his knees, his rucksack still on his back, trying to catch his breath.

"Love?" Mum came out of the living room. "Have you been running?"

He nodded.

"The school phoned. Where were you today?"

"Nowhere." He straightened up. "It doesn't matter."

"Sweetheart, what's wrong?" She reached out, trying to hug him.

"Just leave me the fuck alone! You should've just had an abortion, you could have done. You can't have wanted me, and I've got a really shit life, and I've fucked up yours too."

Tears came into her eyes. He turned away, and stomped up the stairs.

"Edwin, come back!"

He slammed his bedroom door. It was true. Mum should have done it, killed him when he wasn't even a person, when he couldn't feel anything. Then she wouldn't have had to look after him on her own for years and years. She wouldn't have depression.

Whenever he'd asked, she'd said it wasn't his fault, not even a little bit, but now he knew.

He shoved a pile of clothes and magazines out of the way and sat on the floor. He leant against his bed, and hugged his knees to his chest. The anger was slowly seeping out of him, leaving him cold and empty.

"Edwin. Open the door, please."

"No!"

"Is this about your dad? We can talk about it."

There was nothing to talk about. There was no point. Nothing that she said could make anything better.

The door handle rattled. "Edwin, please unlock the door."

"No."

"You're worrying me."

"I'm fine! Go away."

"Well, when you've calmed down a bit, there's chilli for dinner." Her voice sounded almost normal – but he knew she was crying, and he hated her for it, even more than he hated himself.

"I don't want any dinner." He turned the computer on and clicked an album at random: Disturbed's *Down With the Sickness*. It started off quiet, with the drums and words, and then the guitars came in.

As he slumped down on the floor again, the music filled the room, and for a few minutes, it managed to fill his head too. But the thoughts came back in the brief lull between tracks, and he couldn't shake them away again. At eight o'clock that morning – less than twelve hours ago – he'd been living his normal life. And then he'd read Seth's email.

At least Mark had told him the truth. *You were a mistake.*

The whirl of his thoughts slowed and hardened towards resolution. You couldn't go back and undo mistakes, but you could put them right, you could make it so that nothing else got screwed up.

His foot stung with pins and needles. He got up. Opening his wardrobe door, he stared in the mirror at himself. His hair was wild around his face. That T-shirt Seth had bought him was too big: he bunched the material in his hands. His body was just layers on top of layers – skin over flesh over bone. Just a bunch of cells that would all melt back into the air and the soil when he died.

His eyes looked as heavy as they felt. That mark on his forehead was still there. He pushed his hair aside, and a shudder went through him when he saw it properly. It was red and slightly raised, and it hurt when he pressed his fingers to it.

He'd fucked everything up. He'd sent that awful email and Darren was only just out of hospital. And he couldn't tell anyone about it properly, not Mum, not Kay, not anyone. Only Seth knew everything. That weekend in London with Seth had been the best weekend of his entire life. Seth *cared* about him, and Seth had showed him stuff – Oxford Street, the Choking Game.

Edwin could almost still feel the pressure of Seth's hands on his neck. Seth had said it wouldn't hurt, and he'd been right. It'd felt weirdly good, like a rush of happiness and giddiness.

If you wanted to just sleep for ever, maybe that was the best way to do it.

And, online, you could find instructions for anything. He searched for "*Hanging yourself.*"

The first page of results was useless. All the articles had titles like "How to cope when you feel like hanging yourself." He didn't want to cope. There was no way the colour would ever come back into the world. Now that he knew who his dad was, who *he* was, the best thing he could do was end it all. It was like quitting a game which you knew you were going to lose.

The music was so loud that he could hardly focus on the words. He turned it down a bit and jumped through the pages faster and faster. He tried better search terms. *How to hang yourself* and *How to strangle yourself.* He had to get it right.

This time, he found a news story about teenagers killing themselves by pulling belts tight around their necks. He'd do that. He wasn't scared, just relieved. There was a way out.

His mobile rang: Seth's name showed on the screen.

"Hey," he said, and hated how his voice came out shaky.

"Hey, Ed. Thought I'd phone and see how you're doing."

"I'm okay." His voice cracked over the words.

"Yeah? You sure about that?" Seth said.

Edwin switched off the music and slumped on the floor, leaning against the bed again. There were hot tears in his eyes.

"You still there, Ed?"

"Yeah." The tears were starting to spill down his cheeks now.

"What happened? Did you go to see Mark?"

"Y-yeah. It's all fucked up." He was crying properly now and could hardly get the words out. "S-sorry. Fuck it."

"Shh. It's all right. Tell me what happened."

Even now, he didn't want Seth to hear him crying. He took a few slow breaths. And then he told Seth all the things Mark had said: that he didn't want a son, that Mum should've had an abortion.

Eventually, all the words and tears had spilt out of him, and he just sat there.

"Ed. Are you listening?"

"Yeah."

"You're thinking of killing yourself, aren't you?"

Edwin felt dizzy, even though he was sitting on the floor with the hard edge of his bed pressing into his back. "How ... how did you know?"

"Because I know what it's like to be fourteen."

"Yeah, well, it'd be better if –"

234

"Ed, I'm not going to try to talk you out of anything, because I know you don't want to hear it right now – but will you promise me something?"

"I won't promise not to kill myself."

"I'm not asking you to. I'm just asking you to sleep on it, okay? One extra night won't make any difference."

But it would. The night was when the hours were longest and blackest, when his thoughts twisted tight together, all knotting around Darren.

"It will."

"Ed, come on. Do this for me, yeah? Look – I'll drive over tomorrow and see how you're doing."

"Really?" More tears stung at his eyes.

"Of course."

He was quiet for a minute, trying to calm down enough to talk without sobbing. "It's never going to be the same again."

"Not the same, no. But it'll be okay."

Leaning back against his bed, he wiped the tears away on his sleeve. He'd get to see Seth again tomorrow. And Seth actually *cared*.

He put his music back on, and lay on the bed, and let the sound wash over him. This time, it did a better job of squashing out his thoughts. He wasn't going to dwell on anything, on Mark or Mum or Darren or anything bad. Tomorrow, he could talk to Seth, and Seth would know how to sort things out.

He lay there, hugging an armful of duvet. Everything would be better soon. Seth would have a plan. Seth always had a plan.

Chapter 35

Seth glanced again at the arrivals board: Robert's plane wasn't due to land for another thirty minutes. He phoned Edwin, and got a yawn and "Hey Seth."

"Did I wake you?"

"No. I didn't sleep so well. After – you know. Last night."

"Yeah. Feeling better this morning?"

"A bit."

When he'd watched Edwin's string of searches on the spyware, he'd been pretty certain that it wouldn't come to anything – but not certain enough to say nothing. A dead sacrifice wasn't any good to him; he needed to get Edwin to the forest.

"Still happy for me to come over later?"

"Yeah. I don't have anything to do. Mum's on a course at college."

Perfect. "I've got a friend who I think you'd like to meet."

"Who?"

"Heidi."

"Wow, seriously? She's come over from America?"

"Yep. But turns out 'she' is a guy in real life."

"What? No way."

"His real name's Robert. Look, don't mention it to anyone else for now, I don't want to overwhelm him with people. We'll drive over and pick you up. About two o'clock, okay?"

"You *and* Robert, right?"

"Yep." It bothered him that Edwin asked: was he suspicious? Had Kay said something to him?

"Okay," Edwin said. "Yeah. Cool."

Seth checked his laptop: there it was, a short but potentially disastrous conversation between Kay and Edwin, an hour ago:

Kay: Ed? Are you there? Did you get my texts? Listen, if Seth calls you or anything, let me know. Don't go off anywhere with him.

Edwin: What, why?

Kay: Because I'm worried about what he might do.

He should have made a doll after all, tied it, shoved pins in it, never mind that it was probably all nonsense. But it didn't matter. A few more hours, and there'd be nothing she could do, ever again, to get in his way. And he had the doll she'd made of him, safe in his coat pocket: he'd not felt quite comfortable letting it out of his sight.

"Hey! Seth? Right?"

"Yep."

Robert shook his hand. His eyes were shadowed, and he had a baseball cap pulled down to hide his forehead. He was wearing jeans and a checked shirt, the sleeves rolled up, showing tanned arms. They walked through the terminal to the car park, Robert glancing around curiously at everything.

"Hey, neat. Nice car," he said, walking round to the driver's door.

Seth twirled a finger in the air. "Other side."

"Oh, yeah."

As they drove along the M25, Seth explained about Mark and Edwin. Robert shook his head, incredulous. Seth hooked the medallion out from under his shirt. "This was Mark's, then Ed's."

"Like the one the Prince gave Benedict, in the game?"

"Exactly. Down to every detail."

Eventually, Robert broke the silence. "I was thinking, on the way over. We're getting into some deep stuff, aren't we?"

"You could say that."

Robert was quiet for a while, staring out of the window. Then he said, "Seth, how's Edwin involved with all this?"

"He's important to the Prince."

"In the game, the Prince hurt Benedict. I mean, he's still unconscious."

"Yep."

"What're we actually going to be doing?"

238

"Whatever it takes." In the holdall in the boot, he had a torch, a coil of rope, a bottle of vodka mixed with chloral hydrate, and a knife.

There was a long silence.

"So where are we going, once we've got Edwin?"

"To the forest."

"*The* forest?"

"Yes. You trust me?"

"I guess."

They were on the M1 now. Seth stared at the road ahead, and saw the forest at the edges of his mind. Would it have changed at all, in the last seventeen years? The campsite would be deserted in winter, of course; there'd be no-one around for miles.

"This isn't one of the prettier bits of England," Seth said, as the sat-nav led them through Milton Keynes to Edwin's house. It was a shabby terrace in the middle of a utilitarian row, with a patch of scruffy grass in front. Seth parked, got out and rang the bell. After a minute, the door swung open. Edwin stood there, looking rather pale.

Seth leant in a bit closer. "You're wearing eyeliner."

"Um."

"Hey, it's a good look. Very Goth."

He got a not-very Goth grin in response. "Where's Robert?"

"In the car. You left your mum a note?"

"Oh ... hang on."

Seth waited in the hallway while Edwin found a piece of paper and a pen. The stairs were uncarpeted, and there was a crack in the corner of the mirror on the wall.

"Um, what should I write?"

"You've gone out with some friends and you'll be back later. Keep it short."

Leaning the paper against the wall to write, Edwin shook the biro when it began to dry up. Seth read over his shoulder.

"That'll do. Come on, Rob's waiting."

Edwin followed him out, locking the front door behind him. Seth gestured him into the back of the car.

"Hey!" Robert swivelled round. "How're you doing?"

"All right. Hi."

While they talked, Seth reprogrammed the sat-nav, tapping in the postcode.

"Where're we going?" Edwin asked.

"To somewhere I want to show you both." Seth flicked the child lock on.

"Oh right," Edwin said, with false excitement.

"Hey, Ed, relax. We're going to have a good time."

Robert – at a glance from Seth – said, "It's awesome to get to meet you."

"Yeah, it's cool you could come."

"That's a great T-shirt."

Glancing in the rear-view mirror, Seth could see that Edwin had taken off his sweater, and was wearing one of the T-shirts from Metal Militia.

"So, you, like, flew all the way here just to see us?" Edwin asked.

"Pretty much."

"I've never flown *anywhere*. The furthest I've ever been is France, and that was on Eurostar."

"Yeah. Well, I've not been outta Texas much before."

They chattered about the trials of being a teenager. Seth tuned them out, until Edwin said, "When will we get back?"

"In a few hours."

"I should call Mum ..."

He couldn't let that happen. "Ed, honestly. You're telling me she's going to mind that you've gone off on a Saturday afternoon with your mates?"

"No, but–"

"Then leave it, okay? Come on. Grow up a bit."

He glanced in the mirror. Edwin was scowling at the back of his head. But acting like his best friend no longer mattered. They'd got him in the car. They just had to get him to the forest.

"Switch the phone off, anyway," Seth said.

"Huh? Why?"

"Because it might interfere with the GPS."

It was a pathetic lie – but though Edwin was still scowling, he had at least put his phone away.

Every minute, every mile, took them closer to the forest. Would it be the same, viewed through adult eyes? Would it come close to the forest which he'd written about, over and over again, in his journal? He'd written poems about the Prince, about his true domain – a world which encompassed dreams and stories, and all the limitless possibilities of the imagination.

Edwin leant forwards, peering at the sat-nav. "You haven't even told me where we're going."

"The forest."

"What? No! I'm not coming – take me home!"

Robert shifted uneasily in his seat. "Hey, c'mon Ed, we're gonna have a great time."

"I'll call Mum and –"

Seth glanced at the road ahead. There was nowhere to pull in safely, no chance of stopping the car and wrestling Edwin's phone off him. "Okay, Ed. We didn't want to worry you. But I suppose you already know what's going on. You've been more caught up in it than anyone. And after what happened with Darren ... and then that role-play where the demon took Benedict ..."

Edwin filled in the rest. "It's getting worse, isn't it? The *stuff* that's happening."

"That's why Rob's here," Seth said.

"Huh?"

"Tell him," Seth said, to Robert.

"I had a row with my mom and dad. They'd called our Pastor, they thought there was something wrong with me – because of Lycopolis. And I ran off. I heard they'd seen something. It attacked the Pastor. They thought it was a spirit, or a demon. It – it looked like a wolf."

"So you get it?" Seth asked. "You and Robert are *involved* in this. You've made the Prince's wolves real. And we need to go and stop it before it gets any further."

"You think – we're in danger?" Edwin asked.

"You want the truth, right?" Seth asked, and watched in the mirror as Edwin nodded. "Then, yeah, you are in danger. You and Robert. And that's why I'm going to put a stop to all this. I need you to be brave and come along with us. All right?"

"But maybe if we just all go home and ... maybe all this will just go away."

Seth shook his head, slowly. "I'm sorry, Ed. I wish it would too."

"But what're we going to do? *How* can we stop it?"

"By facing it," Seth said. "Look, Ed, all you have to do is come with us, walk into the forest with us. Trust me. We're going to fix everything."

"Even Darren?" Edwin asked, so quietly that Seth could barely hear him. "We can help him?"

"Absolutely." Not that it was worth bothering. He was certain, though, that with enough power, the Prince could alter any aspect of the physical world. It could knit flesh and bone back together. It could prevent cells from ageing and dying.

Edwin just sat there, arms folded, as they drove on.

Robert eventually stretched, self-consciously. "Y'all want some music on?"

"There's CDs in the glove compartment," Seth said: he wasn't about to hand his phone over to either of them. "Fairly limited selection, I'm afraid, they're all ones I bought when I was your age."

Robert riffled through the CDs, then handed a stack back to Edwin, who said, "Don't care."

Robert chose one, and managed to figure out the CD player. Seth recognised the album from the opening chords: Iron Maiden's *Brave New World*.

Both Edwin and Robert were quiet for a while. Edwin leant back with his eyes closed; Robert tilted his head, a slight frown creasing his forehead. The wind was getting up, bending trees at the side of the road.

"Turn the music down," Seth said, and Robert did.

They could hear the wind now, a rush and wail through the trees. It was darker outside, too, the clouds adding to the afternoon gloom.

Gazing ahead at the road, Robert said, "It's so empty. Hardly any cars."

"It's all fields and woods, nothing for anyone to drive to at this time of year," Seth said. The sat-nav led him through the narrow, winding lanes. He coaxed the car up a muddy slope into the empty car park. The music cut out mid-track as he switched off the engine.

242

"Well, here we are." Pulling on his coat, he got out of the car. "Ed, come on."

"Hang on." Edwin reached for his sweater.

Seth walked round the car and opened the boot, taking out his holdall. At his side, Robert asked quietly, "What's in there?"

"The things we'll need," Seth said, equally quietly. "Your job is to keep Edwin moving. We need to get deep enough into the forest."

Robert nodded.

Seth closed the boot. Edwin was still sitting in the back of the car, tapping at his phone.

"Edwin! Stop messing around!"

"I was just writing a text."

"Who to?"

Edwin was silent.

They were in the shadow of the forest now. They were so close. And Edwin could still ruin it all. Leaning into the car, Seth said, "Were you texting your mother?"

Edwin tried to open the other door.

"It's locked. Look, I need to know who you texted."

"Why?"

"Because we're at the fucking forest, Edwin." He let some of the anger into his voice, hoping it'd make his words more convincing. "Because if you're contacting *anyone* from here, you'll be drawing the Prince's attention to them."

Edwin stared at him.

"Did you send the text?"

"I – I didn't know."

"Did you send it?"

Edwin nodded.

"Who to?"

"Kay. She'll be all right, won't she? It can't hurt her?"

Seth wasn't feeling at all merciful. "Let's hope we can end all this before it gets a chance. Turn off the phone. Leave it here."

Without looking up at him, Edwin put the phone on the seat.

"Now get out."

Slowly, Edwin did as he was told. "Brr."

"You should've brought a coat. Come on. You'll warm up walking."

243

The gate was, of course, locked; they scrambled over the fence easily enough – Robert giving Edwin a hand. They jogged across the campsite, which was a bare field now, with a couple of grey brick buildings near the car park. Without caravans and tents, the whole place looked much smaller than Seth remembered.

They came to the ditch at the far end of the field. Edwin stopped, gazing at the trees.

"Come on." Seth jumped across, because he couldn't let himself stand there and wait too long, couldn't let doubts creep any closer.

Robert joined him.

"It's too wide," Edwin said.

"It's not," Seth said, setting his bag down. "We'll catch you."

In the shadow of the trees, Edwin was even paler. He took a run and jumped. Seth caught his hands and hauled him up onto the bank.

"See? Easy."

They walked into the forest, and gradually, the rustle of leaves underfoot gave way to mud. The trees were thicker here, the gaps between them narrow.

There was a long, piercing howl nearby. They all jumped.

"What was that?" Edwin spun round, hands balled into fists.

Seth took a deep breath and steadied himself. "Keep walking."

"But –" Edwin said, at the same time as Robert said, "Was it –"

"Ed, come on. Just a bit further."

Robert was, unhelpfully, silent. Seth gave him a firm look until he said, "Ed, we need you with us."

"But ... that noise."

"Just an animal," Seth said, though his heart was still thumping hard. "It's nearly four o'clock. We need to pick up the pace. Do you really want to be in here when it gets dark?"

They walked for few more minutes, and got to a clear patch between trees.

"Okay. This'll do. Ed, calm down a minute." Seth put his hand on Edwin's shoulder. He was shivering. "It's going to be fine."

Gulping for breath, Edwin nodded.

Seth slung his bag down onto the ground, and took out the bottle.

"Here. Dutch courage." He unscrewed the top, and put it to his lips, tilting it as if drinking. "Get some down you."

Edwin took the bottle and peered at it. "What is it?"

"Vodka. Take a good swig. It'll help."

After a moment's hesitation, Edwin drank a mouthful, grimacing at the taste.

"More," Seth told him. "That's it. Good."

As Edwin gave the bottle back, there was another wolf howl, nearer.

"Shit!" Edwin turned. "I'm going back!"

Seth caught him before he'd made it more than a couple of steps, and shoved him towards Robert. "Hold him."

For one horrible moment, Seth thought Robert was going to refuse – but then he grabbed Edwin's arms.

"Hey! Get off!"

"Edwin, stop kicking! Seth's not gonna hurt you. Right? Right, Seth?"

Seth didn't bother answering. Crouching, he reached into his bag for the coil of rope. "Rob, get him against a tree."

Robert gave a grunt of pain when Edwin kicked him in the knee, and Seth got an elbow in his face as he tried to help.

"You lied! You *lied!*" Edwin yelled. "What's happening?"

Together, they managed it. Seth got the rope around the tree and around Edwin, pinning his arms at his sides. He knotted it tight behind the tree. Pieces of bark flaked from its trunk.

"Stop it!" Edwin was still kicking, uselessly.

Sensibly, Robert had stepped well out of the way.

"Don't take your eyes off him," Seth told Robert. Pulling the knife from his bag, he stooped and etched deep lines into the ground, brushing leaves aside. He drew a series of concentric circles, and cut a line through them to Edwin at the centre.

Chapter 36

Hannah's phone was ringing, dragging her from sleep. She reached for it, blearily, and saw Mark's name on the screen.

"Mark? What's wrong?"

"Come home. Please. There's something I need to tell you."

The sun was streaming through the curtains. She was properly awake now, reorienting herself. Mum and Dad had taken the kids off for lunch and shopping in town; she had laid down for a few minutes that had turned into almost two hours.

She scribbled a hasty note, apologising for landing them with the kids, then drove, too fast, all the way home. Every breath seemed to catch in her chest. Whatever he was going to say to her, it was going to be bad.

As soon as she was through the door, Mark hugged her tight, and she said, "What's happened?"

He didn't look at her, just shuffled into the living room. "Maybe you want to sit down. Oh God. I didn't think I'd ever have to tell you this."

"You're leaving me?"

"What? No. No, of course not."

Tears stung at her eyes. She'd wondered, these past few days, whether she still loved him. Whether she even cared about him.

She did.

"Okay," she said. "Then – whatever it is, just tell me."

"Um. Look, when I was seventeen, I ..." He hesitated. "I got a girl pregnant. Lucy, her name was. She was talking about keeping the baby and – well, I didn't know what to do, I thought my life would be over – so I got out of there."

He'd talked before about a year's backpacking when he was eighteen; she'd assumed it'd been to do with disappointing grades.

"That's it?" she asked, when he didn't say anything else.

"No." He was staring at the carpet. "She promised to keep me out of it. And she did. But the kid knows now."

If Mark had been seventeen, that would make his child – fourteen, maybe fifteen.

"Boy or girl?" she asked.

"Huh? Boy."

"Right." She took a breath, did her best to wrap her mind around this. "Look, you were seventeen. You didn't meet me for four years after that. We all did stupid things as teenagers."

"You don't understand."

She looked at him, felt her stomach turn uneasily. "What? What is it?"

"The kid," he said. "He's Edwin."

It took her a long minute to even understand what he'd said. "*Our* Edwin? From Lycopolis?"

"Yes."

"I – *how*?"

Mutely, he shook his head. But then she squeezed his hand, and he told her about the medallion – *his* medallion – and how he'd once given it, along with mix tapes and painted miniatures, to a girl called Lucy. He glossed over the details of Edwin's conception; she got the impression that a fair amount of alcohol had been involved.

And he told her how Edwin had turned up on the doorstep the previous afternoon. How the secret he'd been keeping for years – to protect her, to protect the kids – couldn't be hidden any longer.

She listened, in silence, and tried to take it all in.

Neither of them had budged from the sofa half an hour later, when her mobile rang. Kay's name showed on the screen. Without any preamble, she said, "I'm worried about Edwin. He's with Seth."

Hannah switched it to speaker, and mouthed "Edwin's with Seth" to Mark. To Kay, she said "Do you know where they are?"

"Fuck," Mark said, "We don't know what Seth might do. You saw what happened in Lycopolis, to Benedict ..."

Kay's voice crackled out from the phone. "It's not just Edwin and Seth. They've got Heidi with them too."

"What? She lives in Texas –"

"It turns out she's a guy. Robert. He flew over this morning."

Hannah blinked and Mark looked back at her, clearly just as surprised as she was.

In the game, it was Heidi who'd backed Remegius – Heidi who'd insisted on taking Benedict to him, and who'd drawn Matilda and Roderic along with her.

"I think," Kay said, "I think they're going to the forest. It's near Cirencester – Ed sent me the postcode, I'll text it to you."

"Can you get to Swindon?" Hannah asked, "We'll pick you up from the station. We need to go after them."

While they waited for another message from Kay, Hannah needed something to occupy her hands, to keep her mind firmly on the moment and stop her thoughts spiralling back into the past and darting uncertainly into the future. She spent the next hour tidying the kitchen, picking up plates and half-empty mugs of coffee, cleaning the grease out of the frying pan, emptying the overflowing bin.

"I was going to sort it out," Mark said. "Sorry everything's in such a state."

She was pretty sure that he didn't just mean the kitchen. "It's okay," she said.

"What're we going to do? About Edwin?" He started drying the plates, unbidden.

"We find out what's going on with him and Seth," she said. "We make sure he's all right. And then we take it from there."

"But what if ... I mean, he'll want me to be his *dad*. And what the hell am I going to say to Lucy?"

She washed the last plate. "Look, let's not get ahead of ourselves. What matters is that Edwin's safe."

Her phone beeped.

"On our way – I've got Brandon with me too. Should be at the station in twenty mins. Edwin told me they're at a campsite. It's quite near you."

Kay had added the postcode. Hannah looked it up on Google Maps. It sat at the edge of a thick forest between Cirencester and Dursley.

"Shit. Print the map," Mark said.

"You don't really think that Seth can –" She looked at him. There was a red mark on his forehead, unmistakable. And she'd dreamt about the forest again last night. "Oh God, Mark."

Quietly, he said, "I – I need to tell you what happened in London."

Chapter 37

Robert leant against a tree, watching. It was an alien world here, uncompromisingly cold, with rain beginning to soak his hair and drip down his neck. The last two days had been like a dream: the airport, the numb flight, the drive to the forest. And now he was thousands of miles away from reality.

"Seth, please, let me go," Edwin said, through tears.

"Shut up," Seth said, coolly. Glancing round, he asked, "Rob. You okay?"

"Yeah. Yep." But his resolve wavered as he watched Edwin crying.

Seth came over to him. "You understand what this means, right? If we succeed ... Rob, you can have *anything*. You can get away from your parents, you can go to college wherever you want, study whatever you want. No-one will be able to stop you."

He nodded.

"Robert," Edwin shouted, "Robert, make him untie me. Please. I want to go home."

"Ignore him," Seth whispered. "Don't look at him."

"Please, j-just stop it. Make Seth stop it."

Seth took a couple of torches out of his bag and handed one to Robert. "Look, we don't have much time. I need you to do what I say without asking questions. Okay?"

"Okay." Robert flicked the torch on and pointed it at the ground. His body and his actions weren't his own. Nothing that happened here was real. Or perhaps it was hyper-real, leaving the rest of his life empty and meaningless.

After handing him a scarf, Seth pointed his torch at Edwin. "Blindfold him."

Robert stepped forwards, trying not to stand on the lines of any of the circles. He could see Edwin's tears in the torchlight.

"Please, Robert," Edwin said, quietly, "Untie me. Call the police."

Ignore him. Don't look at him.

It was hard not to look at someone when you were trying to get a blindfold around their face. Especially when they were kicking you at the same time.

"Get on with it," Seth said, impatiently.

Robert had to lean on Edwin, pressing him into the tree, to hold him still. With some difficulty, he tied the scarf around Edwin's head.

"Stop it! Help!"

As soon as Robert was back at his side, Seth said, "We need to make the Prince manifest."

"Stop it!" Edwin yelled, "It's not funny, it's not."

"It's not supposed to be," Seth said.

"I f-feel sick. I want to go home. Seth, come on, you're my friend."

There was silence for several seconds.

Seth said, "I'm not."

"But, but you are. You like me. You – you bought me T-shirts–"

"I was never your friend."

Edwin was sobbing hard, shoulders shaking.

Robert looked away. "So, what do we do now? To make ... *it* ... come."

"I tell the story of the Prince. We pray. We offer a sacrifice."

The cold stung Robert's skin. "What exactly do you mean, a sacrifice? We're not going to ..."

Seth looked at him, his face in shadows. "No. We're not going to kill him."

It was easiest to just believe that, and not ask any more questions.

"Story time," Seth said. "Ed, are you listening?"

"Untie me. Please. I ... I feel really weird. Dizzy."

Robert picked up the bottle from the ground. It was glass, with a white and blue label: *Eristoff Vodka.* He wondered whether there was more than just vodka in it.

"Sorry we can't offer you a seat, Ed," Seth said, "But look at it this way – you're right at the centre of the action."

Edwin was struggling harder now, but the rope was barely shifting. The knots were tight.

Robert watched.

Standing at the end of the line that he'd drawn through the circles, Seth gazed towards at Edwin. There was a long moment where no-one said anything. The wind was blowing straight into Robert's face and the rain was starting to come down harder. He took shelter under a tree.

Seth said, "This is how it began, seventeen years ago."

Robert listened.

"There was a boy. He was seven. He went camping with his family, one October half-term. Father, mother, brother. He didn't like them. They didn't like him either." A pause. "This boy was afraid of the dark. And on that trip, he found out why."

There was a sound above the wind, like a howl. Seth glanced round. Edwin's head jerked, and he tugged his arms hard against the rope. It wasn't giving.

"The forest called to the boy. It was silent and cool and solitary. He wanted to explore it. Of course, he was forbidden to. But one day, after a row with his dad, he ran off into the trees."

Perhaps it was just the effect of the wind, but Robert was sure that Seth's voice was unsteady.

"The boy was in the mood for a bottle of good vodka and some of the heaviest of metal but, being seven, he'd never encountered either. So, lacking any way to numb the misery of life, he walked on and on through the forest."

Edwin had given up struggling, and was just crying now, little gulping sounds. The rain was coming down harder.

"He wasn't afraid – until it started to get dark. The forest became frightening. The boy was lost. He started to panic. He ran. It got darker and darker, and then he fell on his hands and knees in the mud."

There was another wolf howl, louder this time. Edwin kicked and screamed; Robert shone the torch at him to check that the knots were holding.

"Seth, stop it, please stop it, don't make it come here! Robert, make him stop."

Seth stepped forwards, shining the torch at Edwin's face. Robert watched. Like Heidi, he wanted to observe, to drink all of this in.

253

"Ed, you are going to shut the fuck up."

"No! I won't!"

Seth slapped him, hard, then stepped back out of the circles. Edwin was sobbing quietly now. "Right. Robert, where was I?"

"Um, falling in the mud."

"Yes. A black mist, blacker than the night, wrapped around the boy. It drew him to his feet. He felt his heart beat faster. He felt the pulse of life through his body. There was *hope* in him – and strength. Here was something that he knew was more powerful than his brother and his father and everyone else in the world."

"The mist called itself 'The Prince of Nightmares.' It touched the boy's forehead and it gave him a new name. Seth."

Rain ran down Robert's face. The wind whirled dead leaves up from the forest floor. No-one spoke for several minutes. Then Seth said, "Now we pray."

They knelt in the mud. Water soaked into Robert's jeans. Seth said, "Go on, Rob."

"You want *me* to? I don't know what to say."

Seth just kept looking at him, without offering any suggestions.

There was rain in his eyes. His hands were numb. He found words and felt like they were being spoken by someone else. "Prince of Nightmares. Come here, come to us. Let us *see* you. Be here, in the forest. We all dreamt about it. We're here. Three of us. Robert and Edwin and Seth ..."

"Enough," Seth whispered.

Robert looked up. A black mist was forming in front of them, Edwin at the centre.

Seth got to his feet. "Take him! You chose him, and he's yours."

"No! NO!" Edwin was struggling, the rope starting to loosen around him.

"Come on! Come and take him!" Seth yelled.

The mist darkened. It moved like a creature, obscuring Edwin from view. Robert closed his eyes, suddenly wanting to wake up. But the air was still cold around him, and the rain was still pouring down.

Edwin stopped screaming.

Chapter 38

Edwin was falling into a deep pit, and there was darkness all about. He grasped for memory which wouldn't come. Fog filled his mind; a stone weight crushed his thoughts. He didn't know where he was, hardly knew *who* he was.

He clung on to anger, a dark anger shot through with blood and betrayal. He wanted to lash out, to fight, to smash and break and tear. The anger engulfed him. It defined him. It was all he had.

Slowly, snatches of the world came back to him. He remembered being freezing cold and in pain. He remembered struggling, desperately, ropes digging into his arms. The fog cleared from his vision. He was gazing down at himself, at the back of his head. His hair looked odd from behind, splayed out across the ground. One of his hands was grabbing at the mud. The ropes lay loose around him.

He'd left his body behind, crumpled and empty. And he wasn't seeing normally; he knew what was happening in several places at once, with all of it making perfect sense.

He could see Robert running away through the forest. He could hear Robert's heartbeat, thud thud thud. But he didn't care about Robert.

He could hear Seth saying, "No. You're *mine*. I summoned you!"

Edwin hated him.

He'd thought he hated Darren Miller. That felt so long ago now. He'd thought he hated Mark, for turning out to be his father, for not wanting him. But all of his anger and disappointment and fear had been a thin, pale version of this. This was *hate*. It filled him up so that there was no room left for anything else.

The medallion was round Seth's neck, and Edwin could see the power in it, streaming into the forest like light shining through water. Seth was trying to cut the chain with a knife, but that was almost funny, because Edwin knew how strong that chain was, and how thin and insubstantial the knife was.

He was close, now, close enough to see Seth's face. Seth's jaw was clenched hard, and his eyes were wide and scared.

He wanted Seth to be terrified.

He wanted Seth to run.

The trees blazed a cold blue. They started to move, their roots ripping from the earth. The ground swelled like waves. The wolves howled. Edwin wasn't afraid of them now. He wasn't afraid of anything now.

Seth wasn't running, though. Seth was standing there, the medallion skewed around his neck, a knife in his hand. He was looking down at Edwin's body on the ground.

"What the fuck do you want?" Seth yelled. "I've given you the kid! Look, I'm in charge here, *I* am, and you're going to do what I say."

The world blurred black. Then a dream began, a memory. He was in Seth's flat. The room was warm and fuzzy. Seth was saying something, but Edwin couldn't hear it. He could see Seth's expression though, Seth's eyes, deep and dangerous. Then Seth beckoned him to stand up, to come closer.

The dream sped up. Him breathing fast; the smell of sweat on both of them. A weird lightness in him, like he could think anything, say anything, do anything. Seth's hands round his throat. A jolt through him, electric, and it was like the world had plunged under him and his heart had jumped to somewhere new.

Seth didn't let go. Seth held on and pushed him backwards, into a tree, and he was smiling still, eyes locked into Edwin's, hands around his throat.

The feeling of lightness was gone. There was a sick horror in him which built quickly into fury.

He wanted Seth to *die*.

The dream ended. He was back in the forest.

And Seth was running.

Edwin found that he could move, gliding fast through the air. He watched Robert stumbling through the trees, watched him catch his sleeve on a bramble.

He flowed away from Robert. There was darkness walking through the forest, parting the air. The fallen leaves rippled in its wake. Edwin followed it. He wasn't scared any more. It didn't want *him*, it wanted *Seth*.

He was alongside it, or maybe inside it, seeing just as it saw, a thousand details all at once. Broken spines of trampled leaves, torn threads of cloth on brambles, specks of blood on skin.

Hate tore through him like a wind. He felt it being dragged out of him, but there was more, because this hatred ran so deep that it would never end. He'd trusted Seth, he'd looked up to him, he'd liked him. And all along, Seth had been using him. Seth had never cared about him.

Maybe Edwin was dying. This was death. Or *he* was death, stalking the forest, wrapped in blackness, tearing through the trees, unstoppable.

Seth was still running.

It didn't matter how fast Seth ran; Edwin would always be faster. He saw the flash of silver in Seth's hand, and he felt anger pulse like hot blood. The knife twisted out of Seth's grasp and fell away through the air.

The black mist was thick around him, holding him safe. He leant into it, breathed fury into it, and it grew stronger and stronger. Three wolves leapt out of the mist. They were fierce and beautiful. Two ran towards the edge of the forest. The other went after Seth.

Now he was getting tired, and the anger was still there, but fainter. The cloud carried him along, further and deeper into the forest. Maybe this was the end. He wanted to wake up, he tried to wake up, but sleep was crushing him down.

He hadn't told Mark that he didn't care about everything that had gone wrong in the past, that none of it mattered.

He hadn't let Kay know how much he liked her.

He hadn't said goodbye to Mum.

Chapter 39

The forest was moving. Seth scrambled through the trees, mud clinging to his shoes and ankles. He stumbled over roots which jabbed out of the broken earth. He'd lost his knife.

As he slid on wet leaves, he flung out a hand by reflex, his palm stinging as it hit rough bark. There was a low growl. He shone his torch forwards, the beam wavering so much that he could hardly see. It was a wolf, an actual wolf, with grey fur spiking up in the wind, and cold yellow eyes.

It bared its teeth.

He turned and fled. A bramble snaked around his ankle and he almost fell trying to pull himself free. He twisted round, saw the wolf crouch, and got one arm up to protect his face.

Its claws sank into his coat, scratching his arm. Its breath was cold on his face. Somehow, he pulled free of his coat, and shoved it at the wolf's head. He scrambled up, and ran. Gulps of cold air caught in his throat. He'd dropped the torch – he could hardly see anything through the rain. There was a hard throb of pain up his side, where he'd stumbled into a tree.

Everything had gone wrong, incredibly fast, and he was struggling to breathe, let alone think. He had to get back to Edwin. The Prince was drawing power from Edwin, terrible, terrifying power. He'd find the knife – or smother Edwin in the mud – and finish this. He had to. He had to win. Hell, he had to *survive*.

A branch hit him hard in the stomach, and another swiped at his head, but he pushed on past them. Then something heavy struck him in the chest, and he fell in a tangle of branches, mud below him, rain above, and the wolf snarling at his throat.

"Fuck!" He kicked at it, panic lending him strength. The wolf dug its claws into his shoulder, slicing through clothes and flesh. He yelled in shock; it took several seconds for the pain to hit. The wolf's yellow eyes met his. It growled, low and dangerous, baring its teeth.

Seth lay very still. "Call your wolf off!"

The wolf snapped its teeth horribly near his throat before it sat back on its haunches, watching him.

He didn't try to get up, just lay there, clenching and unclenching the fingers of his left hand. Pain lanced through his arm. He brought his other hand across his body and touched his shoulder. There was blood there, quite a lot of blood.

The wolf turned and trotted away. Seth staggered to his feet, his vision blurring. Then he saw: the trees had shifted. They'd formed a wide clearing around him. The medallion felt heavier. Grabbing at it, he tried to rip it off, fumbling desperately at the clasp. His breath was coming in ragged gasps; there were grey spots in his vision.

Without warning, he was surrounded by black mist.

"Welcome back, Seth."

There was nothing seductive in its voice now – only a cold triumph. He'd forgotten how its words shook him, how they grasped and clung.

"I summoned you. You have to obey me." He couldn't fail. Whatever it took. "I'll give you Robert, okay, him as well as Edwin. Anything!"

The Prince laughed. The sound stabbed into him, gripped at his chest. *"You didn't do any summoning tonight. You didn't bring me into the forest. I brought you."*

"No ..." He'd dreamt this: he'd seen himself walking triumphant out of the forest, the trees parting for him, the air shining with power. It would happen – it had to happen.

"You thought you could bind me with a few circles drawn in the dirt." Its laugh shook him hard, and he almost fell. He started to back away.

"Stand still, Seth."

Turing, he looked for a gap through the trees.

"You won't get anywhere. Edwin's dreaming of you, Seth."

He ran, left arm pressed against his side. From nowhere, something caught him across the legs and pitched him forwards. He landed heavily, the breath squashed out of him, pain making the world lurch.

"He's dreaming for me, Seth."

The black mist drew back – and then there was a hiss all around him. He got to his feet, struggling for breath. And then he saw. He was standing in a circle of dark blue flames. They cast a cold light across the forest.

"This, Seth, is how to bind a human."

The rain poured down, but it didn't quench the flames. He reached for his phone. It shook in his hand.

No signal.

He wasn't going to curl up on the ground with his hands over his head and pray for it all to end. He'd survive. No, he'd succeed. The flames didn't give off any warmth: the cold air was still biting into him. He wasn't trapped, they couldn't burn him.

"Go ahead," the Prince said. *"Oh, this should be amusing."*

Seth hesitated. There was no heat from the flames, nothing except an unsettling sharpening of fear. It was an illusion. There was nothing to be afraid of. He reached out a tentative hand and touched them.

He was five, crying silently in the dark, clutching a pillow for comfort. He was nine, locking eyes with his father even though his knees were shaking. He was ten, screaming his way down a ski slope, the world a terrible white blur.

And it was all at once.

He staggered back, tears spilling down his face with the rain. It hurt, too much fear packed hard together.

The Prince said, *"Quite effective, isn't it?"*

He concentrated on just breathing.

"I spared you for seventeen years. I watched you become the man I needed you to be."

He fought back tears and forced the words out. "I'm my own fucking person."

"You created a cruel and beautiful world for me. You drew others in. You did just what I wanted."

"No."

"It's over. Kneel to me, and all this will end." Its voice was silky and soft now. *"I'm offering you peace."*

261

He shook his head. But it was tempting. He'd spent years denying fear in the day, outrunning it at night. And now he was tired, so very tired.

"There'll be no more pain, no more nightmares, just sleep ..."

"You're lying."

The mist was digging into his skin. *"You'll give in eventually. Why not make it fast?"*

"You can't fucking force me, can you? Or we wouldn't even be talking." The sudden realisation gave him new strength.

"Correct. But there's force, and there's ... motivation."

The medallion around his neck flared blue.

He was ten and his brother was twisting his arm up behind his back while he screamed. He was twelve and terribly lost in a rough part of town, a gang of teenagers bearing down on him. He was thirteen and mouthing off to a sixth former, outwardly glib, inwardly terrified.

With a sob, he grabbed at the medallion, but that only made it worse, the flames darting into bare skin.

He was six, high on a climbing frame, losing his grip. He was eleven and he'd just hit his brother, who was rounding on him, furiously.

It was relentless fear, forced into him.

"Stop it! Stop it!"

The flame died down to a low throb of fear.

"You're not going to serve me. Fine. But – just let me go. Please. I trusted you. You – you were my only friend."

"I'm not your friend, Seth. I was never your friend."

The medallion flame flickered higher again. He struggled for words. "My journal. The game."

"Both very helpful."

He clung on to hope. Edwin had sent a text to Kay; perhaps she was coming ...

"You think she'd help you, after everything you've done?"

Almost certainly not, but then, she'd stood against the Prince; she'd made those dolls. If anyone in the world could help him, it was her.

"She wants you dead. They all want you dead."

He tried not to listen, but it was impossible to ignore the voice as well as the burning fear. Black despair tugged at him. He kept

262

breathing. His arm hurt like hell; that was real, that was something to stay grounded with. This had to end eventually.

"I've got all eternity," the Prince said, *"However, this is getting tedious."*

A line of flame flickered across his body. This time it brought sheer, incoherent terror. He screamed. There was blood in his mouth. The world swam around him, memory packed on memory, nightmare on nightmare.

"Kneel to me, Seth."

Chapter 40

There was a sleek black car already parked in front of the closed gates. Mark pulled up next to it. They all scrambled out.

He took out the carrier bag from the boot; he'd grabbed two kitchen knives before setting off. They weren't sharp enough, or strong enough. He kept the carving knife. Wordlessly, Brandon reached out and took the other – a squat vegetable knife.

Hannah was staring at him. "No. No. They're just boys. "

"We don't know what the hell might be happening." He gave her the spray paint, a silver bottle from the craft drawer. "If we need to mark our way."

Kay was already scrambling over the fence. They followed her, Mark helping Hannah over. It was almost dark now, and Kay shone the torch – the only one they had – across the field. Muddy footprints led right up to the trees at the far end.

"Kay!" Mark yelled, "Don't go running in there alone."

She turned, her hair whipping across her face. "I need to stop Seth! We might already be too late."

The words hit him hard. He'd only just found his son ... and now he might never have a chance to put things right.

"Ed!" he yelled, towards the trees. "Edwin! Can you hear me? Ed!"

The others joined in, calling for Edwin and Robert.

There was no response.

A long howl pierced the air. Mark shuddered. Hannah swung the torch slowly from side to side.

Two wolves strolled out from the line of trees.

"What the fuck?" Mark gripped the knife more tightly. Wolves. Actual wolves. Dark grey fur, yellow eyes, bared teeth.

Hannah walked sideways, alongside the ditch. The wolves matched her pace. Neither of them looked about to attack.

"They're not going to let us into the forest," Hannah said, tightly.

"Get back," Mark said. The handle of his knife was slippery with sweat. "Get behind me. Kay, get the fuck *back*."

He stepped forwards, deliberately, towards the edge of the ditch. One of the wolves stared at him from the other side. Another step. It didn't move. Another step.

It pounced.

He thrust the knife at it, but it wasn't sharp enough, and his hand was trembling too much. The blade barely made contact.

The wolf snarled, snapping at him. He stabbed again, going for the eyes, pushing his other hand against its throat in a desperate attempt to keep its teeth away from him. Its fur was coarse under his hand, and shockingly cold, like it was already dead.

His feet skidded, his ankle twisting under him. He fell. Then the wolf was on top of him, its foul breath freezing his face. It lunged for his throat. He jabbed his feet at it, but he didn't have enough space to get any force behind the kicks. He tried to force its head back.

There were screams. "Mark!"

He was staring into the wolf's mouth, at sharp white teeth. He couldn't hold it off much longer. He swung the knife wildly, over and over, caught it in the leg, which made it growl, low and furious.

His son was in that forest.

Again and again he stabbed, with more strength than he thought he possessed, and finally the blade stuck hard in the side of its head, behind its eye.

Blood rained across his arms and face. The wolf fell across him, heavy and cold. He shoved it away, his hands slippery and red. He gasped in breaths that smelt sickeningly of blood.

More screaming. Hannah yelling "Mark!" and Kay yelling "Brandon!"

He sat up. The other wolf lay on the ground nearby. Brandon, unperturbed, was jabbing it methodically in the head.

"Brandon," Hannah said. "It's dead."

Shrugging, Brandon prodded the corpse with his toe.

When Mark tried to stand, his ankle buckled beneath him, pain lancing up his leg. "Shit!"

Hannah was there, crouching next to him, shining the torch along his body. "What? Where are you hurt?"

"Ankle," he said, through gritted teeth. "Twisted it."

She unlaced his shoe, pulled it off, and touched his ankle gingerly.

"Ow! Fucking hell!"

"You've sprained it," she said.

"Shit." He saw movement, glanced up at Brandon – and Kay, who'd picked up his knife. "Stop! For God's sake, just stay still a second."

Kay didn't take her eyes off the forest.

"I'll be fine," he said to Hannah.

"You can't walk on it. You'll just slow us down. Stay here." She turned away, shone her torch into the forest again.

"Look," Mark said, "We should all stay here. Call the police ..."

"No!" Kay's hair was blowing around her face. "We *can't* wait. You haven't seen what Seth's done!"

She scrambled across the ditch.

Mark grabbed Hannah's arm. "Don't go in there! We'll call the police, they'll sort it out."

"We can't let her go alone," Hannah said, and she and Brandon disappeared into the trees.

A fucking lot of use he was. All he could do was sit in the mud and watch as his wife and two teenagers ran into a forest straight out of nightmare. At least they had the knives, and the torch, and the paint. At least he'd managed that much. And he'd killed the wolf. But wasn't that how he always kidded himself? *At least Lucy can get on with her life; at least I can do my degree now; at least Hannah and Denny and Megan have a roof over their heads.*

They needed *him*. No, they needed someone like him but better. Someone stronger and braver and more patient. Someone who was actually there for them.

The only thing he could do was keep calling for the two boys, and hope that one of them would hear him. "Edwin! Robert!"

The wind threw his words back in his face.

"Edwin! Robert! Ed!"

There was silence. He kept shouting. And kept stopping to listen for minutes at a time, trying to make out any sound at all, any indication that Hannah was safe in there.

"Edwin? Ed. Robert. Oh God, *anyone?*"

They could all be walking to their deaths, and there was nothing he could do.

Finally, an American voice yelled back. "Hello? Hey?"

"Robert? This way! Over here!"

A light wavered towards him, then a silhouette stumbled out of the forest, jumped the ditch and landed on its hands and knees. It stood and ran towards him: a man – no, a boy, really. He was soaking wet, shivering.

Robert half sat, half fell next to him, gasping for breath. When he saw the wolf corpses, he covered his face with his hands. "Oh God, oh God."

Grabbing him, Mark shook him hard. "What's happening in there? Where's Edwin?"

"I don't know, I'm sorry–"

Mark kept hold of him, ignoring the pain coursing through his ankle. "You were helping Seth, weren't you? What the *hell* have you done?"

Chapter 41

Brandon disliked the forest the moment they entered it. Too dark, too closed-in, too full of sounds and scents. He wasn't going to leave Kay, though. She was ahead of them still, but he could see her, and hear her shouting for Edwin.

Brandon listened for an answer, but there was none. He had never seen Kay so upset, or so angry. It was as unsettling as the forest.

"Wait for us!" Hannah called. They ran to catch her up.

"You don't know what Seth's capable of," Kay said.

They kept walking. Hannah sprayed silver paint on every third tree. Brandon watched the shadows, but nothing moved. No birds, no animals at all. That made him very uneasy.

Then there was a scream. Kay and Hannah looked around, wildly.

"That way," he said, and pointed.

Kay was running before he could tell her to wait. He tried to follow her, and so did Hannah, but thick branches rose up in front of them.

"What's – what the –" Hannah said, trying to push her way through.

"The trees are shifting," he said.

They kept trying to press forwards, but the trees blocked them, branches twining to form a wall that Brandon had no hope of cutting through with the knife.

"Oh God!" Hannah spun round, eyes full of confusion. "What – how?"

"Can't you see what they're doing?" he asked. "They're preventing us from following Kay."

Hannah stood very still, and whispered, "I think you're right."

He touched the nearest tree. It was solid, damp from the rain, the bark rough beneath his fingertips. He didn't believe it could be a hallucination or illusion, not when it was so present to all his senses. He sniffed at it, to be certain.

"We can't just stay here," Hannah said.

"Let me have the torch." He shone it on the ground, until he found a disturbed area. "Some trees moved over here."

They followed the path: broken earth, churned mud, branches smashed on the ground.

Hannah stooped, and picked up a stick. A strong, thick one. She weighed it in her hands.

"Look, Brandon," she said, her voice unsteady, "If it comes to it, I don't want anyone getting stabbed. Okay? That's a last resort."

He nodded.

They kept walking. Brandon glanced up at the stars from time to time, and pictured the forest as a map in his mind. They tracked north-west-west, then north-west, then north-north-west, then north.

There were more and more broken branches here, the ground torn as though by machinery.

He saw a shape which jarred, and pointed the torch towards it. "Hannah. Look."

They ran forwards. It was Edwin, lying on his face in the mud.

Brandon remembered being very young, just old enough to count to a hundred. He'd been playing in the wild garden behind the squat, and he'd seen a squirrel lying on its side. He'd never touched a squirrel – they ran too fast – and now one lay unmoving, within reach. He'd crept up to it and touched its body. Cold and stiff. A nothing, a zero.

So he was glad that Hannah was there, to kneel down next to Edwin, and lift his face from the mud.

"Is he dead?" Brandon asked, because he had to know.

"No," she said. "No, thank God. He's breathing."

They turned Edwin onto his back.

"Ed. Come on, sweetheart," she said, "Wake up."

Edwin's eyes were still closed. Hannah shook his shoulders, gently. Brandon stood up and paced around, looking for Kay, looking for Seth.

"Edwin," Hannah said. "Wake up! We're going to get you out of here."

Brandon didn't know how to help. He'd liked Edwin when he first met him, in Nottingham. Back then, he hadn't been able to pin Seth to a number, because Seth was a puzzle. Now, he had a number: *six*, sly and slick, curled between two primes.

Hannah looked up at him, her face pale in the torchlight. "A couple of nights ago, when Remegius brought the Prince into the game, it put Benedict into a supernatural sleep. It was feeding on him."

Nearby, the tree roots were rippling through the soil. The branches were bending, even though the wind had stopped.

Brandon understood. "We need to wake him."

But they couldn't.

"I can carry him," Brandon said.

"Okay." Hannah stood up, and looked around, shining the torch into the forest. "Okay. Let's get him out of here."

Brandon lifted Edwin and put him over his shoulder. And then they heard screams.

"Oh God." Hannah's eyes were wider than usual. "We need to find Kay."

Chapter 42

It was several minutes before Kay paused to catch her breath – and realised she was alone. She looked round. Brandon and Hannah were gone.

"Hannah? Brandon?"

No answer.

She kept calling for Edwin. Kept straining her eyes against the dark, looking for black mist in a black forest. She didn't even have a torch, only a plastic lighter that she'd grabbed from the newsagent's at the train station. It took her several attempts to get the flame to spark.

Had the scream she'd heard been Edwin? Even the best-case scenario was grim: Edwin hurt and terrified. And the worst-case …

He could well be dead. And if he was, that was her fault – she hadn't stopped Seth in time. She should've been ruthless: should've pushed pins into that doll and found a way to live with herself afterwards.

The ground was slippery underfoot, all mud and crushed leaves. The wind was blowing hard again. A branch jabbed her in the leg. The forest was thicker here, and she was scrambling round bushes, treading down nettles, pulling her jeans free of clutching brambles. She almost fell over something, and held the lighter towards it. A coat, soaked with rain.

She crouched. It wasn't Edwin's. One sleeve was badly ripped. She felt in the pockets until she found something.

A doll. The doll she'd made, of Seth. This was his coat, then. When she touched her fingers to the torn sleeve, they came away red.

There were words in the dark air, words which seeped into her mind, like cold thoughts. Maybe she imagined them.

It's too late.

Give up.

Putting the doll in her pocket, she stood, and walked through the mud and the fallen leaves. There was something up ahead, a faint blue glow between trees. Another scream pierced the air.

"Ed? Robert?" she yelled.

The trees were packed tightly together, barely any gaps between them. She could see a flickering blue fire beyond – but no smoke.

Pulling the collar of her coat up to protect her face, she pushed her way through the trees. Her gloves snagged on the rough bark; she yanked them loose and stumbled into a clearing. Her knuckles were tight on the handle of the knife. Black mist drifted around her.

Ahead of her, there was a ring of blue flames.

And a shape lying on the ground.

"Ed! Oh God, Ed?"

It wasn't Edwin. She ran closer. The fire didn't give off any heat, but it was bright.

She met Seth's eyes, through the flames. He was on the ground in the middle of the circle, blue flames flickering over his clothes and face.

"What have you done to Ed?" she shouted, "Where is he? Is he hurt?"

She could feel the demon's voice rather than hear it, a crashing wave of words.

"Seth isn't talking much ..."

"Where the hell is Edwin?" The knife was shaking in her hand. It wasn't going to be any use against the mist.

"Lost in dreams. He's mine now."

"No." A shiver gripped her. "No!"

"Seth gave him to me. Seth sent him down into sleep ..."

The mist was swirling outside the circle of flames. She could see Seth's face now, clenched in pain. He struggled to his feet, swaying. "Kay? Kay – help me."

The anger rose in her like a fever. "Why the hell should I?"

The flames flickered higher. One touched her hand. There was a jumbled flash: monsters, ghosts, noises in the dark. She gasped, stepped back.

The Prince's voice was distant now. *"Game over, Seth."*

She watched, not understanding, as the blue flames that ran across his body flickered and died. She watched him fall to his knees.

Behind her, there was a shout.

"Kay! Kay, thank God! We've got Ed!"

She turned, to see torchlight, and Hannah and Brandon pushing through the trees. Brandon was carrying Edwin. He looked horribly still as Brandon stooped and set him down gently.

"Ed's alive, he's okay!" Hannah said, and ran forwards. "What's happening? *Seth?*"

Kay looked back. The blue circle of fire had died. Seth lay sprawled on the ground. The mist was rushing towards him, surrounding him.

And then it poured into him, and vanished.

His eyes were shut.

Kneeling next to him, she said, "Seth?"

He sat up and his eyes snapped open. The irises were charcoal-black.

For the first time, the forest was silent. The wind was still. No rain dripped from the branches. No-one spoke. No-one moved.

Seth looked at them, and his smile was a horrible parody.

"Oh God," Hannah said, quietly.

Brandon said, "That's not Seth."

Kay watched, horrified, as Seth stood. He moved jerkily, as though he wasn't used to his body. He stretched his arms above his head, experimentally, and smiled at them all again.

"*I win,*" it said, in Seth's voice.

"Get out of here," Kay said. "Hannah, Brandon, get Edwin out of here."

"But –" Hannah said.

"Do it! Quickly! It's drawing its strength from Edwin." They needed to get to safety. And if there was any chance of stopping the Prince, she needed to cut it off from its power source.

"We'll mark the route," Hannah said. Brandon lifted Edwin, and they disappeared into the trees.

She prayed they'd be safe; that the six dolls, huddled in the box in her college room, would have some effect. Around her, the forest was starting to shift again, the trees arching up towards the sky, their branches stretching out like hands. The air was thick and tasted bitter. It stuck in her throat.

The Prince walked in a circle, touching each tree in turn. They moved backwards. A ripple spread out through the forest. Kay grabbed his arm. He didn't even bother to shake her off, just kept walking, dragging her along.

"Seth!" she yelled. "Seth, can you hear me? If I have to kill you to destroy this thing, I will, okay? So fight it!"

'He was fighting me. In case you didn't notice – he lost.'

She clutched at him, desperately and uselessly. He kept moving, pressing his hand against another tree trunk. The branches swayed and curled. She tried to push him backwards, hands on his chest, shoving hard. It had no effect.

There had been no mist inside that circle of flames – and before the Prince had entered him, the fire had died away.

She let go of him, took her lighter, and flicked it hard. The flame seared the darkness.

She pulled the doll from her pocket.

It caught alight easily, the paper inside fuelling the flames. She flung it to the ground.

Nothing happened, for a long, long moment.

And then blue flames, knee-high, surrounded Seth. Screaming, he stumbled backwards. There was nothing human in his eyes.

She jumped at him. He staggered. She grabbed and punched and kicked, and he fought her off, but he was slow, slower than he should've been, and she threw herself on him and pushed him down into the flames.

She fell with him.

And she held him there, the flames coursing up around her arms. Fear flashed through her, fear on fear, images that began at the dawn of time – one brother murdering another; flood waters inexorably rising; kings betrayed; a fleet of longships pulling up to shore; hooded assassins in dark corners; dead bodies piled into carts; fire in the night, gutting street after street of buildings. Wars raging down the millennia, with sticks and clubs and knives and swords and guns and cannons and warships and bombs ...

There was a shriek, unbearably horrible, inhuman – and mist flooded the air, black and thick.

Her face was close to his. Life flickered in his eyes, for a second. "Kay!"

"Yeah." It was hard to talk, the flames digging fear into her skin. "I'm here."

"Make it stop!" He broke off in a gasping yell. "No, please!"

He was struggling, one hand clawing at the ground. She kept him pinned. It wasn't hard, not when she thought about the way he'd stormed into her room with a knife; not when she thought about Edwin.

The world went dark. There was more fear burning into her: a child running into this forest, alone, crying hard. Lying in the dark, hands pressed over eyes, trying to shut out the nightmares. The pictures bled into each other, faster and faster, until they became a lifetime of fear. Being alone, being alone forever. Not being able to trust anyone. Knowing that one mistake might ruin everything. Burying guilt, time and time again. Hurting anyone who got close. Playing for such high stakes that losing meant something worse than death; a hell of never-ending nightmares. Holding onto a name – *Kay*; clinging to a thread of hope, only to have it decisively snapped.

There was another scream. She forced her eyes to open, and met Seth's.

Blue-grey. Human. Wet with tears.

She rolled sideways, and grabbed his arms, and hauled him out of the flames.

The forest was silent. The trees didn't move. The stars shone down, pinpricks in the fabric of the sky.

She sat up and fumbled for her lighter, sparking it again. In the gloom, she could see the scraps of the doll on the ground, charred paper and fabric. It was useless now, its link to Seth gone.

He was curled in the fallen leaves and the mud, the smoke hovering close.

The Prince was whispering again. *"Let me in ... let me back in ... she'll kill you ... just let me in and I'll set you free ..."*

The medallion burnt blue. Seth sobbed, hands pressed over his face. His left sleeve was soaked with blood. It would have been so easy to leave him there. He deserved it. And that voice was inside her head, quiet and relentless. *"Let me take him, let me hurt him, let me punish him ..."*

"Kay." He clutched her arm. "Don't leave me."

"I won't." She reached for the medallion chain, trying to unclasp it – but it was stuck.

"We need to get out," she said. "Can you stand?"

He made it to his feet, and she could see that there was blood on his face too, trickling down from his hairline. Blue flames flickered out from the medallion. He gasped, flinching away from her.

She took hold of his uninjured arm, firmly.

"It doesn't matter how far you run. You're never going to escape. I'll always be there when you sleep ..."

"Just move," Kay said, and tugged him forwards.

They stumbled on through the forest, the mist thickening around them. The feeble flame of her lighter couldn't pierce it. She kept her hand on Seth's arm. He was shivering hard.

Hannah and Brandon had marked a line of trees, the silver streaks just visible through the mist. A few trees had moved out of place, but they were creaking slowly now, branches drooping. The Prince's power was waning: did that mean that Edwin was safely out of the forest?

"We're nearly there." She could just make out the edge of the trees up ahead.

"I can't –" He came to a sudden stop.

She looked at him. "What?"

"This is its last chance. It's got nothing left to lose."

Meeting his eyes, she said, "I am getting you out of here. Even if I have to drag you through that ditch."

He managed a scowl in response.

But they didn't make it much further before he suddenly went down. Thin green brambles snaked around his ankles, holding him against the forest floor.

"Seth. Seth!" She wrapped her coat sleeve over her hand, and pulled at one of the brambles. It came out of the earth, but two more took its place. The mist was heaviest near the ground. "Get up!"

But the mist was closing in on them, and Seth's medallion was blazing blue. There were flames licking up from beneath him now.

"You'll never escape me. Never."

"Yeah?" she said, to the mist. "Well, I'm not leaving him either."

He screamed. Her stomach twisted.

"Give up, Seth. Let me in. It'll be quick. It'll be over. I promise..."

She kept pulling at the brambles, trying to tear them out by the roots, but they kept growing stronger. Her heart was pounding. There was a rush of noise around them, a low roar like water.

"Seth. Open your eyes. Look at me. Don't listen to it." The mist was getting thicker. Every breath she took felt too fast, cold air tight in her throat. "We're nearly out. Come on. Please."

The mist swirled faster, dead leaves caught up in it. *"She's lying, Seth. She's going to run and leave you here alone. Why would she help you? Why would anyone help you?"*

The mist swarmed over his face. And the Prince's voice became louder, inescapable. *"Time to run, Kay."*

"I said, I'm not leaving him."

There was a horrible noise, like the trees were cracking open. It sent a spike of cold right through her. She realised that the demon was laughing. *"You think you're safe. You think you're safe because you don't bear my mark. You're in my forest, Kay."*

The mist engulfed her. The flames were flickering out towards her. She wanted to scramble out of it, to run and run. But that wasn't who she was. That wasn't who she wanted to be. The Prince's attention was on her, and she had to use that. She got up, and began to back away from Seth, deeper into the forest again. "He's not yours. I'm taking him out of here."

The mist slid around her, clinging to her hair, clinging to her thoughts.

She'd been angry earlier. She was still angry. She wanted to hold Seth against the cold earth, and grab a rock, and finish it, finish *him*, so that he wasn't going to have the chance to hurt Edwin or anyone else ever again.

"Leave him for me. Let me take him. Run away, and all this will be nothing but a bad dream..."

"If I can't do anything to help him, why are you so keen to get rid of me?"

The trees leant towards her, branches stretching out. One brushed against her arm. She saw nightmares in the dark: twisted faces, menacing yellow eyes, trickling blood.

"That the worst you've got?" she asked, breathlessly. She could see Seth through the mist; he'd managed to get free of the brambles. She gestured towards the edge of the forest, and mouthed *run*.

The mist thickened in front of her. It brought all the fear and misery of the last weeks, crammed together. Feeling small and stupid at Magdalen. Missing home. Worrying about Edwin. Seeing the black mist for the first time. Nottingham's streets: fog and panic. Confusion turning to fear in a heartbeat when she opened her door to Seth.

And older, worse fears, came rising up again. They crushed every other thought away. Her brother's screaming, on and on; her mother's choked-up sobs, her father's voice on the phone as he asked for an ambulance. Thumping footsteps on the stairs, *her* footsteps, running and running, grabbing that doll and not knowing what to do; pulling the pins out of it in blind panic, wrapping it round and round in cloth, shoving it into a box; she hadn't done this, she couldn't have, and he was her little brother, it wasn't real, only it was; this was her fault, and she was never, never going to be able to make it right ...

The trees were all around. She didn't know which way to go. Her legs wouldn't move. She would die here, in the cold and the dark, alone.

"Kay." A hand reached through the mist, and grasped hers, firmly.

Then she was stumbling, somehow, forwards through the mist with Seth, and they slid and scrambled through the mud, across the ditch, and then they were out, and she could breathe properly again, big sweet gulps of air.

Chapter 43

"Edwin, was it drugs? What did you take?" Hannah asked, as calmly as she could. They sat in the back of their car, Mark on one side of Edwin and her on the other.

"Ed? Ed?" Mark was shining the torch at Edwin's face again, anxiously.

Edwin screwed his eyes shut.

"Shit. He's sensitive to the light, that's a bad sign –"

"You're shining the torch right in his eyes, what do you expect?" Hannah waved him away with a hand.

"I didn't take any drugs," Edwin said, and yawned. "I drank some vodka."

Huddled in the front of the car, Robert said, "I don't think it was just vodka."

She ran her hand over her face. "Seth gave it to him?"

"Yeah."

"Fuck it." Mark got out of the car, leaning against the side of it. "Where the hell are they?"

Brandon, who'd been keeping silent vigil by the fence, turned and glanced at them, shaking his head, then went back to watching the field. He'd managed to break the padlock off the gate, and it now stood open.

"Edwin, sweetheart," Hannah said. "How're you feeling?"

"Tired. Sick. Really tired."

She'd kept up with her first aid certification, mostly to help out on school trips. All she could remember about accidental poisoning was not to induce vomiting. And to get the child straight to hospital.

Which would mean abandoning Kay. And losing their chance to get any answers from Seth.

281

"We're going to be out of here really soon," she told Edwin.

"They're coming," Brandon called.

Scrambling from the car, Hannah yelled, "Are you both okay?"

Neither of them shouted anything back. Kay looked awful: hair tangled and full of leaves, mud plastered up her jeans, coat torn, lip bloodied. Seth looked worse – barely on his feet, one arm draped around Kay's shoulders. He let go of her and slumped against the gatepost.

"Oh God," Hannah said, "Kay, are you hurt?"

Shaking her head, Kay leant against the car's bonnet.

"What the FUCK did you do to Edwin?" Mark yelled, towards Seth. "You piece of shit!"

Hannah caught his arm. "No!"

"He deserves to have his fucking head kicked in. He could've bloody *killed* Ed."

"I know, but he didn't," Kay said, and pulled something from her pocket, and held it out to Mark. "This is yours, I think. Sorry, I had to break the chain."

Mark took it, wordlessly – Hannah saw that it was a medallion.

"Is Ed awake?" Kay asked.

"Yeah. I need a word with Seth." Hannah squeezed Kay's hand, then let go of her and went over to him. He backed away. There was blood on his face and on his sleeve.

She held up her hands, palms out. "We need to know what you gave Edwin."

"Chloral hydrate." He sounded hoarse. "It's a sedative."

"How much? Do we need to take him to hospital?"

Seth shook his head.

"Honestly?" she asked.

"He might throw up. That's all."

"Okay." She looked at his arm; his sleeve was caked with blood.

Kay came up to them. "Hannah – you're taking Ed and Robert back with you?"

"Yes, and you and Brandon and Seth." It was going to be quite a challenge to fit them all into the car – but she couldn't leave any of them.

"No, just take Brandon. I'll get Seth back to his place."

282

Hannah tried to talk her out of it: Swindon was much closer; Seth was definitely in no state to drive, and Kay didn't look much better; they should take Seth to a hospital. But Kay was adamant.

"It's only going to upset Ed if Seth comes with you too. And Mark –" She broke off. "I don't think it'd be a very good idea to have him and Seth under the same roof."

Reluctantly, Hannah said, "Okay. But text me when you get there, won't you? Let me know you're both back safely."

They drove in near silence for several miles, Mark and Brandon in the back, Edwin dozing between them. Robert was silent in the front passenger seat. Once they were on to the motorway, Hannah said to him, "How're you holding up?"

"I'm all right." He sounded surprised that she'd even ask. "I'm really sorry. About Ed."

"It's okay," she said. "Seth's pretty good at dragging people into things. Look, I'm going to need to phone your parents tonight, so they know you're safe."

Robert stared forwards, out the windscreen. "Yeah. I guess."

When they got back to the house, Brandon picked up Edwin and carried him in, wordlessly but somehow insistently – Hannah didn't try to stop him.

"Take him upstairs," she said, "Put him in Denny's room. First on the right."

In the kitchen, she phoned her parents first, and apologised – to Dad, luckily – for landing them with the kids. She told him what little of the truth she could: "Mark had a fall and sprained his ankle quite badly."

Then she called Edwin's mother to say they'd drop him back in the morning. "No, don't drive over. It's late. He's asleep already." She didn't mention anything about Mark. All that could wait.

Robert's parents were, understandably, upset and concerned. She reassured them as best as she could; their son was safe, and she was certain he wasn't possessed. "Led astray, perhaps. That's all."

Soon, Robert was fast asleep on the sofa, and Brandon was sprawled on the rug, looking perfectly content. She tiptoed upstairs to look in on

Edwin – tucked up under Denny's Thomas the Tank Engine duvet. She resisted the urge to take a photo.

Mark was lying down in their bedroom, ankle propped on a couple of pillows.

"How're you doing?" she asked.

"It's just a sprain."

"I meant, more –" She waved an arm towards the door, towards the rest of the house, Edwin and Brandon and Robert. And towards the world outside, the dark, the night. "With all of this."

"I ... don't know. Look, are *you* all right? What the hell happened in there?"

She lay down next to him, and told him, quietly. He held her hand. Her tears surprised her.

"It was scary as hell," she said. "Losing Kay, and not being able to wake Edwin up... and then the Prince, the mist. It was all real. All of it."

They lay there, holding each other, silently. Somehow, it was enough. Having one another was enough.

A floorboard on the landing creaked, followed by footsteps on the stairs. Hannah was instantly alert, attuned to children sneaking out of bed. Except, of course, that the kids were still in Leicester with her mum and dad. She glanced at Mark, mouthed, "Edwin," and got up.

She found him in the kitchen, staring blearily into the fridge. He looked unsteady on his feet.

"Edwin? Are you okay? Do you want something to eat?"

Shaking his head, he mumbled, "Have you got any Coke?"

"I don't think you need caffeine –"

"Yes I do! I don't want to go back to sleep."

"Oh, Ed." She wanted to hug him, but she wasn't sure how he'd take it. "We can take you home, if you want. Your mum said she'll be up for a while."

"You called her?" His voice rose. "She'll be upset – she –"

"It's fine. I just told her you'd stayed out a bit late with some friends, and that we'd get you back to Milton Keynes in the morning. Unless you want us to take you home now."

He shook his head. "Did Mark – did Mark tell you?"

"Yes."

Edwin didn't look at her. "He never wanted me."

"No, that's not true," she said. "Ed, he was worried sick about you, when Kay phoned us to say that you'd gone off with Seth."

"Really?"

"Yes. And ... he told me he said some pretty horrible things to you, and he's really sorry about that."

"Yeah. It's okay." He rubbed his hand over his eyes. "I never – I never thought of my dad having another family. Other kids."

She'd never imagined that Mark had a child by another woman, either. But she didn't say that. She just said, "You're part of our family now. If you want to be."

This time, he looked at her, and nodded.

She leant in and gave him a hug, held him like she'd have held Denny or Megan, and blinked back the tears.

Chapter 44

Seth stood in the bathroom. He needed to do something about his arm. Blood had dried on the shirt sleeve, which clung to the scratches. He tugged at it, gingerly, and winced.

"Let me help," Kay said, from the doorway.

"I don't need any help."

She ignored him, which he'd pretty much been counting on, seeing as she'd already refused to let him drive his own car. "Have you got any scissors?"

"Yeah, in the medicine cabinet there." The shirt was already ruined anyway.

She found them, cut around the sleeve and eased it away from his arm. "Sorry."

"It's fine," he said, though his voice wasn't as steady as he'd have liked.

"Let me get some of that blood off."

The forest still clung to him; he could feel the black mist pressing around the edges of his thoughts. He rested his hand against the edge of the sink. Blood still oozed from the angry red scratches.

"I think you need stitches. And a tetanus jab or something."

"I'm not going to the hospital." That was one thing he could find the energy to insist on.

"They need cleaning – have you got any antiseptic?" She rummaged around in the medicine cabinet and found the TCP. "Sorry, this is probably going to hurt."

The *probably* was rather optimistic. "Yeah. Don't worry about it."

Carefully, she dabbed at his arm with a flannel. It stung like hell, but at least that blotted out the forest for a minute.

"Right – I think that's done. Have you got something I can use for a bandage?"

They settled on one of his clean shirts. She cut strips from it, and wrapped them tightly around his arm. The room swayed around him for a moment.

"Seth? You okay?"

He nodded – which only made him feel dizzier.

"You really don't look too good."

Somehow, he ended up lying on his bed, two blurry Kays peering down at him. She was prodding at his head. "There's blood in your hair."

The trees had reached for him, relentlessly; they'd struck him hard – in the head, in the stomach. And that black mist had swirled around him, merciless … he'd been pushed into the darkness while the Prince took his body.

Kay was saying something to him, but he couldn't hear her properly. He let his eyes close. And sleep was treacherous, quick to take advantage of weakness. He was dragged down, snatched across the border without warning. It was too strong to fight. He was in the forest, terrifying flames high around him, blue light searing into his eyes, the mist thick and tight around his throat.

He was alone. He'd pushed everyone away; worse, he'd hurt them all, deliberately and savagely, and no-one was going to come for him, ever.

He woke up with an inarticulate yell, tears spilling down his face.

"Seth. Seth, it's okay."

Covering his eyes with his good arm, he muttered, "Fuck off."

"Let me help –"

"You've got the fucking record for *helping* me, haven't you, Katherine?" His shoulder throbbed with pain, and his heart was hammering much too fast.

"I –"

"Holding me in the flames." He pulled himself up, leaning against the wall. "That felt good, didn't it? You wanted to hurt me."

He thought she'd deny it – futilely; he'd looked up at her, through the fire, and he'd seen the way she stared down at him, and he'd known.

Quietly, she said, "Yeah. I did. Does that really surprise you?"

288

"No." There was a coldness creeping through him. He had nothing left. No friends – had he ever had friends? He'd lost the Prince; lost any chance of that eternal power.

"Seth?"

He tried to say, "I'm fine," but the words stuck somewhere in his throat. His head hurt, a tight pinch near his scalp. He fought to regain some approximation of composure.

"Seth –"

He didn't want her pity. "It was your brother, wasn't it?"

"You – you saw that?"

"Yes." He realised that she must have seen his fears too, all those nightmares that rose up out of the flames and into his mind. Knowing that, it was easier to continue. "Tell me what you did."

For the first time, she looked as lost and abandoned as he felt.

"Tell me," he said.

"I've never told anyone."

He held her gaze, and she looked away first.

This was an old game, an easy one, something he could win. "You want me to trust you?"

She nodded.

"Then I want your secrets." And he wanted her pain, and her guilt, and her tears.

For a minute, she was silent, then she said, "I was sixteen, and Tommy – my brother – was ten. He was going through this stage of always wanting to join in, hanging around me and my friends. I was just starting sixth form, it was a difficult time."

"You don't need to make excuses," he said.

"No." She looked down at her hands. "There aren't any. One weekend I was bored, fed up of Tommy. I'd been reading up on a load of medieval stuff, for History ... and I'd come across this thing about poppets, sympathetic magic, stuff like that."

"And?"

"And, well, I made one. Of Tommy. I took a couple of pages from his notebook and stuffed the doll with them."

"Go on."

She closed her eyes. She was shivering.

"What did you do?"

"I ... I shoved pins into it. I didn't really want to *hurt* him, I just wanted him to stop being a nuisance –" She broke off.

He should've felt like he was back in control. He certainly shouldn't have felt a twinge of guilt.

"So, what happened?" he asked, as coldly as he could.

"He – he got hit by a car." She had her hand over her mouth, as though trying to keep back the sobs. Tears ran down her face. "You'll say it could've just been coincidence – but it wasn't – I just – I *knew*. And I took the pins out of the doll, I wrapped it up in a cloth, I didn't know what to do. I couldn't tell anyone. I couldn't talk to anyone."

She was crying hard now. Seth couldn't look at her any more. He turned away, towards the bedroom window, at the bright spots of colour in the London night.

He'd hurt her. He'd broken into her room, threatened her with a knife, and hit her. He'd taken a lock of hair from her and if he'd had a little more time, he'd have made a doll and driven pins into it. Yet despite everything, she'd stayed with him in the forest. She'd drawn the demon away from him. If she hadn't been there, he'd still be trapped, imprisoned in darkness while the Prince walked the world in his body.

And now, he'd deliberately made her cry. She was learning forwards and her hair had swung down to shield her face. She said, "If you want me to go –"

"No," he said. "No, stay. If you want."

There was a long moment where he wasn't at all convinced that she would: she'd shifted as though to stand up. But then she brushed her hair from her face with her hand, and turned towards him, her eyes shining with tears.

"Sorry," he mumbled, and hoped she'd understand that he meant it to cover not just the past few minutes, but the past few weeks.

She didn't say anything, just gave him a wobbly half-smile.

Later, he watched her sleep, curled on her side, still wearing her sweater and muddy jeans. He tucked a blanket around her. For a while, he slept too – and he didn't dream.

Acknowledgements

As a young and arrogant would-be writer, I read the "acknowledgements" page of novels and scoffed. Surely, I thought, it only takes *one* person to write a book. What sort of sap needs to note the support of their family and friends?

Having now written four novels (and scrapped three), I know just how vital those family and friends are. *Lycopolis* would not exist without the input of numerous people, and I am incredibly grateful to them all.

My husband, Paul David Luke, read pretty much every draft of *Lycopolis*. Without his support, encouragement and provision of tea, chocolate and regular hot dinners, this novel would never have been finished.

My parents, Gill and Geoff Hale, have helped me in so many ways – emotional, financial, and practical. They've encouraged my writing for many years, and, more recently, have been extremely supportive of my entrepreneurial endeavours. This novel is dedicated to them, with much love.

I started *Lycopolis* in the first month of my Creative & Life Writing MA at Goldsmiths College. Unfathomable thanks are owed to my tutor, the ever-wonderful Francis Spufford, who saw this novel through from conception to second draft. (And had "apocalypse in a forest" written on his whiteboard for at least a term, which kept me heading in the right narrative direction...)

My other tutors, Pam Johnson and Blake Morrison, also provided insightful feedback and proved extremely willing to engage with a novel that was far from their usual genres.

The members of my workshop group saw Draft 1, Scene 1 of *Lycopolis* (plus later pieces) and tackled it with bravery and rigour. Thank you all: Andrea, David, Frankie, Gill, Graham, Jon, Julianne, Rachel, Sybilla, and Tom. Especial thanks to Andrea, Gill, Graham, Julianne, and Rachel, as well as Anna and Jenny, all of whom provided feedback via informal workshopping sessions. Your suggestions made this novel so much stronger than it would otherwise have been and, in several cases, prevented me from going off in completely the wrong direction.

My writing group in Oxford has a special place in my heart. They welcomed me when I was a very young novelist – I joined when I was 14. Current members have provided a helpful fresh perspective on the later drafts of *Lycopolis*: thank you to Ann, David O., David S., Eve, Jenny, Kate, Mike, and Robin. Especial thanks to Robin who read the whole of *Lycopolis* and provided very welcome feedback. I'm also particularly grateful to David Olsen, who took an interest in my writing when I was a student and saw potential that I didn't know I had.

Several friends read early drafts and responded enthusiastically. Thanks to Andrew, James and Tracy for keeping me going. Big thanks to Nick Bryan, who bore with early drafts and provided ample distraction on Twitter.

Two talented friends, both named Lorna, played a key role in the final production of *Lycopolis*. Lorna Cowie read the whole novel, then came up with the concept for, and designed, the fantastic cover. Lorna Fergusson edited the entire Draft 5 manuscript – a Herculean task – and didn't shy away from advising drastic revision. Without her, this book would be 50,000 words longer and considerably the worse for it.

Of course, any astute reader of *Lycopolis* might suspect that I have first-hand experience of the subject matter. No, I've never summoned any evil demons. I do, however, owe a very great debt to an online game rather like Lycopolis, called *Wolfenburg* and then *Kingdom of Heroes*. Not only did it give me the inspiration for *Lycopolis*, it was also where I met my husband.

I won't name everyone who played Wolfenburg between 2001 and 2007, because I will inevitably forget someone (and count someone several times under different character names). But thank you, a huge thank you, to all who knew me as the inept thief Juxquin, for giving me a place to belong.

Ali Luke
November 2011

Enjoyed Lycopolis?
Here's What You Can Do Next...

I'd love it if you'd tell a friend about *Lycopolis*. Or if you're feeling really generous, you could write a short review – on Amazon, on your own website, or both. This really helps would-be readers who are trying to make up their minds. Thank you!

And ... the fun doesn't end here. *Lycopolis* is the first novel in a planned trilogy. The second, *Oblivion*, is already out (you can buy it from Amazon).

To make sure you don't miss out on the third book, pop on over to the Lycopolis website and join my email list. I'll let you know when it's nearly ready to arrive on the virtual shelves ... and I'll also have some free advance copies to give away.

www.lycopolis.co.uk/emails

You'll also find some short stories on that site – completely free. These take place before the events of the Lycopolis trilogy. Enjoy!

Ali x

Printed in Great Britain
by Amazon